Karen's

BP
GP

Dorothy Uhnak

VICTIMS

A NOVEL

SIMON AND SCHUSTER   NEW YORK

Copyright © 1985 by Mighty Minkey Production Company, Inc.
All rights reserved
including the right of reproduction
in whole or in part in any form
Published by Simon and Schuster
A Division of Simon and Schuster, Inc.
Simon & Schuster Building
Rockefeller Center
1230 Avenue of the Americas
New York, New York 10020

SIMON AND SCHUSTER and colophon are registered trademarks of Simon & Schuster, Inc.
Designed by Eve Kirch
Manufactured in the United States of America

10 9 8 7 6 5 4 3 2 1

Library of Congress Cataloging in Publication Data
Uhnak, Dorothy.
    Victims.
    I. Title.
PS3571.H6V5 1986   813'.54   85-26246
ISBN: 0-671-45237-1

This book is dedicated with love and deep affection to three of the most constant, supportive and dependable people in my life:

To Dennis Power

To Sam Schmerler

And especially to my dear old, forever young Swanie

Prologue

She had forgotten to lock the door on the passenger's side. Even through the pounding headache, Anna Grace followed routine procedures. She slipped the key into the lock, gave it a quick half turn, checked the door handle, then let the car keys fall into her shoulder bag. In her right hand she held the house keys. The key to the apartment was positioned between her thumb and forefinger.

She sensed him before she heard or saw him: a heavy-smelling damp physical mass, large and ill-defined. He crowded her, forced her without actually touching her with his hands, just by his presence, moving into her, against the warm metal of her car. She twisted around to face him, to face the barrage of unintelligible words, directed at her. He was talking, whispering, leaning into her, ferociously insistent.

"What? What is it? What do you—"

His voice dropped to a growl as he grabbed her shoulder. Her hand went up automatically, to protect her face.

"Money? Do you want money? Here, take this—"

He slammed her across the face, but it didn't feel like a blow. It was a sharp clean tearing sensation. Her hand caught the next peculiar pain: so sharp and intense across the palm and down her arm.

She pushed at him, pulled herself away from the car, from his grasping hand, his slashing hand. She swung out with her shoulder bag, swung wildly, felt the impact, heard him roar, screaming at her, furious that she had struck back.

"Oh my God help me help me help me please someone he's hurting me . . ."

His hand, strong, incredibly strong, clamped on her neck as he leaned into her. He was talking to her: she caught a word, a phrase.

"No, no. A mistake. I don't know you, please you're making a—"

There were a series of blows, each thud felt dull and strangely without pain. And yet she knew he was stabbing her with a sharp long-bladed knife, his arm rising, punching down at her, delivering new and unimaginable wounds.

She screamed as loudly as she could. That would stop him. The noise would frighten him. They were standing in the middle of the brightly lit street. She cried out to all the people at all the windows in the apartment buildings on both sides of the street. From the bottom of the canyon created by the buildings, she called out to them.

They heard her. She saw them, watching. She pushed at the heavy wetness covering her face, knew that it was blood, that he was ripping at her with each new blow. She was beginning to feel oddly hollow. Shell-like. Empty and emptier, lighter and lighter, flowing and fading away.

He was making as much noise as she was. His own screams of rage, anger, fought hers of anguish and terror. And then, in one surprisingly quiet moment, he backed off and let his hands dangle at his sides. He lowered his head, glared at her, studied her as though deciding what to do next.

In that silent split second, Anna Grace felt a scream of

agony rise from some reservoir of life-force energy. It was her final cry for help, and it was electrifying.

He froze, listened, looked around as though for the first time aware of where they were—in the middle of a well-lit street, surrounded by apartment buildings, people at the windows, watching. Seeing everything.

He turned and ran and was gone.

Her cries were low-pitched now, very soft, but audible in the stillness of the night. She raised her face, looked around, saw the buildings shimmer and blur. She moved carefully toward the lamppost. It was her immediate goal, and she reached it, leaned against it, cried softly, then felt her body slide down slowly, carefully, landing in a sitting position. She brought her knees up, felt her head fall back, heard one last softly mourning cry: a final animal sigh of despair and sorrow.

Then Anna Grace felt her head fall forward, and her last thought was about all the blood she was losing. Someone better start applying some pressure pretty soon. . . .

Anna Grace was a nurse, so it was logical that her last thought should be of the medical action necessary to save her life.

1

If Mike Stein had waited until morning to drive home from the beach house in Bridgehampton, he would never have become involved in the case. He would simply have added the name Anna Grace to the body count of violent deaths in New York City in the lower right-hand corner of his twice-weekly column in the New York *Post*. The details would have been left to whoever was covering Queens that night.

Queens, to Stein, was a place to drive through on the way to the Island, or to hurry past in the back of a cab on the way to the airports. It was almost as unknown as Brooklyn, though a little less remote than Staten Island. The Bronx of his boyhood was memoryland: it had been burned and pillaged and systematically destroyed beyond recognition through the years. Occasionally, his column was a sad, nostalgic journey into what it had been like to grow up in the Bronx in the thirties. It read like ancient history.

New York was Manhattan, and Manhattan was home, and he was gratified by the light traffic on Grand Central Parkway. It would take him no more than twenty to twenty-five minutes to reach his apartment. His ex-wife, Julie, had given him a week to come up with a solution. It was his fault. His attorney had told him ten years ago, when he bought the beach house in both names, "You want to give your child bride a gift, make it jewelry or a car or a new wardrobe. But not half interest in a house. That is serious stuff: a well-meant gesture that will one day blow up in your face."

This was the day. Julie, just turned thirty, twenty years his junior, had come in from California. She had the West Coast look, thin but firm, long loose blond hair, tanned skin, free of even the most ordinary lines—not even a laugh wrinkle.

Her new lover made *her* feel old, she confided. He was four years younger than she was. Mike could sympathize with that. In theory.

He had two choices, she told him. First choice, put the house on the market. She'd checked around. They could ask for three hundred thou. Probably get two hundred and fifty thou. Or, second choice, he could buy her out. She would be more than fair. For a hundred thousand dollars, he could make the house all his. Which was what it should have been all along.

He did not want to put the house on the market. It was the only place he had ever truly loved. It was where he went when the alternative was to go crazy.

What Julie could not understand was why he couldn't come up with a hundred thousand dollars. He'd made a killing on his novel about the Korean War. The movie sale alone had been in the six figures, plus the book club rights and the paperback. And what about all the money he'd made a few years ago, when he won the Pulitzer Prize for that book about that murder—or whatever—in Vietnam? Didn't that book make a lot of money?

Yes and no, he said. The novel about Korea was a long time ago. Okay, he'd made a lot of money. And spent a lot. He had four kids to support before he met Julie. And the Pulitzer—that bestowed more prestige than cash. The timing was wrong; no one wanted to read a horror story about a young American soldier murdered by other Americans who passed it off as a war death.

Listen, did she think he wrote two columns a week because he loved to wallow in the slow and certain destruction of life of the New Yorker? Yes, he was syndicated in over a hundred newspapers. Yes, she did read him in L.A. But it did not pay enough for him to do anything but meet expenses. That was why he did the lecture circuit from time to time: for money. She didn't forget, did she, that they, between them, had a nine-year-old son? That Mike had to pay his tuition, among other set responsibilities?

Now Julie, who had been his response to turning forty, had a new man in her life. He was just getting his production company together, and she wanted to buy in. The hundred thousand from the beach house would do for openers.

As though she could not bear to let it pass, she mentioned his upcoming birthday casually. Fifty, Mike. Wow!

But what Julie really wanted to talk about, what she talked about incessantly, was money. Why hadn't he stayed in L.A. when he was hot? Did he realize how much money was floating around?

The two-day stay at Bridgehampton ended the way it began, and what he had to do was find a way to come up with a hundred thousand dollars to buy back from her what was already his.

He hadn't been listening to the blips and static and metallic drone of information being broadcast over the police radio. It was his background music, the way kids who walked around with earphones clamped to their heads became oblivious to the sounds being forced into their brains. It was purely coincidental that within two miles of the Grand Central Parkway exit to Forest Hills Mike yawned and decided to not think about Julie or money or the Hamptons or Hollywood or young producers who made his former child bride feel old, because what the hell did that make him?

"On Barclay Street, Forest Hills, between Sixty-ninth Avenue and Sixty-eighth Avenue, female on sidewalk obviously injured described as covered with blood. . . ."

Once he caught the first few words, the message seemed clear of distracting noise. A long time ago, he had wondered how cops could ever understand any of the messages directed toward them, but it was something subliminal. When it was meant for you, you got it, and this message was directed to him. Acting on it, Mike swung to the right and followed the ramp which led to the Sixty-ninth Avenue exit.

He knew where he was going, but he didn't know where he was. Years ago he had attended the tennis matches at Forest Hills Tennis Stadium, which was more or less the location given on the police call. The area had been all low buildings and empty lots, but that was more than twenty years ago. Driving across Queens was like drifting through an unknown, unimagined city. Queens Boulevard looked like a reasonable facsimile of Third Avenue. It had that new-town quality, as though all the buildings had been put up within a month of each other.

He remembered, vaguely, that the eight- or ten-lane Queens Boulevard had been lined with six-story apartment buildings set between large used-car lots. It had crossed his mind, years ago, that a great deal of valuable land was waiting to be developed. Now it was all twenty- or thirty-story buildings. The six-story buildings had been plowed under and the vacant lots had been built on, and for a moment it was difficult to tell exactly where he was. No landmarks until he spotted Continental Avenue: gateway to the real, old Forest Hills Gardens.

He drove down past the crowded collection of shops that

lined both sides of the street, until he reached the underpass of the Long Island Railroad, and then it came as a surprise. It was like driving into a still-existing past: there was the cobbled brick square around which had been built the Forest Hills Inn. He sat for a moment and it was as he remembered it. Archways led to quiet streets of large, expensive houses. It was all still there, had been preserved as if existing in some sort of time warp. It was intensely quiet, and the old-fashioned lanterns on the privately owned streets glowed brighter than he remembered. There were signs warning that Forest Hills Gardens was not a parking lot; violators would be towed away.

Now on every other privately owned lamppost was a neat metal sign: THIS AREA IS PATROLLED BY GUARDIAN SECURITY PERSONNEL/TRAINED SECURITY WATCHDOGS. That took the Disneylike cast off the setting; it was indeed modern times.

He made a right turn onto Barclay Street, which was one long uninterrupted stretch along the deserted fenced-in tennis courts on the left. On the right was a slightly raised embankment leading to the fenced-in Long Island Railroad. Barclay Street continued right out of the elite, private, Forest Hills Gardens. As it made a turn and swung into Sixty-ninth Avenue to the left and continued Barclay Street to the right, it was just plain Forest Hills, and it was as he remembered it.

Barclay Street was lined on both sides with pre–World War II six-story apartment buildings with Tudor façades. Courtyards faced courtyards. There were neat little lawns, low, precisely clipped hedges, clean sidewalks. It formed an old-fashioned enclave of a middle-class neighborhood. The past was sitting on a fortune of real estate that someone had missed for the time being.

Mike Stein drove slowly past the collecting crowd, getting

a quick overall view. There was only one patrol car on the scene, although the night was filling with those awful wailing, rising and falling sounds of approaching cop cars that reminded him of movie Nazis. He pulled up and parked and walked slowly back up the block.

He stood back in the crowd, carefully getting oriented to the event at the center of which was a small, bloody body, seated, leaning in death against the base of the lamppost. She glowed under the orange light, which was designed to simulate perpetual daylight so as to discourage crime on the streets. After a quick glance at the body, he turned his attention to the crowd.

This wasn't the normal scene of a normal everyday, every-night killing in the city of New York. The difference wasn't in the victim. She was bloody enough and dead enough. The crowd was made up of *white* faces—that was the immediately discernible variation from the norm. Street crime scenes are usually dark brown in color.

There was an absence of children at the scene. This was a white middle-class street. Children did not stay out on the street alone at night, not even on a summer night. They were not habitual witnesses to casual violence. The few children present at the periphery of the crowd were held fast by a parent's hand and were hustled away once the reality of a bloody death on their sidewalk faced the parent with a problem of explanation.

The street sounds were different. Instead of heavy and continuous noise from shoulder-resting ghetto blasters, loud voices, inappropriate laughter and hooting, an occasional scream echoed by some cruel imitation of expressed anguish, there was a palpable silence. The soft and far-off sounds of television sets or indoor radios, the hum of air conditioners, provided a low-keyed background for the arrival of the police cars. The motors being sharply shut off, doors opening and being slammed shut, could be clearly heard cutting through the near-silence.

Overhead, the surprisingly close-you-can-almost-touch-it sound of jets, unnoticed by the residents of Barclay Street. This had always been a pathway to both Kennedy and La Guardia. This was normal and accustomed noise, as was the low rumble of the Long Island Railroad train which could be felt vibrating through the soles of his shoes.

Mike Stein turned his attention to the policeman guarding the body. Technically, he had to be at least twenty-one years old, but with his smooth cheeks, light-yellow hair, thick light eyelashes blinking nervously, tongue darting out over dry lips, hands shaking slightly, he looked no more than twelve. He tried to be cool. He stood tall and straight, unaware of how incongruous his skinny six-foot frame appeared inside a police uniform. But he did his job, which was to keep the neighbors away from the body. He lost his supposed cool for one split second as two other police officers arrived, older, more settled into themselves and their responsibilities. He actually said, the young cop, what he had been thinking. It was doubtful he was even aware of having spoken. What he said was, "Thank Christ! Am I glad to see you guys!" It was a thought spoken aloud, and it seemed improbable to Stein that anyone else actually heard him.

On command, the gathering crowd did what it was told to do: stand back, make some room here. As if to allow the victim some air, a chance to breathe. Then the crowd did as expected. They leaned forward to see the effect. There was none. The young woman was unquestionably dead.

This was a crowd of neighbors, and it was easy for Stein to drift around, pretending to be one of them. He looked enough like someone you'd see every day walking the dog, waiting for the elevator, checking the mail, carrying a bag of groceries. He could fit in and be mistaken for the neighbor

18

down the hall whom you saw occasionally, nodded to maybe, but never really noticed. That's what neighbors were: vaguely familiar faces or forms, people who were seen but rarely known. People you never actually talked to except on special occasions: an accident, a blackout, a car slamming into another car in the middle of the block, an elevator caught between floors, an ambulance pulling up, a heart-attack victim hustled out expertly by the professionals who handle such things, a death of an elderly lady who used to sit in the window on the ground floor. A few older women and some retired men knew more than they let on. They could put names to the faces and weave relationships: married sons and daughters, college students who dropped out or graduated; a job lost, a career changed. They were here, too, the older people. They didn't press too close. They stayed together and waited and watched.

"Who is she? She's familiar a little bit."

"I thought she was, you know, that girl who . . ."

"Yeah, that's who I thought, but now . . ."

"When she cried out . . ."

"Did *you* hear that, too?"

The question was directed toward Mike Stein, and he shrugged vaguely and gestured over his shoulder, indicating he lived at the other end of the street.

"Even across the street they could hear," a man told his wife. She pressed her lips together and nodded and he said, "We thought at first it was a dog. You know, hit by a car."

Yes. That's what it sounded like at first. There was some agreement as to the sound: a high-pitched, far-carrying, wounded-animal sound which had carried up and down the canyon of Barclay Street. A sound repeated many times, it seemed. The information was offered and affirmed by people first from one side of the street and then from the other.

"We turned the sound off on the TV, we thought it was

interference of some kind, from the radio waves, you know, those CB radios that sometimes get into the TV."

Yes, it sounded like that. At first.

Stein looked toward the dead body. The young woman had at some point been alive before sliding down and tilting in death against the lamppost. Many people could bear witness to that fact. They had heard her voice.

"I thought she was drunk, you know, or drugged, staggering like that."

And now the crowd had her staggering. Had watched in life what they all looked at from time to time in death.

"The way she moved, hunched forward . . ."

"Not at the end. She threw her head back and . . ." The young man's demonstration brought forth some agreement and some contradictions.

"That was when she screamed the last time, she threw her head back and . . ."

"No, that was before she fell."

This crowd was filled with witnesses, and there was a relaxing, an almost relieved atmosphere, a freewheeling unloading of information they wanted to be rid of; they unburdened themselves by comparing impressions of the dead girl's last moments.

An unmarked police car pulled up alongside several patrol cars. The driver was unmistakably a police officer. The gold shield pinned to the lapel of his jacket gave him authority on the scene. His manner would give him authority anywhere. He let the uniformed officers come to him. He turned his back on the crowd and spoke in a deep, quiet rumbling voice, lifted a hand and snapped his fingers. He was taller than everyone except the young blond officer, whom he outweighed by about fifty pounds.

"Torres," he ordered, "go over there and take a look. And don't touch nothing."

A tall slender young woman, her face obscured as she adjusted the detective shield on the chain she had slipped over her head, nodded. She pinned a plastic ID card to the collar of her lightweight linen dress and checked to see that it wasn't bunching the fabric. She moved so quickly, so efficiently, that she provided her audience with nothing more than a flash of the coppery-red-gold muted colors of her dress. She worked methodically, ignoring everything but her assigned task.

The Crime Scene Unit arrived, and from their van they quickly brought out wooden horses with paper signs: CRIME SCENE: DO NOT CROSS THIS LINE. The crowd of observers moved back, pushing itself in place as these barriers were quickly and expertly set in place.

"Who's that? That girl, who's she?"

"The sister, maybe?"

"No, they wouldn't let the sister near the body yet, would they? Look. She's got a police badge around her neck."

"Imagine! She's so skinny, that girl, and she's a policeman."

She was a slightly built girl and she moved carefully within the periphery of the victim. Without touching anything, she observed and noted the position of the body. She jotted down whatever information could be discerned. Alongside the body was a shoulder bag, large canvas, similar to an airline carrier. Contents were scattered where they had apparently fallen. She noted a wallet, apparently filled with bills; a cosmetic case, a pillbox, small sealed brown envelope. It was more of a contents count; nothing could be touched or examined until Homicide said it was all right.

"I thought she was the Spanish girl's sister. She looks a little like her."

"They all look alike."

Mike Stein registered the remarks; filed them away for

21

later examination. He studied the woman police officer as she stood up and glanced around at the crowd, which was now focused on her.

In the orangy glow of the streetlight, Miranda Torres' face took on a deep burnished color: warm, cinnamon brown with a strong underlay of red. Her high sharp cheekbones caught the light, which accentuated the hollows of her cheeks. Her fine jawline was clean and tight. Her eyes were large and dark, her brows black, her lips turned up slightly at the corners into less than a smile. Her black hair was cut very short, very boyish, and framed her face in strong silky wisps along the temples and the forehead. She stood and gazed through the crowd, her face revealing nothing. She might have been staring off into empty space, but a quick pull at the corner of her lips gave her away. The calm expression, the placid veneer, hid a rigidity that was costing her a great deal. She was tall and slender to the point of fragility and there was something proud and tribal in the way she held her head, high and slightly tilted; her back absolutely straight, her body centered like a dancer's.

The homicide men arrived. Stein could spot homicide people under any circumstances. They were grim without being horrified. They approached a murder victim prepared for any atrocity, and in some minute corner of their minds they focused on some perverse incongruity in any death scene, something they could all laugh about later. Morgue humor; saving grace. No matter what it was, there had to be *something* funny about the human condition. They were generally very careful, however, about keeping their jokes, wisecracks and observations "within the family."

The crime scene widened considerably as the technicians spread out in the search for a weapon and any other physical evidence. Chalk circles were drawn around blotches of blood which led to the other side of the street. They conferred,

22

pointed, measured, took blood samples from within each circle and photographs from various angles to trace the route and action of the murder.

There were enough stories coming from the crowd, and detectives moved in, chatted up, looped an arm around a shoulder and let themselves be led along the row of parked cars. They nodded and noted and questioned and listened as witnesses to the event pointed and explained.

One man pointed out what might be the victim's car. He had been looking out the window to wave goodbye to a friend, had stayed there for a moment, had seen the yellow Toyota pull into the space his friend had just vacated. Pretty sure, yeah. Anyway, a girl, a woman, got out and locked the car and started across the street and no, he didn't watch anymore, he went to take a shower so he hadn't seen or heard anything more until there was all this noise and police sirens and he got dressed and came down and then he realized that the woman who parked the car might—maybe, must be—the woman who got killed. Think so, maybe?

Maybe. The detective went to check on the ownership after advising a uniformed man to stand guard on the Toyota.

A small, graying man in a dark suit, carrying a doctor's black bag, approached the dead woman. They all knew who he was—they'd seen it all before in the movies, on TV. He had to be the medical examiner, and sure enough he was. He greeted a few of the homicide cops before he even looked at the victim, then finally he turned and stared.

"You got all you need, Ed?" he asked the crime scene photographer.

"Gimme two more minutes."

The photographer circled, aimed, flashed, photographed from every angle possible. It seemed a waste of time; from any angle, the girl was dead.

Finally it was the medical examiner's turn, and the neighbors could not see what his work entailed because the detectives were all standing around blocking their view.

Stein moved back and mingled again with the older people. They were not so anxious to catch every word or to identify every new arrival. Death was there under the streetlamp and it had visited a very young woman. They stayed somewhat apart from their neighbors.

"Do you think it is the Spanish girl?" a woman asked her neighbor, who merely shrugged: I don't know. Who knows?

"Where does the Spanish girl live?" Mike asked quietly, turning, searching the apartment building.

"No, no," a woman told him. "Over there, in the first building."

"Not just one girl, two sisters I think live there."

"Stewardesses, that's what they are."

"The third girl, the youngest sister, she goes to school. She's the troublemaker, she has boys over and plays that music so loud. Her sister, the stewardess, she comes and goes, very quiet."

There was a sound, a communal moan of surprise, of shock. Stein turned and watched the medical examiner slide the body from its sitting position. Under the glare of the lights that had been set up, the reality of bloody, violent death was revealed to people who had not seen it before. It was not exactly like a movie or a TV event, after all.

There were great wide slashes on both sides of the woman's face. Her chest and arms were covered with blood to such an extent that it was impossible to immediately verify other wounds. It didn't take the M.E. very long before he finished his job and packed up.

Stein wandered among neighbors; stopped; listened. They had finished, for the time being, comparing what they had seen and heard. He moved closer now to the body, as close as the police lines permitted and then a little closer. He lis-

24

tened to one detective ticking off to his partner information to be included in their initial report: no apparent rape or sexual mutilation; no apparent robbery—wallet and credit cards intact; victim holding house key in right hand.

Other detectives were moving through the street, now turning their attention to the crowd of people who were watching and waiting for something more to happen. The police were very good at what they did, and careful not to turn people away or frighten them off. They moved and spoke and questioned with great tact and consideration and awareness of who these people were: middle-class Barclay Street, Forest Hills, neighbors who had never seen such a thing before, ever.

The police had picked up the situation, of course. Stein stood quietly watching, listening, catching the surprise and the carefully controlled reaction to the fact that there were people here who had followed every step of this crime: had watched and heard and seen it all from beginning to end. For an estimated twenty minutes.

He glanced around and selected the young blond police officer, who was earnestly watching the detectives and the technicians. He came alongside the young cop with the assurance and authority of a superior officer.

"You first on the scene, Officer?" he asked.

"Yes, sir. Well, me and my partner, sir. We picked up the call at about eleven-thirty or eleven-thirty-one. I have it marked in my notebook, sir."

"Who made the call? Was it called in on 911 or what?"

The policeman glanced around carefully, leaned closer to Stein and confided, "See the bus driver, sir? Well, you should hear what *he* got to say."

"Suppose you tell me."

"Yes, sir. Well, it seems that . . . well, all these people are telling me about how they saw this girl, this man grappling with her, hitting on her and yelling and all, and some of them

25

seen him slashing at her, and then they seen him take off and all and watched and all and . . ."

"Officer, get to the point."

"*Nobody called 911.* All these people, well, some of them, a lot of them, they all watched and they all can tell you what went first, but . . . no one called. No one . . . did anything."

"And the bus driver?"

"Oh, yes sir. He completed his run down at Metropolitan Avenue, and as he turned onto Barclay Street he saw her, he could tell, just the way she was sitting, leaning, like he could see she was dead. And he pulled the bus up, and got out and couldn't believe it. He says from the amount of bleeding, he could see she'd been there awhile—you could see she was dead. And nobody did anything. But watched from the windows. So he starts yelling and all and got someone to call 911."

"How many calls were there?" The cop looked blank. "Never mind. That's okay. Thanks, Officer."

Stein moved back and moved carefully, not speaking to any of them. He watched the detectives work the crowd: friendly, easy, helpful. They knew. They were trying to get enough witnesses to give the whole scenario, beginning to end, and they knew that the information was available. The whole thing had been witnessed by an audience of movie and TV experts who seemed to have anticipated each move and were surprised only now by the fact that this was real.

He tried not to study the faces too closely, because he began to see things he did not want to see. He wanted to keep a calm distance from this really ordinary street crime. From what he'd heard, it seemed like a lovers' quarrel. It had been done without stealth, right out in the middle of the street, under lights and before witnesses. That added up to a great emotional upheaval.

But it wasn't an ordinary event. If the killing was nothing

26

really unusual, the fact of the witnesses, standing around, comparing notes, giving a minute-by-minute scenario to the detectives, was more than unusual. People at the crime scenes he usually covered were silent or said things like "Hey, I don't know nothin', man, I don't even live here, I just lookin', like everyone else. Hell, ain't nothin' to me."

He felt a sense of fleeting despair at their earnestness. He turned away from the neighbors for a moment and tried to go blank, to suspend judgment, but he could not suspend a familiar if long-dormant charge of electricity that sharpened all his faculties, energized him totally. There was something terrible here on this street, among these people; the spotlighted dead body was merely the most visual evidence. A pervasive sense of outrage swept through Mike Stein. He had been numbed by so many years of observing all the horrors people daily inflicted on each other, he had been desensitized by the ordinariness of crime, the lack of significance and meaning. The electricity crackling through him sharpened and widened his point of view. The greater crime was here, among these good people, in their telling of how they watched. And watched. And waited, while the girl lay dying.

He turned and faced the apartment house directly in line with the lamppost, and he registered the clicking, clicking, clicking from the air conditioner that was balanced on a carrier outside the center window of the apartment just above street level. It was the sound of an old air conditioner that had been turned off: the kind of sound that on a quiet night becomes intolerably loud and steady. There was movement behind the sheer white curtains, a strange apparition: a person standing, watching, listening, leaning against the window frame, nearly invisible. Except, by concentrating, he could make out that the person watching was swaddled in bandages. The whole face seemed hidden.

As he narrowed his eyes and moved closer, the person disappeared, seemed to vaporize, and for a moment he wondered if he had imagined the whole thing.

It was something that made him feel uneasy and he didn't know why.

There was a commotion coming from the vicinity of the bus. Apparently the bus driver's supervisor had arrived, and this gave the driver his opportunity to express his opinion of the people on Barclay Street. He had, up till then, been very quiet, conferring only with the detectives.

"Ya know what kinda people they are, Jimmy? I'll tell ya. They stood around at their windas and watched this girl die out here on the street, right in front of them, and not one of 'em even picked up a phone. Not one of 'em called 911 and tried to get the kid some help. How about that, huh?"

His supervisor tried to quiet him down, turned him toward the bus, but the man was warming up to his moment.

He began to use the kind of language he knew would offend these people; he insulted their conception of themselves as good people. A few voices in the crowd called out that he was wrong; that he should just shut up and go home.

"Ya deserve what happened here," he shouted back wildly, "all of you—you don't look out for your own daughters! What kinda people are you?"

"No, no, don't say that," an older man said softly. "We didn't know that the girl . . ."

The voices around the bus driver were quietly protesting, explaining. He didn't understand, he had it wrong, it wasn't like that at all.

"It *was* like that, ya bastards, ya all stood at ya windas and watched her and ya did nothin' at all. Ya let her die—you're all fuckin' bums, all a ya!"

An older man put his arm around his wife's shoulder, turned her away. They'd seen and heard enough for one night. They didn't need this man's crazy yelling and bad language.

A broad-shouldered guy in a gray sweatshirt and blue-jean cutoffs, his face damp and red with anger, pushed through the crowd and confronted the bus driver. They were matched, bulk for bulk, eye to eye.

"Hey, you loudmouth, wadda ya yellin' about, huh? You didn't do nothin', you just kept goin' first time you passed the girl, so you just watch your mouth around here, ya bum. You're someone to say something to anyone! Jeez!"

The bus driver pulled away from his supervisor's grasp and jutted his chin forward. His eyes blazed and his fists tightened.

"I didn't do nothin'? *Me?* I didn't do nothin'? I'm the one got down on my knees to help this kid, to tell you people to get the cops. She'd still be there I hadn't stopped and—"

"Ya didn't stop the first time, pal," the big guy said. He turned to face his neighbors. "He didn't stop the first time. He come past her, made a quick stop at the sign and pulled around the corner." He turned back to the bus driver, "You finished your goddamn *route,* so don't say you fucking *helped* her."

"What? *What?*" The bus driver turned to his supervisor, letting him grab at his shoulders, take him under control, restrain him.

"I saw that, too," a short round gray-haired man standing next to Mike Stein said to no one in particular.

"Yeah. He did."

"Yeah. I saw that."

"Yeah."

Others in the crowd had watched not just the assault and the dying. They had also watched the bus driver complete a pass without stopping. Had seen him return finally and get out of his bus. When it was too late.

29

All of these remarks, these accusations, these retellings, were noted, registered, filed away for future examination, not only by Stein but by all the plainclothes detectives now circulating in the crowd.

The bus driver, shaking his head, sorry for himself—no matter what you do, it's the good guy gets it in the end—let himself be led back to his bus by his supervisor. He had seen enough of these people. What could you say to them, people who had let a young girl die like that?

Without helping her.

"You know who I thought it might be?" an old woman asked Mike. "That woman, Mrs. Hynes, who lives on the first floor? Her daughter, the one who became a nurse. When Mrs. Schroeder said it looked like one of the Spanish girls from the top floor, I thought no. It looked to me, when she was sitting there— My eyes aren't so good anymore, but I remember the girl, Mrs. Hynes's daughter, the nurse. You think it might be her? I hope not."

"I hope not," Mike said.

"I hope not," the woman repeated. She grabbed her husband's arm, and he said, "It's about time, about time, we should go home. This is terrible. You'll be up all night now upset from this terrible thing. It's not safe anywhere, anywhere."

Acting from automatic signals, from unexamined intuition, from too many years of experience, Mike walked into the courtyard leading to the building at 68-35. He entered the vestibule and was struck immediately by the cleanliness of the hallway. The brass rectangle of apartment buttons was shiny. The floors were clean without the smell of dirty mops. He studied the names of the tenants.

Apartment 1-A, Mrs. Hynes.

He walked outside and studied the setup and took a guess:

that would be, he felt certain, the apartment immediately overlooking the lamppost where the dead girl now lay under a light blanket. The apartment with the clicking, turned-off air conditioner; the apartment with the apparition peeking through sheer curtains.

As more detectives arrived and moved among the witnesses, taking names and addresses and phone numbers and information, the homicide man finally signaled that it was all right: he was finished with the body. He pulled back the cover that had been tossed lightly over the dead woman.

"Anyone know her?" he asked, allowing a few of the more curious to glance at the bloody face.

Miranda Torres' partner was carefully going through the contents of the victim's wallet. Stein had come into the proscribed circle and stood alongside Torres. No one questioned his presence.

"Anyone know a woman named Anna Grace?"

No one did.

The address given was in Little Neck, and some police officers were dispatched to get her husband.

He read out the "in case of accident" information: husband, William; employer, St. John's Hospital. This girl a nurse? Anybody know her?

Another card: similar information.

Anna Hynes Grace: anybody know her?

Stein looked around quickly. The elderly woman and her husband were gone. No one seemed to register the information.

Moving quickly, Mike Stein grabbed Miranda Torres by the arm. She turned, surprised.

"Officer, come with me. We'll get an ID on the victim."

He spoke to her in the tone of voice she expected to hear, had been accustomed to hear, from superior officers. She followed him without question. It was an order not open to discussion. She had to take running steps to keep up with him. Apparently he knew exactly where he was going and what he was going to do.

She couldn't really see what he looked like in the dim hall light. She didn't recognize him, but it didn't surprise her when he addressed her by name. She wore an identifying name tag just above her detective's shield. She was a little surprised when he took a plastic credit card from his wallet and used it to open the locked door that led to the hall. He saw her surprise and he shrugged.

"Look," he said. "There's a lady in there who's going to need you. All you gotta do for now is be there, okay?"

He stepped back and let her enter first; his hand on her shoulder directed her to apartment 1-A. He took a deep breath, then rang the bell. It set off a long, soft chiming sound.

There was silence after the sound stopped, and then there was a long, low moaning sound: a wounded-animal sound. Miranda Torres looked at Stein in alarm, but he was watching the door intently.

"Come on, Mrs. Hynes," he said softly. "Open up."

They heard chains fall away and locks being undone, and the door opened onto a long dim hallway. The woman stood there, arms dangling at her sides, large black-lensed glasses set into her bandaged face.

Mike Stein called her name again.

The woman shook her head, and her voice was a whispery, painful sound and she said, pleading, "Oh, no. No, no. Don't come here to tell me this. Please. *Please no!*"

She reached out and grabbed at Miranda Torres' arms and said in a terrible whisper, *"I thought it was the Spanish girl!"*

2

Bill Grace stared at the two uniformed policemen standing in his doorway.

"Yeah, I'm Bill Grace, Officer, what's up?"

"Listen, Mr. Grace, can we come inside? It's real hot out here."

"Sure, gee, sure. C'mon in, I got the air conditioner up high. Want a brew or something?"

When they both declined, Bill Grace extended his hand, indicated the couch. He tried very hard not to let them speak. Whatever they had come to tell him he did not want to hear. He realized that he was doing all the talking, his voice pitched soft and low, his words tumbling over each other, as though he were creating a screen around himself, to protect him from whatever they wanted to tell him.

"I work for the city, too. Fire Department. I'm a fire fighter. We used to call ourselves *firemen,* but you can't do that anymore. Not with women's lib and equal opportunity and all that."

He stopped speaking abruptly. His mouth went dry; he couldn't swallow. He could feel his heart accelerate. He saw the younger cop glance at the older cop.

33

He had been in this situation God alone knew how many times. Bringer of bad news: Mr. Jones, I'm sorry, but your wife didn't make it. Asphyxiation. If it's any consolation, she went very fast, like falling asleep. But the kids, Mr. Jones—Jesus, that was a tough one. Incinerated. Burned up. How did you soften that one? Whatever these guys were selling, he did not want to buy. No way.

"I'm sorry, Mr. Grace, but there's been a terrible accident."

The young cop, his first experience in this kind of situation, caught on: You start out slow and easy. An accident; they'll find out the details soon enough.

"Your wife, Anna, Mr. Grace. She's dead and we need you to come and identify her body. She's in Forest Hills."

The fire fighter shook his head and let his breath out with relief. It *was* a mistake. *Jesus, what a mistake!*

"Look, my wife is a nurse. She's on duty at St. John's Hospital in Elmhurst right now, late shift. Hell, I'll show you."

He reached for the phone, dialed and began to speak.

"Yeah, hi, Miss Parson. Bill Grace. Okay. Listen, can I speak to Annie for a minute? Something's come up."

He knew she wouldn't be there. But he had to try to make things right. He knew guys like these didn't make that kind of mistake any more than he did.

Speaking very carefully, he asked, "Well, what time did she leave?"

He caught the young cop's expression: he had been afraid that maybe they had been wrong. The older cop's face was blank and cool.

He checked his watch. "She left about eleven? Two hours ago? Thank you. No, no. Nothing's wrong. Nothing."

He replaced the receiver, turned and said, "What are you guys telling me?"

All the way from Little Neck to Forest Hills, Bill Grace talked nonstop. About his job, about risks they had taken and how many people they rescued. He was aligning himself with the cops. They were on the same side of things. They were not among the victims.

Abruptly, he spoke about his wife.

"Miss Parson, her supervisor, said Annie had a headache. Jeez, she's been getting a lot of them lately, migraine, they're real tough, ya know? But she takes something for it, and that helps. Look, she wouldn't have gone to Forest Hills, because her mother's down in Florida. My mother-in-law, she's visiting *her* mother in a retirement community in Florida. . . ."

He kept talking until they got out of the car and he was led through the crowd into the wide-open area designated as a crime scene. Someone uncovered Anna Grace's face.

Bill Grace knelt down.

"Hey, babe, what the hell? What's happened here?"

He embraced her, and the blanket fell away. He held her close, combed her long dark hair with his fingers. Finally a hand pressed his shoulder hard, and he looked up, surprised, puzzled.

"Mr. Grace," a detective said softly, "I'm sorry, but I haven't asked you officially. Do you identify this woman as your wife?"

He turned back to her and for the first time realized that she was covered with blood. Her face and arms and clothing were covered with blood.

"Annie?" he called softly. "Annie?" This couldn't be Annie. "My God, Christ, Annie, what happened?"

The detective nodded to the men with the stretcher: Okay, she's been identified.

"C'mon, Mr. Grace. C'mon, Bill," a voice said with easy familiarity. "Let's go inside your mother-in-law's apartment and see what we can get sorted out, okay? It'll be okay," the man said senselessly, because nothing would be okay, but Bill recognized it as the kind of thing you say and he nodded and walked away from the body and went with the detective.

There were a lot of people in Mary Hynes's apartment. He looked around for his mother-in-law and saw her standing in the doorway to the kitchen. She looked like the Invisible Man in the movies. It was a joke of some kind; her face was hidden behind bandages, and she whirled away and ran into her bedroom and slammed the door. He could hear her sobbing.

He accepted now that something terrible and irrevocable had really happened.

He asked the strangers in her living room, "Who did this to them? Who hurt them like this?" He called, "Mary, who hurt you? Who hurt Annie? Mary, for God's sake!"

He pulled open the bedroom door and could not believe how small she looked. She was lying on the bed, her back to him, her knees drawn up, her bandaged face in her hands.

"Oh, Mary," he said. His voice was as hoarse as if he had entered a room filled with smoke. His mouth tasted of ashes. "Mary, my God, what did they do to you? How did . . . what . . ."

It was so confusing. It made no sense. Annie out there covered with blood; Mary in here bandaged. There seemed to be no time sequence. Nightmare time, events crossing and slipping and merging.

He was astonished at her rigidity. His hands seemed to be pressing on stone as he tried to turn her toward him.

"Mary, please, Ma, tell me what happened, please!"

There was a soft, muffled sound coming from beneath her bandages, a gagging, choking, anguished sound. Someone pulled Bill Grace away. A doctor. Someone had sent for a doctor.

"She's in pain, son. Let me take it from here."

"But what happened? I don't understand. Who did this to her? Why is she bandaged? What happened? It doesn't make sense."

He turned to a familiar face, a neighbor, a friend of his mother-in-law. "Mrs. Ferris? What's wrong with Mary?"

"Billy, come into the other room. Come, please."

He walked with her, focused on her so intently that others milling around Mary Hynes's living room were background.

"She told us she was going to Florida, Mrs. Ferris. Why is she here? Who did this to them, to Annie and Mary?"

"Billy. Mary didn't want you kids to know. She . . ."

"To know? To know what? What?"

"She had some . . . cosmetic surgery done yesterday morning."

"Cosmetic surgery?" He repeated the words carefully, phonetically, as though he had never heard these words before. They made no sense.

The neighbor went on. "She was going to go down to Florida next week and then come home and you'd see how good she looked. Rested. She wasn't going to say anything. She had the surgery yesterday morning. That's why she's bandaged like that."

"But . . . but . . . Annie? Someone hurt my wife, out there, right out there, in front of Mary's apartment."

He turned abruptly to the triple windows, pulled back the filmy curtains, raised the narrow-slatted blinds. The crowd on the sidewalk turned and looked up at him.

"There. Right out there. It doesn't make sense. Why was Annie here? Did she know Mary was home? Did Mary see . . . out the window . . . Did . . ."

For a split second, he thought he saw his brother's face, out there, on the sidewalk, in the crowd, and then, time whirling, spinning into an incomprehensible sequence, his brother was in the room, beside him, wrapping his arms

37

around him, holding him. His eyes closed tight. He knew it was all a mistake. He was at the scene of a fire; the room was gutted and charred and black and the corpses were strangers. All he needed was a whiff or two of oxygen and he'd be fine.

But no one seemed to realize that, and for the first time in his life, Bill Grace passed out.

3

Captain William O'Connor, squad commander of the 112th Precinct detectives, rubbed his eyes. It was 10 A.M. and he had been on duty since he was called to the crime scene at 1 A.M. He was alert and sharp, but his eyes ached. It was the new glasses. He couldn't see with them and he couldn't see without them. He opened the top drawer of his desk and found his old scratched glasses. They didn't have sharp focus, but they were comfortable and familiar.

Detective James Dunphy brought him a mug of hot coffee, set it down carefully on the desk blotter.

O'Connor took a cautious sip, smiled and said, "See, there are compensations working with a girl. Your little lady out there make us a fresh pot or what?"

He was kidding. Everyone was careful these days about what women should or should not do around the squad room. No one even suggested they take their turn at the coffeepot. Hell, who wanted to hear from their damned indignant female lawyers yelling male chauvinism?

Dunphy jutted his chin toward the report on the captain's desk.

"Hell, I'm grateful the girl likes to type. And is good at

it. My brother John, at the Forty-sixth, in the Bronx, he got a woman partner, first thing she says to him, *first thing,* she tells him, 'I been a secretary for five years, buster, and I don't type anything anymore for anybody except myself.' "

The men had been friends for twenty years, had gone through the Police Academy together and had watched the changes take place not just in the outside world, but within the Department. They agreed, however, and without discussing it at any great length, that Dunphy had gotten lucky. If he had to work with a female, he couldn't do better than Miranda Torres. She was good; she was tough; she didn't make waves; she didn't hold back information; she understood the partner relationship. In short, Torres seemed to be a stand-up-guy kind of girl.

The only mystery surrounding her was who the hell was her rabbi. She'd been on the job six years. She had a degree in criminal justice from John Jay. She'd been assigned right from the Academy to undercover narcotics work in East Harlem, and she'd made third grade by the end of her second year on the job. That was legitimate. That was not unusual. But, one week before being transferred to the 112th, Miranda Torres was promoted to detective second grade. This was guaranteed to cause hostile feelings among her new colleagues. Her promotion canceled the squad's vacancy in that grade. Not only had she used up the available promotion, but some guy in plainclothes lost a slot in third grade.

Everyone knew that these days it wasn't necessarily an individual who was transferred to a prime assignment, awarded a promotion, given a medal. The recipient of these Department perks was more often than not a representative, a statistic to satisfy the endless demands for equal opportunity, affirmative action for the underprivileged and overlooked of history.

By squad calculation, Miranda Torres was someone's idea

of a triple whammy: she could be cited as being female, Hispanic and black. However, when O'Connor asked around, it did not add up. Torres was no activist, and the organizations were not pushing loners.

The black organization would not settle for Miranda because in her case black was questionable, at least visually. She was bronze with a high-cheeked American Indian look. And she had been born a woman. If the women wanted in, they had to take care of themselves. And she was a Puerto Rican Hispanic. Let them claim her.

The Hispanic organization wasn't backing her or even settling for her. They were also concerned with male promotions. Women were taking jobs away from men. Women didn't need any help.

The women's group wasn't happy with Miranda's promotion. Let the Hispanics claim her, or the blacks. Their ideal candidate would be someone no other organization had claim on.

She was not a member of the Holy Name Society or any other religious organization affiliated with the Department. She was floating out there alone, unattached in a department that was virtually run by its separatist organizations.

No matter how much discreet and serious inquiry was set in motion, the only word on Miranda Torres was, Who the hell knows? Which in police parlance meant, Watch out. She's connected somewhere, somehow, in some way to someone apparently strong enough, big enough, to maintain not just a low profile but no discernible profile. The available information on Torres, the official record, proved her an excellent narcotics cop with an outstanding activity record. However, word was that she and her partner had been made or were in imminent danger of being made. That, in itself, did not explain her transfer to the 112th. Rumor was that her partner was an alcoholic who was drying out for a while before reassignment. Whatever the story, Torres maintained a silence about anything that wasn't strictly official knowledge.

For which, of course, she had to be respected. Obviously, this did not make her popular with the guys at the 112th. What they knew they didn't like; what they *didn't* know bothered the hell out of them.

There was a light finger-tapping at his door, and Miranda Torres came in and took a seat next to her partner. She had that alert, wary look, her head held just slightly to one side, as though she was listening for more than just what was being said. She was a beautiful girl and she made the captain uncomfortable. He wondered if Dunphy had had any thoughts about her: fantasies, daydreams. He doubted Dunphy would make any moves; he was too smart for that. Probably.

"Good report," he said to Torres. She waited politely. "Okay," O'Connor said, "what the hell are we dealing with here? No signs of robbery or attempted robbery. No signs of sexual assault or attempted; guy stalks her and attacks her right out in the middle of the street, under the lights. No attempt at concealment. The guy is yelling his head off at her, like they're arguing." He flipped through the report, then narrowed his eyes, adjusted the distance until he could see the typing clearly. "The guy was yelling at her in Spanish?"

"We're working on a translation, Captain," Miranda said. "No one we spoke to understood Spanish, but it seems, phonetically at least, that he was calling her names: cheat, liar, thief. And a few . . . sexual references."

Her delicacy was natural, as if she sensed O'Connor's discomfort at her presence in his squad. There was a ladylike quality, a fine line that she had drawn around herself, an unspoken demand that she be accepted and respected on her own terms.

O'Connor nodded. "So. Maybe we're dealing with a lovers' quarrel. Who the hell knows. The girl thought her mother was in Florida, but she's coming to her apartment anyway instead of going home from the hospital where she works. Claimed she had a sick headache, so she left work two hours early. She's got a key to her mother's apartment in her hand. Which seems to indicate she believed she was heading to an empty apartment."

O'Connor gazed over the top of his sliding-down eyeglasses and waited for comments.

Miranda sat, pen poised over a notebook.

Dunphy said, "That might indicate that she had an arranged meeting with the guy. A couple of hours of bliss, maybe, then home to hubby. Who the hell would know the difference. A possibility."

"But why wouldn't the guy wait until they were in the apartment if he was planning to attack her? Why in hell was he so out in the open about it?"

Neither partner answered. They waited as their captain continued thinking out loud.

"The consensus, so far, seems to be that this has nothing to do with the other murders. That this was a one-on-one thing, whatever else the hell it was. That makes sense, right?"

"The circumstances of this killing are in no way—not one single way—similar to the other killings," Dunphy said.

"There is nothing to indicate a similarity," Torres said. It registered with O'Connor that her answer was tentative and open-ended.

The other three killings in Queens County seemed to be random sex murders. Within the last nine months, there had been three late-night attacks by an unidentified rapist-murderer who had followed women from deserted subways or bus stops, dragged them into alleys or bushes, raped and murdered them. He had been named in the headlines "The Beast of Queens."

The first victim had been found in Elmhurst at the end of

43

January. She had been a sixty-three-year-old practical nurse. The second attack in April had been in Long Island City; a twenty-one-year-old factory worker on her way home. The third victim, an eighteen-year-old on her way home from night classes at Queens College, had been brutalized and killed two blocks from her home in Queens Village in June. There were definite similarities in all three attacks. Each victim had died from a puncture wound in the jugular. Very messy. There were certain other reasons to believe that the crimes had been committed by the same person.

"I talked with Jaffee, over at Homicide, a while ago," O'Connor said. "He's anxious to keep this one separate and apart. Hell, all we need is a fourth unsolved serial killing on the streets of beautiful safe Queens County. He's letting out a low, casual word through the PR people that this is very possibly a lovers'-quarrel kind of thing. Of course, if we find the guy within the next twenty-four hours and he confesses to all four murders, we'd be the first to announce we got the Beast himself. At any rate, we're separating this killing out for logical reasons. It doesn't connect with the other murders."

O'Connor took off his smudged, scratched glasses, blinked rapidly, then focused on Miranda Torres. She was an outline, sitting absolutely motionless, her face tilted, waiting. He put the glasses back on and flipped through the report.

"Well, we don't have to search too hard for witnesses," he said. "How many people we got in the field, Jim?"

Dunphy closed his eyes for a moment. This was his case—his and Miranda's—and they were working with Homicide. It was his first homicide in many years. When he was transferred from downtown Brooklyn to Forest Hills, his job had changed drastically. He had to get back into gear.

"We got eight squad members—nine, what's-his-name is back from vacation; he's fielding the phones. And Homicide has a crew. And we've got about six uniforms doing interviews."

"This guy had a regular audience," O'Connor said. Dunphy shook his head in disgust. Torres did not react in any way. "Their statements are pretty consistent, too. Just slight differences depending on the perspective. Jeez, *this* one takes the all-time cake, doesn't it? *The mother.*"

They let it sit there for a moment. There was genuine hostility coming from Dunphy. He still wasn't sure how the hell Torres had gotten to the mother before anyone else had. Along with Mike Stein. What the hell was that connection, anyway?

There wasn't too much to say about a mother whose daughter was being murdered right outside her window. She hadn't denied knowledge of the fact: just of the identity of the victim.

And no one had called 911. No one had done anything at all. They had just watched.

O'Connor flipped through the report, ran his finger quickly, then held it under the words he had been seeking.

"What's this about 'I thought it was the Spanish girl'?" he asked Torres, as though she would understand and have an explanation.

"According to several other witnesses, besides the mother, there was an assumption that the victim was a young Hispanic woman who lives on the top floor of the corner building."

"So then we have a possible mistaken identity," O'Connor said. That was a starting point. "You checking her out?"

Dunphy answered. "I've got a meet with the manager of the building. In about an hour. Torres and I—Miranda and I are splitting up interviews. Doubling back. You know, clarity with the light of day."

"Yeah, well, here's a little fog on your clarity." O'Connor

searched through the collection of papers on his desk, then pulled out a telephone message slip. He glanced at it, then leaned forward. "Detective Torres, do you know Mike Stein?"

"I've read his work. I didn't know who he was last night. He acted like brass, and so I . . ." She stopped, shrugged.

"Acted like brass. Yeah, he's got some brass, all right," O'Connor said. "You don't know him, then?"

Dunphy turned toward his partner. There was an accusation in the captain's question. He had worked with Torres long enough to catch the stiffening of her spine, the movement along her jaw as she clenched her teeth.

"Is there some question you want to ask me, Captain? Some specific question?"

There was a sharp tense silence in the room as the men exchanged glances. There was a mixture of anger, tempered by respect. This girl didn't pull her punches, and she either didn't have the slightest trace of common sense or felt so protected that she didn't bother with games.

"I just asked you a specific question, Detective Torres."

Dunphy was an interested observer. Despite twenty years of friendship, he never crossed the official lines of O'Connor's authority. It was one of the unwritten rules: the boss was, after all, the boss.

It wasn't really that Torres was challenging the captain, although it seemed that way. It was more a let's cut the crap and ask me what you want to ask me. Which took guts, no matter who was in her corner.

"I never met Mr. Stein before last night, Captain. When I went with him to Mrs. Hynes's apartment, I had assumed he was a superior officer. He didn't actually say that, but he . . . acted in a certain way. I did not know he was a journalist until later on. When my partner told me who he was."

"Uh-huh." O'Connor leaned back in his chair, glaring at

her. "Then you wouldn't know why Mr. Mike Stein put in a request—through certain channels that make a request more than a request—that you be assigned to him? That you be his 'liaison officer' during this phase of this investigation."

Her surprise was genuine. Dunphy, who liked the kid, was glad.

"Well, then I will explain it to you. *Specifically.* Apparently, this case has interested Mike Stein. He plans to do some articles about it. About the witnesses who watched this girl die and didn't do a damn thing to help her. For some reason or other he felt that *you* would be a good liaison for him." O'Connor reached his hand to the telephone, tapped it, then said, "Stein has selected out this case for himself. There will be very low press coverage. No one else gets anything. He has permission—*absolute permission*—to see every report in every phase of the investigation. Including Homicide's findings, the technical findings, whatever. He also wants you to accompany him—or maybe the other way around, he wants to accompany you—on some of your interviews with the witnesses."

O'Connor studied her for several seconds, then asked, "What's your reaction to this, Detective Torres?"

"If that's what my assignment is, then that's what my assignment is."

"Uh-huh," O'Connor said. "I guess I don't have to tell you to be careful. To be very careful. Mike Stein is an unknown quantity. One day he's for us, the next day he's on our case. Be aware of that and act accordingly."

Damn, O'Connor thought; she resents being told. But was smart enough not to say so.

"Yes, sir, Captain. I shall be very cautious with this Mr. Stein."

For the first time, he caught what Dunphy had told him: when she was very uptight, when she was exerting a tough control, her speech patterns changed. Sounded almost as though she were speaking in translation.

He handed her a slip of paper with the information she needed: where to meet Mike Stein. She had a free hour and she said she would use the time to organize her material and to set aside copies of reports for Stein.

O'Connor glanced quickly at her as she left the room: great figure, if a little thin. He shook his head and said to Dunphy, "You got yourself a hard case for a partner, pal."

"She'll be okay with Stein. What the hell is he up to, anyway?"

O'Connor shrugged. "Whatever he wants, we know who *his* friend is."

Nearly fifteen years ago, Mike Stein had accompanied the Police Department's Chief of Operations, Arthur Cordovan, to Vietnam. Cordovan's only son had been sent home in a body bag: accident victim; run over by an Army truck. The son, an intelligence officer, had written his father a series of letters describing a huge illicit market operating with the knowledge, approval and participation of some high-ranking Army personnel. He had gotten in over his head. He had nowhere to take his information. He had turned down lucrative offers; he had fielded various threats by trying to take his information higher. He had been run over by an Army truck. Accidentally.

Cordovan had contacted Mike Stein.

The two men spent weeks investigating, and their findings were described in Mike's Pulitzer Prize–winning series of articles about corruption, graft and murder. He named the names that Cordovan's son had uncovered. Together, the two men were responsible for congressional hearings, for a massive shake-up within the Army hierarchy, for several courts-martial and convictions. The murderer of Cordovan's son, however, could not be located. There was reason to assume he too ended up an "accident victim."

Stein, despite the fact that he was known to write the truth, however he saw it, despite the fact that several of his recent articles had ripped Police Department personnel and procedures, had carte blanche through Cordovan's office.

He had in the past written in defense of police officers when the action they had taken on the scene was characterized as brutality and racially motivated. He was known to drive a straight line, to write what he found to be fact and to let things take their course from there.

Jim Dunphy sensed the easing of tension, the relaxing of his old friend. It was safe to make a joke that he wouldn't have made five minutes ago.

"So tell me something, Bill," he said. "What if Torres didn't want to 'work liaison' with Stein? What if she went to *her* 'friend'—whoever the hell he is—and said, 'Hey, do something, I don't want to work with this journalist'? You think her friend would be able to cancel out Chief Cordovan?"

Captain O'Connor blinked through his smeary glasses. There were times in a police department, just as in the real world, when it was wiser to just stand mute and leave things alone.

But it did bother him. How the hell did Miranda Torres, from the South Bronx, acquire a rabbi so heavy that no one seemed able to get a line on him?

4

When she was a little girl, her mother used to tell her, "Miranda, speak softly, nice and quiet. When you talk to the sisters in the school, when you talk to the grocery man, when you talk to that nice library lady who lets you take home all those books. It shows respect, Miranda, and they will see you are a good girl."

Her mother thought that all the people she came into contact with were in the position of dispensing or withholding gifts: knowledge, food, information, opportunity. Nothing came about directly because of what Miranda herself had accomplished but because of how people in positions of power viewed her accomplishments.

To a degree, her mother was right.

Miranda could not decide, however, whether it was because of herself and her actions or because of the most totally unanticipated good fortune that she, Miranda Torres, for the first time in her life, had a powerful protector.

When they worked together, Miranda Torres hadn't even known that her partner, Kevin Collins, had a brother. They rarely discussed family. He knew that she was divorced; that her son lived with his father in Florida. He knew that there was a man in her life, some trouble recently, and that she lived in a small, neat apartment in Astoria, Queens. She knew that he was a widower, that his children were grown, married, scattered across the country.

She liked working with Collins. He was very different from the hard-nosed Irish she had encountered before. They were an exceptionally good narcotics team. There was a great deal of the actor in Kevin. He played his various roles with such zest, he seemed to truly *be* whoever he presented himself as.

There were times when Miranda felt a little tense with Kevin, a little worried. There were times when he seemed more than just into his role, more than enthusiastic—times when he seemed so excited, so exuberant, so taken with whatever game he was playing, that he forgot the danger, the realness. He seemed to slip over some invisible line, then quickly pull himself back again, very close to the edge. It had been happening more and more lately, and when she tried to talk to him about it he brushed it off and told her to stay loose and play the game.

Of course it wasn't a game. It was very real, and people got killed. One careless slip was all it took, and Kevin brought them perilously close at times. Close, but Kevin always managed to pull off the caper.

They were a great undercover team. They made contacts, connections, gathered intelligence and floated off. They set things up and drifted. There was enough territory and they took on enough identities to build up an extraordinary record.

Then Kevin began to quiet down. And down and down until he became almost motionless.

At first, Miranda thought he was on something. It seemed unlikely, but always possible. She approached it directly. She had an absolute right—her life was literally in his hands. She couldn't work with a partner on drugs.

No. He was fine. Just down in the dumps. Nothing special. Probably needed a vacation. It would be okay.

They had a long weekend off. Miranda had spent the whole time alone, thinking, trying to come to some decisions; she was at a crossroads. She was at the end of four years with a man she no longer wanted to know or be with, and she had mixed feelings of sadness and relief.

The knock on her door was very soft, almost a scratching sound. The voice wasn't familiar.

"Miranda. Open the door. Please, Miranda. I need help."

It was Kevin. He had never been to her apartment before. He looked terrible. The forty-three-year-old man seemed to have aged twenty years. The look in his eyes was one of terror. He had seen something so horrible that his eyes seemed forever fixed on it: he had seen his own nightmares.

"Take my gun," he said in a grating voice, drawing his .38 snubnose out of its holster and handing it to her, butt first. "Just take it. I came so close. I don't even know why I'm . . . Get Johnny. . . . Or give me the gun. I'll leave. . . . I'll leave." He was agitated, plucking at his clothing, then at his skin, seeming not to realize the difference.

"Kevin, what are you on? Just tell me and I'll get help." She broke open the revolver and dumped the cartridges onto the floor.

He reached for her, his hands bit into her shoulders. "No. Nothing. You don't understand, Miranda. Here. Wait. *Here!*" He dug out a scrap of paper with the name "John" and a telephone number on it. "Call John. Tell him. Miranda, where can I hide from . . . from myself?"

He looked around wildly, pulled open the bathroom door, closed it, found a closet. He crept quietly to the floor of the closet and whispered, "I'll stay here. It'll be all right, won't it?"

"It'll be all right, Kevin. It'll be all right."

52

She dialed the number, and on the second ring a sharp, tight, suspicious voice answered. It sounded like a cop's voice.

"Yes? Who is this?"

"Is this John?"

"Yes. Who is this?"

She wasn't sure how to get into this. She didn't know whom she was talking to or what was wrong with Kevin.

"This is a friend. Of Kevin's."

"You're a friend of Kevin's?"

"Yes."

"Just a minute."

She heard some off-the-phone conversation. The person who had answered was obviously in charge. He dismissed someone and then he got back to her.

"Where are you?"

Again she hesitated. Then she took a deep breath. "Look, I don't know who you are. Or . . ."

"It's all right. I'm Kevin's brother. Kevin Collins, right? That's whom you're calling about, right? Well, tell me where he is and I will get there."

She gave him her address.

"What's his condition?"

He didn't sound surprised when she told him. Miranda had the impression that this was something he had been expecting or had gone through before.

"All right. Wait a minute. Astoria. Where the hell is that, in Brooklyn? No, in Queens, right? How do I get there? From the East Side."

He was at her apartment within twenty-five minutes. When she opened the door and looked at him, she felt a thrill of recognition. She knew she knew him from somewhere, from television, the movies, newspapers, from somewhere.

Then she realized. She had voted for him in the last elec-

53

tion. Kevin's brother was the junior U.S. Senator from the state of New York: John F. Collins.

An aide came with him, and they took Kevin away. The Senator told Miranda, "I'll get back to you, Miranda, as soon as we get Kevin settled in."

"Settled in? Where? What do you mean?"

"I'll explain it later. May I . . . may I come back later? You're entitled to an explanation, and I want to tell you exactly what's going on with Kevin."

"Yes. Yes, I'll wait."

Kevin Collins was a manic-depressive, presently in a severe depressive swing. He had been functioning for years without serious problems, under medication, and in the care of a psychiatrist. For some reason, he had recently stopped all medication. He had first gone through a modified manic cycle, then gradually he had slid down down into a despair he could never describe. It took a great deal of desperate, forced energy and determination for Kevin to go to Miranda. For whatever reason, he could not bring himself to call his brother. The Senator got him into a discreet treatment program upstate, and the word was that Kevin Collins had a drinking problem and was drying out.

The Police Department could understand and accept alcoholism. That was the way things were. Psychiatric problems, on the other hand, could not be admitted, condoned or accepted. Jesus, imagine getting on the witness stand and having some attorney ask you, "Officer, when was your last visit to the nut house and what was your problem? And what does your shrink say about your condition now, you screwball?"

The Senator told Miranda that he and Kevin had the same father, different mothers. No one knew that Detective Kevin Collins was the older half brother of the popular, respected, ambitious Senator. It had been Kevin's decision, and John had respected it. Any smoothing John ever had to do to pro-

54

tect his brother had been done through complicated channels. No one knew the connection.

Except Miranda, now.

The Senator was a chain smoker. He lit a fresh cigarette from the glow of his last. Inhaled deeply, blew the smoke up and away from his face. He was a handsome man, a more carefully sculptured version of his brother. There was something theatrical about him. He was accustomed to being watched closely, and his gestures, his pauses, his quick smile and studied attentiveness were all very effective. He was an energetic man, but suddenly he seemed to run out of effort. He seemed to collapse with weariness, to lose the easy ability to display a certain, particular façade. In Miranda's small neat apartment, exhausted by the emotional demands made on him this night, he realized he had no need to present any particular aspect to this girl. He stubbed out his latest cigarette, and when he looked up at her Miranda was startled by his resemblance to his brother. The Senator had a wounded, vulnerable look.

"Miranda, I am in your debt. Totally."

She sensed his anxiety and told him, "Kevin has been my partner and my friend. We learned to trust and rely on each other. There is a matter of great discretion involved. It is always that way: trust and discretion. I wish only that he becomes healthy again, that he does not suffer the way I saw him suffer tonight. And," she added carefully, "I consider that a private and confidential matter altogether."

"Miranda, the telephone number that my brother had you call. It is unlisted. He is the only one who uses it. It is his direct line to me. I have a system, a feed-in, so that, wherever I am, if that number is activated the fact is revealed to me and I pick up the recorded message and get back to him. Until tonight, Kevin's was the only voice I ever heard on that line." He pulled a business card out of his wallet and wrote

55

the number on the back of it. "I want you to have the same access. If, at any time, for any reason whatsoever, you feel the need of my friendship, call the number. Whenever, Miranda, day or night, twenty-four hours a day. I will return your call. Because I know that *if* you call, it will be a *very serious matter.* And I will be privileged to respond."

She took the card and nodded. Her mouth went dry. She had never been in the presence of such power before. She had never been the recipient of such a gift before. She had never expected anything like this—never.

His voice, his tone, his manner changed. He became crisp, light, as though merely mouthing polite words as he asked her: What were her ambitions? What would she like her life to be like if given a choice? He understood she had a bachelor's from John Jay. Was she interested in perhaps teaching in the field someday?

Law school, she said softly. Surprised at herself. It had been in the back of her mind, never had she said it.

"That's a good thing, to get a law degree. What are you doing about it?"

"Well, not yet. Not for a while. There is time."

"Yes. Right. Well, Miranda, when you decide to apply to law school, let me know." He waved his hand casually. "You leave a message at my *office* for that, and I'll get back to you." He made the distinction between his office number and his private number sharply clear.

"Senator," she said carefully, "I will never use the number you have given me except for some very . . . *very* special reason." She paused, shook her head. "I will *never* use it, but I will know that I *have it* and *can* use it. And that gives me a very special feeling."

He slipped out of his public character again as he took her hand and looked down directly into her eyes.

"Miranda. Thank you. For my brother's life. You use the

56

phone number whenever you feel you must. Without reservations. I promise you, I will be there for you as you were there for my brother."

She had never spoken to him again. About anything.

She was told in her squad office that Kevin Collins had gone on sick leave. After a few weeks, she heard he had put in his papers. Twenty-two years on the job were enough. She had been assigned to office duty, awaiting a new partner and a new assignment.

Her promotion to detective second grade, while deserved, was not really expected. It was handled routinely, with other squad promotions. No one behaved in any particular, special manner toward her. There was the usual squad griping, complaining, gloating, puzzling, gossiping, muttering and congratulating.

Immediately after the promotion ceremony, Miranda was reassigned: to Forest Hills. The land of the decent people, as safe and pleasant and clean and convenient an assignment as anyone could wish. She was near home. Her working hours fell into a regular pattern, so she could begin to think about taking some courses. Prelaw; possibly at St. John's. A whole new opportunity had opened up and she wasn't sure. She was certain, but not certain. She didn't know whom to thank, or whether thanks were appropriate. She studied his card a few times, thought about it. She knew there was a certain protocol in these matters, but she had never been privy to anything like this before. She played it by instinct. She accepted her good fortune without comment. For the time being.

The 112th Precinct in Forest Hills had no relation to previous assignments. It was a different world: what was taken for granted in East Harlem was a big deal in Forest Hills. She sensed the air of excitement, the energy, the newness among her colleagues. This was an unusual case: a murder.

This was not just another dead body, routine assignment, routine questions and routine answers; routine games, blank stares, monotone denials, whispered requests for a deal. This was Forest Hills, and most of the people she was working with—at least the younger police officers—had little or no experience with this kind of violence. The Homicide Squad was another matter—death was their business. But the squad men, even those with a long time on the job, were not familiar on a daily basis with this kind of violence.

Miranda sorted copies of all the reports to which she had access into a neat file. To give to Mr. Mike Stein.

She wondered, absently, what that was all about.

5

They sat in a coffee shop and she wondered how Mike Stein could take such large swallows of the steaming coffee. She sipped her iced tea and watched him.

He had a strong weathered face with heavy dark brows over pale-blue eyes, a strong nose, a wide mouth that seemed on the verge of grinning, if not with amusement, then with secret knowledge. He had the kind of white hair that must have happened very early in his life. It was thick, casually styled, falling over his wide forehead. Despite the heavy frown lines, there was something boyish about him, a sense of expectation, adventure, discovery. He was an attractive man and a smart man and she knew she must be very careful with him. Careful in many ways.

She had read his novel about Korea and the book based on his Pulitzer Prize–winning articles about the murder in Vietnam. There was a hard blunt honesty in his work that was admirable if sometimes alarming. His twice-weekly columns about crime in the city were harsh and cold, generally lacking the passion of his earlier works. At times, however, he took a stand head on against popular opinion, sometimes surprising the Department by his vehement defense or living up to their worst expectations by his attack. When a matter aroused Stein's interest, he went straight for the center of truth, and when he found it he wrote it. It was what Miranda Torres admired about his work.

She was uncertain of Stein, the man across the table from her. All her protective signals were fine-tuned. He was a handsome and a charming man and she did not know what he wanted of her.

Not yet.

"You mad at me because you thought I was brass last night?"

She didn't answer. A slight shrug of her shoulders was all he was going to get. It was inconsequential: a matter of no importance.

She was a real beauty. He had noticed that in all the commotion and horror of the night before. He'd made a quick mental note and now he spent a few moments confirming an impression. Her cinnamon skin was tight and flawless over high cheekbones and a strong, determined chin. She held her head tilted slightly in a provocative position. Or so he felt. There was just a touch of gloss on her lips; she had true black hair and brows; black eyes, really black, the color of midnight. Not a flicker as he examined her. Her eyes went blank: she was accustomed to being stared at. Some guys at the counter were taking quick glances: this kid a model, an actress, a whore? Long, tall, thin, fragile, but tough somehow. Something strong about her, streetwise—an attitude.

The waitress smiled widely as she offered Stein a second cup of coffee, a freebie, then flickered a quick, unpleasant glance at Miranda Torres. Who noticed but ignored it.

"Your captain—O'Connor—tell you I asked that you work with me for a while? On this case?"

"What is it you'd like me to do?"

I would like: oh, Miranda, I would like.

60

"For you to come along with me on certain interviews. And keep me up-to-date on all other aspects of the investigation. A sharing of information. All cleared with your boss. You give me what your people have, I give your people what I have. But no outside press people. An exclusive for as long as possible."

"All right. As long as the captain cleared it."

"Just like that? All right? Not curious about my interest in this case?"

"I presume you're going to tell me. Do you really want to play question–answer? What's the point?"

The softness of her voice was not the respect her mother had advised. It was the street quality, the low deep voice of someone who knows the score.

"Let me ask you something." He placed his elbows on the table, leaned toward her, watched her closely. "What is *your* reaction to what happened last night? Not the murder of the girl. That was pretty routine. The people who watched and did absolutely nothing, how do you feel about *them?*"

"Are you starting with *my* statement, Mr. Stein? What's the phrase—'is this off the record'? Is that what one says?"

Is that what one says? For the first time, there was a slightly musical, slightly Spanish cadence to her speech. A different rhythm; a different knowledge.

"Miranda, everything you say to me, or I to you, will be off the record. So, what do you, personally, think about all those witnesses? How they let the girl bleed to death and didn't do a goddamn thing."

A stillness surrounded her for a moment before she broke her silence. Then, "Why do *you* seem so surprised? You've been around."

"You saw where we were last night, right? In the heart of Middle America?"

"Mr. Stein," Miranda Torres said, "I worked narcotics in

Spanish Harlem for many years. Out on the street. Everyone up there witnesses everything. Everyone knows who's buying, who's selling, who's wheeling and dealing, who's cheating and who's going to get hit. And who will do the hitting. When someone gets wasted, it's never a mystery who did it. It's all out in the open, even if it happened behind closed doors or in a dark alley. You follow? If we ever close out anything, make a collar, make a case, it's because of a good stoolie, or a not-good stoolie who badly needs a favor. Everything is witnessed by everyone, but no one says anything about anything. No matter who gets hurt, the word is, 'Hey, it wasn't me, man, I don't know nothin'.' No one comes forward to help some guy bleeding or some girl convulsing from a bad shot, because no one 'sees' it. 'It ain't me, it ain't happenin', dig?' An almost Hindu attitude, isn't it?"

"Jesus," Stein said. Her last words seemed to take the harshness, the implied agreement, out of what she had been saying. Her voice had had one quality as she told him the street version. She became someone else at the end, someone distanced, bemused, observing without fully understanding and without judging. "I wish I could do an article or two on you."

She shrugged and smiled. "But you can't. It would be unethical."

"Ah. Unethical. Would that bother you very much, Miranda? To be the victim of an unethical action?"

"I would move heaven and earth to preserve what I consider ethical, where I am personally concerned. It is what I live by. You seem so surprised by this thing of last night. That no one came forward to help this girl."

"And you seem so unsurprised. These people are not East Harlem junkies or dealers or street people. Survival is not an issue when you dial 911 from an apartment in Forest Hills. The risk in Harlem is very real, and violence is ac-

62

cepted as a part of everyday life. Everyday death is a fact. Tell me, what was at risk last night on Barclay Street in the heart of civilized Forest Hills in the mysterious and grand borough of Queens?"

"Isn't it possible, Mr. Stein, that each person, each witness, had something, as you say, at risk?"

"At the cost of a girl's life? What's the big deal about dialing 911, giving the information and hanging up? No one asked them to go out and tangle with the guy. Tell me."

"I don't know," she admitted.

"Well, *I want to know.* There might be some surprises. Why do I have the feeling that it would take a lot to surprise you? I would think, Miranda, that you would have strong feelings about this. All these decent white middle-class citizens watching a girl of their own bleed to death."

Quietly, firmly, with sad conviction, Miranda Torres said, "It's all East Harlem, Mr. Stein."

6

It was a ludicrous situation. Miranda and Mike Stein and Mrs. Kirschner sat in the living room and stared at the grotesquely fat poodle. "Pudding" sat on a pink velvet pillow placed on his favorite chair.

"That's his favorite chair," Mrs. Kirschner told them for the third time. Her gray fluffy hairdo was a pretty close duplicate of her dog's. Her eyes were dark and small and beady. So were Pudding's. Her voice was an annoying whine. So was Pudding's.

"He's been through a real trauma, you have to believe me," Mrs. Kirschner assured them. "It was my fault, you see. I never, never miss his ten-o'clock outing, but I've had the flu and last night I fell asleep. I heard him telling me it was time, but I just couldn't get up."

Mike Stein nodded.

Miranda silently stared first at the dog and then at Mrs. Kirschner.

"But I slept through. That's why I took him for his ten-o'clock walk so late." She leaned forward and stuck her face inches from the dog's. There was a mean growling sound. It was hard to tell if it came from the dog or from Mrs. Kirschner.

"What time did you go out, Mrs. Kirschner?"

The woman turned and looked directly at Miranda. Whoever she spoke to received her fullest attention. Even the dog. Especially the dog.

"Well, I would say between maybe about eleven-fifteen and eleven-twenty?"

She checked it out with the dog for a moment, then nodded. "Before eleven-thirty, anyway. Somewhere in there. Wasn't it?" She seemed to be asking the dog. He whined a little.

"And you walked him right past the young woman, who was slumped against the lamppost."

"I never even *saw* the girl, believe me. If I had noticed her, I would have crossed the street. But I was so sleepy. The flu, it really knocks you out. Now, don't you still be angry with Mommy," she instructed the dog.

"Mrs. Kirschner, you're the only person who went anywhere close to this young woman," Mike explained. He leaned forward, put his hand out and waited for the dog's reaction. He withdrew his hand swiftly when the growl was backed up with a wicked smile. The dog was small, but his teeth looked pretty big.

"Now, now, don't shame Mommy," Mrs. Kirschner said. "He's still angry with me."

Mike smiled and held the microphone toward the dog in an attempt to curry favor with his owner.

"Want to say a few words for posterity, Pudding? I guess not. He in a bad mood, Mrs. Kirschner?"

She warmed up to Mike. She told him exactly how it was: she, ashamed and apologetic to the dog, still sleepy and dazed by the flu, walked him toward the end of Barclay Street, his usual spot being around the bend in the tangle of weeds along the fenced-in railroad tracks.

"All of a sudden, Pudding just came to a stop, didn't you, precious? Then I noticed the girl. She was sitting on the sidewalk with her head down, leaning against the street lamppost. I thought, What a shame. Right here on Barclay Street. I thought she was drunk, you see. She certainly *looked* drunk."

"Was she making any noise, was she crying or talking or anything?"

Mrs. Kirschner blinked at Miranda, then spoke to her dog. "Was that lady saying anything to you, Puddy-boy? No, she wasn't, was she. She just sat there and scared my little love, didn't she?"

"How did she scare your dog, Mrs. Kirschner?"

"Why, just by being there, I suppose. But you know, dogs are very clever. Pudding knew more than he was telling. Didn't you?"

Stein had the crazy notion that they were all three of them waiting for the dog to pick up the story.

"What happened was, I told Pudding to come away from that lady. Come away. After all, who knows what a drunken person might do?"

"She wasn't drunk, Mrs. Kirschner."

The woman spoke to the dog. "Well, *we* didn't know that, did we? Or *I* didn't know that. But Pudding has an extra sense about these things. He just edged a little closer to her, sniffed a few times and then he began to shake. I've never in my life seen such a terrible thing. He started to cry and shake—not tremble, mind you, but *shake*. I picked him up and, poor baby, he was so upset he wet all over me. I know *that* upset him, because Pudding is such a nice, clean boy, aren't you?"

The dog never took its eyes off Mrs. Kirschner. Every time

she stopped speaking, it began to whine, but every time she reached out it snapped its teeth at her.

"If I'd been awake at ten for his regular walk, this wouldn't have happened, would it? I mean, she wasn't sitting there at ten, was she?"

"What did you *think* was wrong with this young woman, after you realized she wasn't drunk?" Mike Stein asked.

"I had this poor hysterical shaking sobbing little creature to worry about. As soon as I got him upstairs, I put him down on his pillow and checked him carefully. There was some blood on his front feet." She shuddered. "So I washed him with cool water. And tried to quiet him with a brownie—one of his favorite treats. You can imagine how upset he was when I tell you he wouldn't even touch it!"

"Did you wonder, Mrs. Kirschner," Miranda asked, "what had happened to the girl? After you saw the blood on your dog's front paws, did you wonder about the girl? Why she was bleeding?"

"I want to tell you something, miss. Pudding and I, we are all we have. Each other. I didn't know who that girl was. Still don't know. I had a very disturbed little doggy on my mind, and I did whatever I could to calm him down."

"Was the girl dead or dying when you saw her?"

Mrs. Kirschner waved a hand at Miranda. "Ask Pudding. He went right up to her. He'd know more about it than I would."

They sat again, three human beings staring at a fat gray poodle.

"There were other people all up and down the block," Mrs. Kirschner said. "I saw people at the windows. Any one of them could have helped her. I am the only one in the world who could have helped Pudding. So you tell me, do you think what I did was wrong? To bring my dearest friend back up here, and try to calm him. Was that wrong?"

"Was that *right,* Mrs. Kirschner?" Mike asked.

"You just don't understand, do you? We thought the girl was *drunk.* What should I have done? Now you say she was *dead.* So actually, what *could* I have done?"

And then she gave the line that Mike Stein had been waiting for.

"My responsibility was to my dog, not to some girl sitting on the sidewalk, drunk or dead, or whatever."

7

Anna Grace had worked on the surgical floor of St. John's Hospital. By ten o'clock, the quality of the nighttime noises echoed down the long hallways of the new wing, which was still settling in. Television sets had been turned down, music was contained within individual rooms, patients were dozing, nurses on duty were catching up with paperwork. The nurses' station was quietly busy as charts were checked, medications prepared for delivery. An occasional cough, an occasional blare of noise as radio stations were changed, the rubbery padding of nurses' shoes on waxed floor: typical hospital sounds. The tempo would remain until the next shift of nurses arrived: wide-awake, energetic, prepared for the next eight hours.

Dr. Philomena Ruggiero was a short, round woman with wiry dark hair cropped neatly to frame her face. She acknowledged Miranda's presence with a quick nod, but did not interrupt herself as she dictated facts and information into her recorder. With a wave of her hand, firm, explicit, she indicated a chair, bear-with-me-for-a-moment, and then she put away the recorder, the papers on her desk were slid into a folder, the folder was slipped into an open drawer.

"Now," she said, ready. "You are Detective Torres? How do you do?"

She stood up, leaned across the desk. Her handshake was strong and her eyes went directly to Miranda's, studied, measured, examined. She was making evaluations, entirely aware that Miranda was doing the same thing.

"What is it I can tell you? What is it you want to know about Anna Grace?"

Miranda wanted, first, time of arrival and time of departure Wednesday night. Reason for not staying through her tour of duty. And some general information: what kind of woman was Anna Grace, had she been having difficulty with anyone, any enemies, any love affairs? Any reason, no matter how improbable, why anyone would want to hurt, attack, kill the young nurse.

On Wednesday, August 17, Anna Grace reported for duty at 10 P.M. Her normal tour was midnight to 8 A.M., for this week Anna Grace was putting in two extra hours to accommodate a friend.

"One of the nurses' husband is an entertainer. A singer; he got a gig at the Bottom Line," Dr. Ruggiero said casually. "That's big time; even *I* know that. Janice, Janice Young, wanted to be sure to be in the audience, so Anna covered for her last two hours. The nurses do that. They are a good group here. Very close. They are devastated by what's happened. No, Anna Grace had no enemies. It seems a cliché, what everyone says about a person who's died, but in Anna Grace's case it is the truth. She was one of a kind. A warm, loving, concerned, caring . . ."

Dr. Ruggiero dug her fingers into her eyes, shook her head, sniffed. She shrugged.

"There have been a lot of tears shed around here since we heard what happened. Okay, in answer to your question: no known enemies; no difficulties with anyone; and possibility of a lover, unknown to anyone, no way. Positively no. That girl was so in love with her fireman. They were very special, Detective Torres. A team. Very square kids for the eighties. Engagement; church wedding; didn't live together until it was legal. A religious girl; dedicated nurse; a loving and loved young wife. A wonderful daughter."

Dr. Ruggiero stood up suddenly. Her hands plucked restlessly at the snaps on her white jacket. She moved to the window, turned her back on Miranda, dropped her face to her hands. Just one sob escaped, then she turned around. All her movements were fast, efficient. She leaned her hands on her desk and waited for Miranda's questions.

When Miranda asked why Anna Grace had left the hospital after less than an hour on duty Wednesday night, Dr. Ruggiero changed before her eyes. Her face stiffened, her mouth drew back, her eyes glared and her voice was filled with anger.

"If *I* had been on duty Wednesday night—which I wasn't because my daughter was giving birth out on Long Island—Anna would have spent the night here, in the hospital."

Miranda was surprised. Dr. Ruggiero continued quickly, brushing aside any questions with a wave of her hand.

"She would have spent the night in bed, under observation. Dr. *Ahmed,* who filled in for me, is, in my opinion, *careless.* He floats off on some mystical trips of his own. Forgive me. The relationship between us is very bitter. So accept that as a given. But his carelessness in allowing Anna to leave, *knowing* she was going to drive a car, in her condition—this is a professional observation—was inexcusable."

"I'm sorry, I don't understand. My information is that Anna Grace developed a bad headache and asked to be excused. That she stopped off at her mother's apartment in Forest Hills rather than continue to Little Neck."

"Yes. All right. On the face of the available information, perhaps I'm too hard on Dr. Ahmed. I don't know. What happened to Anna is so terrible, so ironic. Dr. Ahmed says 'it was written.' All right? Get the picture?"

"No. Not really. Why would you have been so concerned about a headache?"

Dr. Ruggiero shot back, "Because the headache was indicative of a possibly serious problem. Because Anna had been having certain symptoms: the headaches, which were increasing; a certain loss of feeling, momentarily, in her arms and legs; a stiffness in her neck; blackouts lasting no more than a few seconds, but which left her confused and out of sync. All right, I'll be fair, Dr. Ahmed didn't know about *all* of these symptoms, but I'm willing to bet that as Anna presented herself Wednesday night, had he been paying attention, had he *really* looked at her . . . No. It wouldn't have mattered, I suppose. . . . You see, our Dr. Ahmed doesn't particularly care for American 'girls.' He probably thought she was just trying to get a night off. I'll bet he never even *attempted* to examine her. And I'll tell you, it would have to be a pretty intense headache for any of our nurses, and particularly Anna, to ask to be relieved after less than an hour on duty. *That* he *should* have known."

"Dr. Ruggiero, what was your concern, about Anna's headaches?"

Dr. Ruggiero raised her hands, palms up. "What difference does it make now? Maybe he's right, that bastard, maybe it is *written* somewhere, but what a rotten entry for Anna. All right, I knew about her symptoms and I was trying to talk her into taking these headaches and the other symptoms more seriously. I wanted to schedule her for a CAT scan. Something was going on."

"What did you think you might find?"

Again, the shrug. What difference now? What difference? Who knows?

"Actually, what does it matter?"

"I'm curious," Miranda admitted.

Dr. Ruggiero sat back, laced her hands over her flat stomach, regarded Miranda thoughtfully.

"Not idle curiosity. I can see that. Well, I was concerned about a brain tumor. I think Anna was concerned, too, but even the most intelligent, knowledgeable person in the world sometimes doesn't really want to know. Maybe yes, maybe no. If yes, maybe operable, maybe not. A lot of maybes, and now it's all just one big so what? Right?"

"Why do you suppose she stopped off in Forest Hills, instead of continuing home?"

"I imagine she realized she was in big trouble, or else she would have continued home to Little Neck. Instead of stopping off in Forest Hills. Where some lunatic rendered the whole thing academic."

Miranda started to speak, then stopped.

Dr. Ruggiero said, "Go ahead. Ask."

"As you say, it's academic. But . . . do you think, if she *had* gotten to her mother's apartment . . . what do you think *might* have happened?"

"If this monster hadn't attacked her, if she had arrived safe and sound in her mother's keeping—there very well might have been a medical emergency for Anna Grace Wednesday night. Maybe a . . . small explosion in the brain. An aneurysm. Something bad was under way." She paused. "I guess it is indeed written. I just don't happen to like the book."

8

As they sat in his car, parked on Metropolitan Avenue, Miranda waited while Mike Stein checked through his notebook, adjusted his tape recorder, then glanced around. This was new territory for him. He wasn't exactly sure where he was. Finally he caught her expression.

"Something on your mind, Detective Torres?"

"Yes. I want to clarify something before we continue."

She ignored his expression, the patronizing, indulgent smile.

"Mr. Stein, you do not have any interest at all in who killed this woman. Am I correct? This is not a matter of any particular interest to you."

"Absolutely not. It doesn't make any difference to me, in any way. The girl is dead. Someone killed her. That happens all the time; every how many minutes? How many every hour? Someone somewhere can quote the numbers. My interest is not in the crime or the victim. My interest is in the witnesses."

"All right. Then let us understand something, between us."

74

Again, his slight smile.

"My job," she told him, "is to find answers. First, who did this thing. Second, why it was done. And, with the knowledge we gain—the police officers on this case—to help see the perpetrator is apprehended. And then turned over to the 'system.' *That's* where my responsibility lies."

"I won't interfere in any way in your investigation, if that's what's on your mind. We won't be working at cross purposes. Is that what you wanted to clarify, or are you curious, Detective Miranda, about my interest in the witnesses exclusively?"

She opened the door on her side of the car, but before she got out into the bright sunshine she turned back to him.

"I have enough things to be curious about, Mr. Stein, without spending time trying to understand *your* motives. Whatever interests you about this death is your business. So long as your interest doesn't get in the way of my doing my job."

Without waiting for his reply, she stepped out of his car and slammed the door.

Mike Stein liked the old-fashioned quality of Metropolitan Avenue. All the buildings were two-story-high taxpayers: shops of all kinds at street level with small apartments upstairs. There were food shops, a grocery store with merchandise arranged somewhat haphazardly, a fish store with a variety of glassy-eyed fish lying on beds of ice in the window.

There was an Italian bakery next to the pharmacy. Its window was stacked high with an assortment of golden loaves, long and narrow, lying against baskets of rolls which were set next to a large aluminum tray overflowing with small seeded cookies and cakes.

There were also craft shops. An upholstery store with a few bolts of faded material in the window. A stained-glass store with a legend in the window: REPAIRS AND ORIGINAL DESIGNS. A carpentry store with the sounds of machinery and activity.

Elderly women with string shopping bags walked along the hot sun-soaked street with younger women who pushed contented children in carriages or strollers. Every child seemed to be chewing or sucking on something. There was an air of timelessness, contentment. An air of innocence.

"Is this really part of Forest Hills?" Stein asked Miranda. "This street is in a time warp of some kind."

"This is a borderline section," Miranda said. She pointed down the street. "Richmond Hill is that way." She turned. "Glendale is that way. But this is still a part of Forest Hills."

"It has a certain charm, doesn't it?"

If he noticed that Miranda was not impressed, he didn't comment.

"I wonder how long ago the shop owners around here installed all these security gates."

At the end of the day the street would look like a deserted prison with steel gates covering storefronts and entrances. As they approached the pharmacy, they were not certain if it was open. The security gate was down and the window and the door were nearly obscured. Mike peered inside, then pushed the button and waited for the release click.

A man in a white jacket came to the door, his head thrust forward, his eyes searching. He looked from Mike to Miranda and hesitated, even though they had telephoned before arriving.

Miranda Torres displayed the detective shield she held in her right hand. The pharmacist nodded, pressed a release and allowed them to enter.

"Can't be too damn careful," he explained. "Come in. I just gotta finish typing up this label. One minute, okay?"

Mike checked out the high tin ceiling, the old-fashioned

globe lights, the built-in wooden shelves behind the counter. Even the small-tiled floor seemed in good condition. The place had to be sixty, seventy years old. There was an elusive, evocative odor he remembered from when he delivered packages for his neighborhood drugstore. The only thing missing was a soda fountain: that would have made it perfect.

"Okay. There. It's ready whenever they pick up." The pharmacist, Edward Farmer, leaned his forearms on the glass-topped counter. He was a large, heavy-boned man, a little sweaty in his stiffly starched jacket. He glanced at the tape recorder which Mike Stein set next to his arms, then at Mike, and shrugged. Sure. It was okay with him.

"Mr. Farmer," Miranda began. "You live at 68-43 Barclay Street in a front apartment? You witnessed what happened last night?"

Mike admired her—no kidding around. She got right to the main event.

Before he could respond, there was a buzzing at the door. Farmer stood up straight, came around the counter, went right up to the door and peered at the woman outside. Then he nodded, held up a finger: just a minute. He got the prescription, released the door, exchanged the prescription for the money, then reactivated the lock.

"Nice, isn't it?" he turned from the door. "Isn't this terrific, all these gates and doors and buzzers? Twenty years ago, when I bought this place, it was so nice. A real neighborhood pharmacy, like a small town. You get to know everyone, everyone knows you. They came here for advice, for reassurance, sometimes when they really couldn't afford a doctor, they just wanted a little reassurance. That was all part of the business. You know, on days like this, in the afternoon when things were slow, shopkeepers used to pull up old kitchen chairs in front of the stores and sit and sun themselves and gossip. This place, this section of Metropolitan

77

Avenue, you know why I bought this place? It was a trip back to my childhood." He caught the expression of Mike's face.

"Right, Mr. Stein? Like the thirties."

"It still has that feeling, Mr. Farmer."

Mr. Farmer had a round shiny face; a dampish fringe of dark hair surrounded his bald skull. There was a peculiar indentation from the front of his head to the back. He returned to the present and stationed himself behind his counter.

"Mr. Farmer," Miranda said, "could we get to last night, on Barclay Street? I'd like you to describe what you saw and heard."

"No," he said. "No. *First* I want to tell you something." He pointed to the dent in his head, ran his forefinger into it. "I wasn't born with this, right? *A bullet did this to me.* In the last few years, this place was held up I don't know how many times. So okay, they took some money, they were disappointed they didn't get much. They took some drugs, no big deal. So last year, a year ago February, I was held up by two *schwarzer* punks with guns."

He glanced at Miranda, raised his eyebrows, shrugged. She didn't react.

"They were a pair of nasty bastards. They took the money, some drugs, but they weren't happy. Not enough loot. So one of them hit me in the mouth with the butt of his gun."

He rubbed the front of his mouth, then lifted his lip to show them. "Cost me a fortune, not to mention the agony to get fixed up. Okay, so I report it to the precinct, and what do they tell me? Same thing all my neighbors up and down the street tell me: Lucky the bum didn't shoot you. You see, you gotta find something to be grateful for, so that's what I was supposed to feel. Gratitude that he didn't shoot me.

"Okay, so a couple of days later, I'm having some soup in the deli across the street, and there is the bum who held me up and knocked out my teeth. He's having a frank and

78

a knish, nice as you please. So I grab him. I'm a big man, right? Someone calls the police and they come and arrest him and we go to the precinct and then we go to court. The whole long miserable day—it was when we had those sleet storms last February, a year ago, so the whole day I spend in court waiting. And what happens? They set a date for pleading and they let him walk out. No bail; nothing. On his own recognizance. He's such an upstanding citizen."

As he got closer to the worst part, the pharmacist's voice went softer and lower. He was asserting a great deal of self-control, but his hands were trembling now. There was a dry clacking sound from his mouth.

"He had a long record, this man. The judge looked it over, pushed it aside and lets this bastard out. So we ride in the same subway car, this bum and me. He sits himself across from me and he keeps staring and smiling. So I get up and I say, listen, you garbage, you stay away from me. You're a little punk and you belong in a sewer somewhere. And while I'm talking, my words hardly make sense." He pointed to his front teeth. "So he thinks it's funny, that I can't talk right. He's laughing and I'm dying and we're both out free to ride the subways.

"The next day, *the next day,* this bastard comes back into my store. No steel gates at the time: just open-door, come-on-in policy. He doesn't say one single word to me—nothing. *He just points a gun at my head and shoots me.*"

Somehow, the bullet skidded across the pharmacist's skull. The gunman turned and walked away. In the hospital, Farmer told the police he knew who his assailant was. The police arrested him. The man provided four witnesses, including a counselor on duty at the time in a city drug-rehab program. They all swore he had spent the entire day with them, never out of their sight.

79

"He walked. He walked again. He shot me in the head and walked. I was laid up for four months; had to learn things all over again, from the shock and . . . what the hell. So you know what the police told me? I mean, they were very sympathetic and they told me in a very nice way, like some friendly advice. Two choices, they said. One, I should get a gun and shoot first, or, two, I should sell my shop—who'd buy it?—and find a safer location. Except, of course, no one has any information as to where the safer location might be."

He ran out of words and breath at the same time. He began to choke and cough, but held up his hand. He disappeared behind the half-wood, half-glass barrier to the section where he made up his prescriptions. A moment later, he was back with a Dixie cup of water.

"I'm okay, I'm okay."

Mike waited. Miranda, her face a mask, her voice steady and calm, said, "It *is* terrible, Mr. Farmer. What happened to you."

"Hey, look," he said, "if I offended you, what I said about this guy . . ."

Miranda's chin went up an inch. "You didn't offend me. It was a terrible experience. *Now.* Tell us what you observed from your window last night on Barclay Street."

"I saw whatever I saw, who can tell from the fourth floor up? Identify the man? Describe him? He wore a light-colored suit and he was dark, that's it, that's all."

He answered each question. He offered no opinion as to what the relationship, if any, of the victim and the assailant might have been. He had no further information. He could be of no help.

Miranda Torres tapped her pen on her notebook, then flipped the pages and made a check against the name of Edward Farmer.

Mike Stein asked him, "Mr. Farmer, why didn't you call 911? Why didn't you at least call *after* the man left?"

The pharmacist spread his arms, shrugged his shoulders. "For what, Mr. Stein? What good would it have done?"

"*You* understand the situation, Mr. Farmer. You're a trained professional, don't *you* understand? The girl died. *She bled to death because no one cared enough to make a phone call.* Her life was in your hands. In the hands of all of you people on Barclay Street, and none of you helped her."

"Look. I didn't call the police because maybe they would catch him and then they would let him go. And maybe he would come after me. Why not? They do whatever they want. *We're* the *prisoners;* locked in our shops, our apartments. *They* roam the streets, *they* own the streets, not us."

"That doesn't answer the question, Mr. Farmer. What happened to you was one thing. That girl, lying on the street, *bleeding to death,* that's another matter. What *did* you do, after the man left the girl alone?"

Edward Farmer traced the path of the bullet wound with a fingertip, from the front of his head to the back. He exhaled a deep, heavy sigh.

"I went back to bed. I went to sleep. I treated it as though it was a nightmare."

9

Miranda was uneasy and uncomfortable with her immediate assignment. She was doing this at the request of Mike Stein. To background a suspect or even a victim was one thing. To background the mother of a murder victim for the exploitative purposes of a journalist was something entirely different. Miranda Torres presented her credentials to a suspicious, tight-lipped assistant supervisor of personnel at the Forest Hills branch of the New York Telephone Company.

"Yes, we heard the terrible news about Mrs. Hynes's daughter, but I'm afraid, Detective . . . er . . . Torres? that I don't understand what it is you want."

The nameplate on the desk identified the tall, thin woman as Mrs. Celia Simpson. She had a pale, dry, bitter face. Her frown lines and downturned mouth were more a matter of expression than of years. This was a not a very happy lady and she squinted hard at Miranda Torres. An intruder, uninvited.

"It is a very sad thing, what happened." For some reason Miranda never understood, in the presence of a certain kind of person or in a particularly stressful stituation her speech patterns shifted: became Spanish. "What we try to do, what we must do, no matter how farfetched or foolish it might seem, is to find out as much as we can about the victim. In hopes that it will lead us to the perpetrator."

"But Mary Hynes wasn't the victim," Mrs. Simpson pointed out shrewdly. There was no fooling this woman.

"Other investigators are doing background work on Mrs. Hynes's daughter, and her husband, and her relatives. It is very unlikely, but we must make no assumptions. There are so many crazies out there."

This Mrs. Simpson knew. "Oh yes. I could tell you about that. I ride the subways every day. Enough said, right?"

"Since Mrs. Grace, the victim, was killed right outside her mother's apartment building, it is natural that we do a background on her mother. Was there anyone who might have been angry at Mrs. Hynes? Angry, crazy, whatever, so that he would try to hurt her by hurting her daughter?" Again, the shrug that said, These days, anything can happen, yes? "And since Mrs. Hynes is a supervisor here—she is your superior here? Yes—well, we have to eliminate the possibility that perhaps some employee who might have had some difficulty with Mrs. Hynes . . . Unlikely, but this is my job. To eliminate all possibilities."

Mrs. Simpson nodded. She glanced around her own small glassed-in compartment and confided to Miranda, because Miranda was so sympathetic and understanding.

"Years ago, what you're saying, my God, you wouldn't even say it, right? But nowadays. Well. In my time, when I started with the phone company, it was, oh, it was wonderful. Right from high school. Like belonging to a club. All *parochial*-school graduates. That way, they knew what kind of girls they were hiring. There was a real status connected to the job. Mrs. Hynes and I, we're old-timers. I guess I shouldn't complain. If they hadn't opened up, I suppose neither of us ever would have been promoted to positions of authority. Only men had these jobs in the old days."

"In the good old days?" Miranda prompted quietly.

Mrs. Simpson frowned. "Maybe we didn't have the kind of opportunities we have today, but we had other compensations. But nowadays, of course, the phone company had to open up and . . ."

"Ah. Yes. I do understand. A similar thing happened in the Police Department. All sorts of people began to enter the ranks."

Mrs. Simpson took a deep breath, and in a soft and confidential voice she told Miranda, "I can see that you are an intelligent girl, not one of these *equal-opportunity* appointments. It must be very hard on someone like you to have to be included with . . . oh, you know what I mean."

Miranda's large black eyes froze and she raised her eyebrows and spoke quietly. "No, please. I'm not sure what it is you mean."

Mrs. Simpson locked her jaws and pulled her arms close around her body. Those eyes focused on hers were burning holes right through her. Mrs. Simpson's short eyelashes batted up and down like frantic bugs trying to get out of a trap.

"I suppose you will want to talk to Alice Peterson. She's Mrs. Hynes's secretary. You'll get on fine with her."

"Is she an equal-opportunity person, too, like myself?"

"Yes, as a matter of fact," Mrs. Simpson said coldly, "she is. She's part of the 'new look' the Telephone Company is obligated by law to adopt. Along with male telephone operators. Along with a lot of other things. Which I'm sure I don't have to tell *you.*"

Miranda impaled her for one more split second and then

dismissed Mrs. Simpson as surely as though the woman had been incinerated.

Alice Peterson was thirty-five years old; heavyset; slow-talking; suspicious; upset. And black.

"Mary Hynes is one of the sweetest, dearest, kindest ladies you will ever meet in your lifetime."

Miranda sipped at her iced tea and glanced around the cafeteria at employees on coffee breaks. A few of them stopped by their table and asked about Mary Hynes.

"She'll be okay, Mary's a fighter, God bless her," Alice Peterson informed them. It sounded more like a prayer than a promise.

"I don't know why you're interested in Mary's background, Detective Torres. What you've told me doesn't make sense, but I guess you've got your job."

Miranda did not respond.

"You want to know about Mary Hynes, about what kind of lady she is. Well, look at me. They think they did us a big favor around here, 'letting' us in. In. That's a laugh. Most of those bitches upstairs are still proud of being the first in their family to be high-school graduates. I have a degree from Hunter and the only reason I'm here and not teaching is that the only assignment I could get was in Harlem, and that's where I'm from, not where I'm going. Understand? Sure you do. I was in the typing pool and I did some work for Mary Hynes, and four years ago, when she got promoted to supervisor of personnel, the first thing she did, her first official act, was to assign me as her secretary. I'm going to tell you, I was cruel. Here was another 'high-school graduate,' you know, going to have a Hunter College girl working for her."

Miranda smiled. She knew the scene. Alice Peterson smiled, too.

"Sometimes you can make some pretty dumb mistakes, right? Well I asked her right out, 'Am I to be the phone company's poster black girl? Will this cover you? Are about ten little black girls not going to be hired as operators because you can point at me?' "

Alice Peterson shook her head. "Oh boy. If you could see the look in Mary's eyes, like I had hit her in the face. She sat looking at me like she never saw me before in her whole life, and do you know what? That lady was crying, tears just running down her face. Which of course made me feel just terrific, to know I'd hurt her so badly. Just that fact alone says it all, doesn't it? Finally she said, 'Alice, I don't know what you're talking about. I asked for you because I think you're the best and I always had the feeling I could rely on you. And,' she said, 'I thought maybe you'd be able to *help* me in a lot of ways.' "

Alice Peterson bit on her lower lip; her eyes were brimming with tears. "Mary is a genuine lady. We have worked together—*for* each other, she says, and it's true—for four years now. Mary Hynes has made the difference for me in this job. And I can't think of one single person in the world who could say an unkind word about her or even be angry at her for anything at all."

The two women had several things in common: both were widows, each had raised a child alone.

"I married a second time when my boy was just a child. Mary didn't make that mistake. She just lived for her girl and it's only recently that . . ." Alice Peterson stopped speaking abruptly. She took off her glasses and began to clean them with a paper napkin.

"Is that why she had the surgery? The plastic surgery? Has she recently met a man?" Miranda asked.

Mrs. Peterson went hostile; her face locked; she jerked her chin up. "I wouldn't know about that. Now you tell me, Detective. Why are you really interested in all of this about Mary Hynes? What has any of it got to do with what happened to Annie?"

"I don't know," Miranda said.

The dark heavy face stiffened and the head shook once in resolve. Miranda would get nothing further from her. She tried anyway.

"Who is Mrs. Hynes's friend? Is he the reason why she had the plastic surgery?"

"Is that any of your business?"

"No. Not really. Not personally," Miranda admitted quickly. Then, slower, more official, "However, I am conducting an investigation into a murder. I have to ask questions that may not seem to connect to anything. Sometimes the most vague, far-out things begin to form a pattern." She shrugged. "Sometimes not. Often, I'm left with a lot of information that doesn't mean anything at all. But it is my job to try to form a picture. You see that, yes?"

Mrs. Peterson put her glasses back on and glared across the table at Miranda. "If you want any information about anything personal in Mary Hynes's life, you can just go and ask Mary Hynes."

"Yes. I think you are probably right," Miranda agreed.

"Well, then. I'm sorry if I came on strong just then. But Mary is a friend, you understand. And . . . what happened to her daughter, it's so terrible. So terrible. Well, I've been here long enough. I've got to get back to my job."

Mrs. Peterson pulled herself away from the table, and Miranda stood up and offered her hand. They exchanged a firm grasp.

"Thank you, Mrs. Peterson. I appreciate your time."

"Yes. Yes, and . . . and . . . that's all."

Miranda watched Mrs. Peterson walk with heavy firm steps across the cafeteria. Then she disconnected the small microphone from the flap of her shoulder bag and wound up the cord around the tape recorder and wondered how much of what she had learned about Mary Hynes was pertinent. To anything at all.

10

Miranda skimmed through the reports that had been com-
piled by the squad members, making sure both she and Stein
had copies of everything available. The witnesses corrobo-
rated one another; they told more or less the same story, if
from various perspectives. Nothing different or new or very
helpful at this point.

Dunphy came out of the captain's office and handed her
a slip of paper.

"Here's the name of the tenant in apartment 6-A, 10-43
Barclay. Arabella Vidales, a stewardess with Avianca. I'll
leave this for you—unless you want to come out to Newark
with me?"

Miranda shook her head. "No, thank you very much."

There had been a rape-murder in Newark, and a suspect
was in custody. Nothing unusual or spectacular except that
the guy had been spending the hours since his capture the
night before informing the Newark homicide cops of ten
other murders he had committed in New Jersey and in New
York.

Including that woman, that nurse, that girl in Forest Hills,
in Queens. Yes, he insisted, he did that one too. God told

him to. He couldn't remember anything at all about it, except that he had done it.

He was a six-foot-six-inch very dark black man dressed in his old high-school basketball uniform. Background check confirmed he was a psycho: in and out of mental institutions for the last ten years. There was no doubt about the rape-murder he *had* committed moments before he was apprehended. There was considerable doubt about the long list of other crimes he was claiming.

There had been four other confessions to the murder of Anna Grace. One from a seventeen-year-old Iranian student who called the police to his apartment on the Columbia campus and lectured them on the politics of murder. Two others from a pair of chronic confessors who had been taken to Bellevue and Kings County, respectively. A fourth from a lunatic calling from some phone booth, demanding that a limousine pick him up and take him to City Hall, where the Mayor was to appear with him for a televised confession. "Don't think the Mayor doesn't know more than he's telling," the hysterical voice informed an unimpressed desk sergeant in mid-Manhattan. "Yeah—yeah, right, pal, " the sergeant said, "you come on in and we'll set it up with the Mayor. He'll be glad to do it. He loves TV interviews." The caller hung up. He wasn't heard from again.

"Okay, Miranda. You come up with anything, leave a message. I'll call in a couple times. How you doing with Stein? Where is he, by the way?"

"He's gone out to talk with the bus driver. A mucho-macho. Mr. Stein thought he would feel more comfortable talking man to man. I don't think he'll come up with anything more than what he said in his initial report." She looked up at Dunphy. "Jim, you aren't worried about anything, are you? About Mr. Stein? He's writing a series of articles about the witnesses. He's not interested in anything but the witnesses."

"I just hope he doesn't scare them off, in the event we find the guy. They've all given a damn good general description. I wouldn't like them to fade away because Mike Stein gives them a hard time."

Miranda thought it very unlikely that they would have an opportunity to make an ID. If this was—as it seemed at this point—a random killing, with nothing to connect victim to murderer, the odds were with the killer. Unless Anna Grace knew her murderer, the possibility of apprehension was bleak.

At first, the personnel director at Avianca was reluctant to answer Miranda's questions on the telephone.

"As you wish," Miranda said, and then, in Spanish, she told him, "You will make it necessary for me to escort you to my office. You will lose time. There would be gossip from your co-workers. It would all end exactly the same. You *will* give me the information. We are questioning nearly two hundred people who live on Barclay Street. Ms. Vidales happens to have an apartment whose windows face the street. So, if you don't want to tell me her working schedule, now, over the phone, please have the information ready for me when I come out to your office. Only, you see, I won't accept it there. I'll insist you come back here with me. Silly, no?"

Ms. Arabella Vidales was on a layover. She was not due to report for a flight until Saturday—tomorrow morning. At 9 A.M. According to the record of the personnel manager at Avianca, Ms. Vidales, along with a group of other stewardesses, rented an apartment at Parker Towers, a large luxury housing complex on Queens Boulevard in Forest Hills. There was nothing to indicate that she had rented an apartment on Barclay Street.

"So you see, you have misinformation, Detective Torres. A group of stewardesses get together, they take large apartments in different cities. The way their schedules are, the apartments are used in rotation, so after all this, you see, it would appear that Arabella Vidales *doesn't* have an apartment on Barclay Street at all. Or we would have this in our records." There was a silence and then the Avianca man's voice went a few pitches higher with suspicion. "And I am curious as to who, exactly, you say you are. And what this is all about."

Miranda never deserted someone who gave her information. There was no point to do what she had seen colleagues do—cut the man off and let him worry. She restated her name, her office phone number. She calmed him. She might need him again.

"So you see, there is nothing to be upset about, yes? Thank you so much, you've made my job easier. Apparently there was a mistake and you have saved me much time, for which I thank you."

That calmed the personnel man down. He became polite and helpful and confidential. He offered her a deal on an eight-day tour of Colombia.

Miranda sat and studied Dunphy's notes. According to the apartment manager on Barclay Street, the two-year lease, signed a year ago, was in the name of Arabella Vidales, employed by Avianca Airlines.

She had no idea what the discrepancy meant.

Parker Towers was literally across the street from the 112th Precinct. It was a huge, circular grouping of buildings that stretched along Yellowstone Boulevard, and that had been built with a carefully tended expanse of grass and shrubbery and garden statues at its center. The lower levels of the twenty-two-story complex contained a variety of professional offices: dentists, doctors whose nameplates suggested various specialties; psychologists; someone who had a small discreet sign designating herself as "Naomi—Fashion Consultant." There was a brightly painted door in the lobby leading to a nursery school. Miranda stood back out of the way as a small mob of screaming sunburned little kids, waving some sort of paper constructions over their heads, threw themselves at a group of young mothers. Miranda smiled and waited until things quieted down.

She went over to the security officer at the desk. She couldn't resist pointing out to him how lax his security was.

"I just walked in, with the group of young mothers. I could have been anybody. I tell you this so that you will maybe get a little angry. But with yourself."

Her criticism was not appreciated, but, before he could answer, Miranda held her gold shield toward him.

"There are a group of stewardesses in this building? What apartment number, please?"

Even with the obvious morning-after look, Miranda would have taken the young woman for a stewardess. There was a perfection just under the sleepy surface: tall, slender but curvaceous, a body that would keep the male passengers interested but not too aroused, a manner that would make even the most tedious flight somewhat pleasant. The smile was automatic. Miranda wondered if the woman was even aware of the fact she was smiling.

"How may I help you?" she asked. Coffee, tea, a pillow? "Come on it, sit, excuse the mess. We've been partying—just a little bit." She glanced toward a partly opened door, excused herself for a moment. "Be right back. Please, get comfortable. This chair—oh, you settle down here, you'll never want to get up."

Miranda sat on the edge of a contoured leather chair and scanned the large room. It was furnished the way a good hotel suite is furnished: everything right, everything expensive, everything coordinated by a decorator accustomed to providing a neutral, bland decor. A room that would not intrude on or interfere with the occupants: comfort without hominess; style without statement. Leathers and suedes and rough-textured fabrics, all pale and colorless. Bright pillows, large and lush, silks and linens. The sweep of window, overlooking Queens Boulevard, was covered with narrow fabric-covered blinds. Someone had come into this huge room, made a quick drawing, gotten immediate approval, and with a snap of the fingers the transformation from empty space to up-to-the-minute décor had been accomplished. There was no trace whatever of any individual occupant.

The place was filled with the residue of an all-night party. From what was left over on various tables, on the shiny bar top and in the dining area of the room, Miranda made a quick calculation: the party had been airline style. There was a collection of small bottles—scotch, gin, vodka, liqueur. She wondered whether they also walked off with little dishes and trays of the pseudo food. Or would it spoil between Kennedy and Forest Hills? Or would anyone notice after a couple of the small bottles?

"There, okay. We got a full house and I've got to check the time. A few girls are working tonight. Is it hot out? We keep the air conditioner way up. So, can I get you anything?" The bright, white smile was automatic; the words were by rote.

"Is Arabella Vidales here? I'd like to speak with her."

"Ara? No. Wait a minute." The girl ducked her head down: the perfectly straight-cut shiny black hair fell over her face. She flung her head up: the hair swung back neatly.

"No. That was last week. Ara . . . no, she isn't here. But I think she *is* on layover. Yes . . . but she isn't here."

"Have you any idea where she is? Where I can find her? I'd like to talk with her."

"Ara? No. I think . . . Could you tell me again, please, what it was you said when you came in? I'm a little groggy. We had a big thing here last night."

"Are you sure Ara wasn't here last night? Could she have been here, if you had a big party, maybe she was here?"

Something in Miranda's voice, her tone or manner, alerted the stewardess. The smile froze, and for the first time she really looked at and saw Miranda.

"You say you are a detective? With who?" She glanced around, her eyes darting about the room. She reached out and palmed a small bottle with a tiny Dewars label.

Miranda leaned forward. "Relax, I don't care about that—or anything like that. I'm with the New York City Police Department. I'm investigating a murder and my job is to interview possible witnesses. That's all; nothing to do with anything else at all."

"You want to talk to Arabella? About a murder? My God, what would she know about a murder?"

"Probably nothing at all. Look, she's just a name on a long list of names. My job is to see each person, to make a check alongside each name, the way you do against a passenger list."

Yes, Arabella Vidales was one of the eight stewardesses who rented the apartment. At any given time, there were usually four women using the apartment. Very rarely, the apartment was empty, but for no more than a night or two. Even more rare were the times when all eight were present at the same time. Their schedules were such that generally one group arrived as the second group left. No, she, Jeanine Feliz, did not work with Arabella. Wait, maybe once or twice, but not as a general thing. Christine Valapo, yes, that's who Ara worked with. They're good friends, and no, Christine Valapo was not in the apartment, either. But yes, Christine had a piece of the apartment.

"But they are on layover," Miranda said. "Have you any idea where they would be, if not here?"

Jeanine Feliz shrugged elaborately, and her smile was not the automatic smile of the stewardess. It was one woman to another.

"Say, the ideal layover is not here, in this apartment. This is a check-in place, no? You can always hope for something better. If nothing better turns up, sometimes we party here. I don't know Ara or Christine too much, but maybe they had plans. Sometimes you get an invitation to a beach house, out on Long Island, you know. There are a lot of nice parties, on Fire Island, the Hamptons, you know? Nice, not wild or anything. People get the wrong idea, but let's face it, you could go crazy spending so much time in an apartment with girls you work with. Maybe they went to Long Island or someplace nice. You know, this Queens, it is . . ." Jeanine rolled her large dark eyes, raised her arched brow and shook her head.

"Does Arabella have any family here, in Queens? Do you know anything about her renting a small apartment here, in Forest Hills?"

"Here. She shares rent here. You mean *another* apartment? No. I wouldn't know. Wait. She was partners last year with Sonyia Garcia. If you would wait for a moment, okay?"

After about ten minutes, Jeanine came back into the living room with a young woman who looked like her twin sister, only sleepier. The forced smile, the pleasant inquiring tilt of her head, the fall of her shiny, tangled but clean black hair, were identical: part of the stewardess uniform.

Arabella Vidales had a younger sister: Maria? Maybe Maria. A college girl. Queens College? No. No, wait: St. John's College. Yes, a Catholic university. Sonyia remembered that last year Ara had rented a small apartment for the girl, somewhere in Forest Hills. Close by, so that she could keep an eye on the girl when she was on layover. Was that helpful information?

Miranda thanked the Avianca stewardesses and left her phone number with them.

"If Arabella turns up, please have her call me. It probably isn't at all important, but when I talk to her I can check her name off my list. We all have our lists, yes?"

It wasn't a long walk, even on a hot afternoon, to Barclay Street. Maybe Miranda would get lucky. She'd check out Arabella Vidales' apartment. Maybe she'd come up with her college-girl sister.

It would seem that Maria Vidales was the only Spanish girl living on Barclay Street, and enough people seemed to have thought she was the victim of last night's attack.

Miranda wondered what Maria, or her sister, would have to say about that. If anything.

It was a waste of time. No one was in the top-floor apartment. Miranda rang a few bells and left her card with neighbors, who promised to call should anyone return to "the Spanish girl's" apartment.

11

Mike Stein had made an intuitive decision to interview Frank Palermo, the bus driver, alone. He had seen him briefly at the murder site and had read his initial police interview.

Frank Palermo led the way into the cool neat interior of his small house. There was a group of women seated around a dining-room table. They were too intent on their activity to look up.

"Hey, Ange," Palermo called, "bring a coupla cold ones into my den."

One of the women sighed loudly, shook her head with annoyance and left the table.

"Here we are," Palermo announced, "my den."

It had once been a garage, and despite the renovations it still looked like a garage.

"So wadda ya think? My game and communications room."

He pointed to various items: a large-screen TV, a VCR, a collection of video games, a music system, the works.

"They got real sophisticated, ya know, not like when they first came out, these video games. I got the games all catalogued to sort of, you know, trace the progress these game-makers come up with. They keep you on your toes, these electronics whizzes. And then, when I wanna relax the old brain"—he pointed with pride—"I just lean back in the old contour chair. Only old thing in the room; like it just fits my body, ya know? And I play an old movie or sometimes just put on an old record, stretch out and reeeelax. Ya know?"

"Yes. I know," Mike said.

There was an impatient kicking at the door. "Open up, Frank, I got my hands full."

He yanked the door open, and his wife put the tray down on the large desk that dominated the wall opposite the entertainment center.

"Watch my papers, jeez, watch it," Palermo told her.

"I didn't touch your papers. There's your beer and your cheese puffs and your pretzels, so that's it, right? I can get back to my own business now?"

He gestured toward his contour chair, but Mike declined with thanks. The hard wooden desk chair was better. He put his tape recorder on the desk, in full view but without mentioning it. That would be up to Palermo. It was his den.

"So," Palermo began after a good gulp of beer. "I seen you looking at my street map up on the wall and the schedule. I'm the coordinator. For the Neighborhood Watch Committee. And treasurer. Not that we have any money; just expenses, like for flashlights and ID cards and things like that."

"Why don't you tell me about it," Mike suggested.

"Yeah, well, I'll tell you." Palermo was serious now. He leaned forward from his contour chair, dangled his beer can between his legs. "What happened in Forest Hills last night would not happen in our neighborhood. We take care of our own. We take care of each other. We don't need to hire some fancy paid security service like they got in some places, like Forest Hills Gardens or Jamaica Estates. We . . ."

"Forest Hills Gardens? You mean they have a private security patrol there? Where the hell were they Wednesday night?"

"Nah, nah. You don't know Queens too good, right?"

"I don't know Queens, period."

"Okay, so here's the story. Forest Hills Gardens is that ritzy section around the Forest Hills Inn. You know where that is? The square?"

"Right. I know the square."

"Okay, so all those streets startin' there, they give 'em names like Deepdene and Greenway Terrace, ya know, all that phony Old English stuff, so anyway, once you're past the Forest Hills Tennis Stadium you're out of the Gardens. In just plain old Forest Hills. Got it?"

"No private security patrol in just plain Forest Hills."

"Right."

Frank Palermo was relaxed and expansive and in a confiding frame of mind. He glanced at the tape recorder, admired it and kept talking.

"See, we provide our own protection here. Eighteen signed-up members."

The Neighborhood Watch Committee kept to a tight schedule. When Palermo worked nights, his next-door neighbor came over to babysit the phone and keep the records. Two cars patrolled in the daytime; four cars at night. No one, not anyone at all, not family friends, friends of the kids, cousins, invited guests, not even clergymen, entered the neighborhood without his presence being recorded and his movements monitored. All this within an eight-block sector of Howard Beach. They maintained close contact with the police department, and no one messed with them. Not anymore. Before they organized, there had been break-ins, muggings, and one very serious beating and attempted rape.

"We got a coupla punks when we first got going. Boy, I'll

tell ya, we was a little too enthusiastic. They were *glad* to see the cops by the time they got here. Word gets around, ya know? They keep clear of us now." He gestured over his shoulder with his thumb. "They move on, keep going until they're clear of this neighborhood."

"Operate in the next neighborhood over, huh?"

"You got it," Palermo said with a grin.

After a few seconds of silence, Mike Stein leaned forward and shook his head. "Terrible, about that poor girl on Barclay Street."

Palermo made a small grunting sound, carefully dropped the empty beer can into the waste-paper basket next to his contour chair. "Jeez," he said.

"So, Frank. What's the story? You see the guy or what?"

Palermo flexed his heavy shoulders and rubbed a rough hand over his face and shook his head.

"Hell, no. I seen the guy, I tell you that guy would be sitting in a cell right now. Or in a hospital. No. What I seen was the girl . . ."

"You saw her staggering around, or what?"

He looked up and said sharply, "*No.* Uh-uh. She was down, sitting there against the lamppost, when I seen her. Hey, you read my statement—what I said at the police station?" His small dark eyes, set close together at the bridge of his large nose, focused on Stein. Mike nodded.

"Lissen, can I level with you?"

"Absolutely."

Palermo glanced around, checked the walls, then back to Stein. "They let that girl sit there and bleed to death, ya know?"

"That's how I figure it, too."

"What kind of people would do a thing like that?"

"I don't know."

"You know how long my run is from Barclay Street to

Metropolitan and back again? Oh, yeah, you don't know the neighborhood. So Metropolitan is the turnaround, the lay-over; then I head back over my route the opposite way, right?"

"Right."

"So okay, a good fifteen minutes from Barclay to Metro. God alone knows how long she was there before I come along."

"A while, I'd guess. She wasn't screaming or crying out when you saw her, right?"

Palermo shook his head.

"No, I mean the *first* time. She was staggering. A lot of people thought she was drunk."

"Hell, they knew she wasn't drunk. The kid was crying. Like she was—" Palermo tensed; his large face froze for a moment. He licked his thin lips and moved his head slightly as though to focus better on Stein.

Stein's voice was reasonable and reassuring: a pal. "Hey, Frank, look. The whole thing took place over a certain time period, right? So, if it takes you fifteen, twenty minutes to pass Barclay Street, go to your turnaround and come back to Barclay Street, it figures, right? Hell, look, the first time, whatever the hell was going on at the moment, you were just driving the bus, doing your job. You weren't in a position to find out what was going on, right? It must have been a real surprise to see the girl *still* sitting there, against the lamppost, and no one around her. That must have really knocked the hell outa you."

Palermo hunched forward, and his tone was confiding. "Look, I'm not even sure I actually seen anything the first time, ya know? I mean, so you pass by some girl and she looks a little drunk, ya know? So she's yelling a little, right? Hell, she's right outside all these buildings, all these people

102

can see her and hear her same as me, and I'm just passing through."

"The guy was gone by then?"

"Like I tole ya, if I seen him, he'd be in a lotta trouble right now."

"But the girl was in a lot of trouble when you first saw her, right?"

The bus driver stood up with some difficulty. It was hard to jump up from a contour chair.

"Hey, listen, I thought you was a nice guy. I read your column sometimes, how you keep track of all the crimes in New York City and all, and I thought you was a good guy."

"I am a good guy, Frank."

"Yeah? Well, what I told you, everything what I told you, that's . . . 'privileged information,' right? Like between a doctor and a patient or something. I mean, I'm just trying to be helpful. I told the cops all I know, and that's it."

"Why didn't you stop and help the girl the first time you saw her, Frank? When she was still alive. She was screaming and staggering and bleeding. Why didn't you help her then, Frank?"

"*Me?* I was the only one who *did* stop, never mind *when.* In all that time, nobody from her block helped her, not even to call the cops. If it hadn't been for me, that girl's body would still be propped up there and they'd ignore it, ya know?"

"She bled to death because no one helped her, Frank. You might have saved her life."

"Me? Me? I might have saved her life? Me? Hell, I had a schedule to keep. I was just passing through."

12

She accepted his casual invitation to supper after a long and tiring day. "There are some pretty good restaurants in this neighborhood. Greek, Korean, Cuban, Italian, Chinese—"

He grabbed her arm and led her toward his car. "It's Friday night. There's only one place to eat on Friday night. First, I have to stop off at my house, check in with one of my kids. It'll take about a minute and a half, and then you'll see where we eat on Friday nights."

He double-parked in front of a wide brick-and-limestone town house on Seventy-third Street off Fifth Avenue. He inserted a key into the lock in a heavy grilled door, stepped aside for her to enter the narrow marble-floored vestibule guarded by another door: a heavy oak with a wide viewing panel.

"This one no one could slip. Guy I know, used to be a burglar. Now he's consultant to a security company. This lock is his invention."

Mike worked several heavy odd-shaped keys in a particular sequence, then pushed the door open onto a magnificent interior.

The huge room was paneled in rich dark wood from floor

to shoulder height; from there to the high beamed ceiling it was covered by an expensive brocade. There were paintings on the wall in heavy frames, lit by brass lamps which made them look old and valuable and important. Set among them, there were modern glass-covered posters which you could buy for under fifty dollars in any of a hundred places. There were chairs and sofas and tables: it was a room without definition so far as Miranda could determine. To one side, a wide curved staircase; directly ahead was a cagelike elevator, big enough for two or three people. The sliding grill door was brass and gleaming.

"Your apartment is in this building?" Miranda asked.

"Well, sort of. Wait a minute." He stood still, listening. Voices could be heard from somewhere upstairs.

He went to the elevator shaft and yelled, "Hey. Dennis! That you, kid?"

A young man's voice answered, "Yo, Pop. Up here. Third floor."

Mike led her to a library off the main entrance. "Here, Miranda. Make yourself comfortable. This'll take about four minutes. If anybody looks in on you, just wave. It'll be one of my kids. Or one of their friends. There's a gang using the house this week. Relax." His hand swept the room. "Enjoy."

He caught the expression of enchantment that transfixed her face into the unguarded pleasure a child might show.

Miranda moved slowly into the most wonderful room she had ever seen in her life. The walls were bookcases, floor to ceiling, continuing around doorways and windows, every inch available for books. There were magazines piled on library tables, books, periodicals, manuscripts. There was a huge, beautiful partners' desk set into the wide alcove topped by a triple stained-glass window that went from shoulder height to the high ceiling. The furniture was English: leather couches and chintz-covered old comfortable lived-in easy chairs, all with tables near to hand, lit by brass lamps.

But it was the books that drew Miranda, intoxicated her, transfigured her. She stood in awe; reached out, dropped her hand, shook her head with pleasure. Her eyes swept the titles: classics, old and leatherbound in matching sets or first editions; textbooks, encyclopedias, history, art, politics. And hundreds of current books, best-sellers, novels, self-help books, cheap romances; even shelves of paperbacks. He had collections of everything.

He watched her for a moment before he spoke. "Help yourself," he told her. "I mean it. It's a standard offer to any true book lover who gets invited into this room. The first editions you get to borrow, anything else you want you keep. So?"

"This is *your* room?"

"This is *mainly* my room. My kids have been known to use it. And my wife."

"Your wife?"

"Ex-wife. Mother of my four firstborn. This is her house."

"Her house? And you live here? And she lives here, too, and your . . . four children live here, all of you here?"

As he encouraged her to make a collection of books, he explained: At twenty-one, he had married a college classmate whose family owned one of the most successful chains of department stores in the country. The founding grandfather had been a Russian immigrant who had believed in real estate.

"This town house has been in the family since it was built. Turn of the century. The old man had four daughters; each one was left a piece of property with the proviso that it be kept in the family. My wife was an only child. This house, someday, will go to my kids. And their kids. It's practically a commune. We all use it."

"And you have four children?"

"Five. My youngest son you might call my forti-eth-birthday celebration." Mike shook his head, and his smile was sad. "My wife and I had been leading separate lives for a long time. She's a very active VP in the family business and we decided on a friendly divorce, meaning no significant changes in lifestyle. Until one of us got married. She did first, so she relocated to a condo in midtown. But she keeps a stu-dio on the fifth floor. Our kids are all grown. The oldest is a GP in Vermont. And the father of my three granddaugh-ters."

"You are a grandfather?"

He ran his fingers through his thick white hair and hunched forward. "I am a grandfather. Had no say in the matter. My kids come from a heritage of kids. So this house is usually pretty busy. Two are still in college. Right now, my son-the-actor is in from the coast shooting New York background for a TV series. He's staying here along with his girlfriend and a couple of the crew members. Beats a hotel."

"And your youngest son? What did you say—your forti-eth-birthday celebration?"

"I did two things to celebrate turning forty: first, I married the scriptwriter who was helping me turn my novel into a movie; and I fathered my last-born. Who is rapidly ap-proaching ten. And who is living with his Vermont brother while *his* mother copes with turning thirty by marrying a Hollywood stuntman turned producer four years younger than she is." He suddenly realized that she hadn't been col-lecting or selecting books. "Hey, c'mon, Miranda. You picked out only three so far."

He reached out, ran his finger along titles, slid some out, stacked them on his desk. He picked a book off the shelf, turned the cover toward her. It was a copy of his Korean War novel.

She reached for the book, held it, smiled and handed it back to Stein.

"I have a copy of your novel, Mr. Stein. I read it when I was in high school. And I've reread it—parts of it—over the years. It is very fine. I also have a copy of your book about the murder of Chief Cordovan's son. You are a very good writer."

He was surprised to realize how important her approval was to him. "Well. How about that? Well. Hey, are you going to just stand there or are you going to grab some books? Here, let's put them into this satchel. It belongs to somebody in the house. Anything around here is up for grabs."

He loaded the satchel with books and slung it over his shoulder. "Come on, kid. It's about that time. And it's Friday. So let's go eat.

The restaurant wasn't what she expected, and Miranda felt a slight letdown followed by a certain relief. It was a somewhat shabby, rundown, overcrowded, extremely noisy and smoky establishment in Little Italy. Mike pulled her through a series of small, dark, narrow rooms.

"We go to the back, a private room," he said.

He stopped at the bar, which was oddly located in the rear of the restaurant. From the street, passersby wouldn't know that Pisani's had a bar. It was a small, dark, narrow enclave backed by a dark-blue mirror which cast sinister shadows on the faces of the men who stood, in groups of two or three, holding drinks but not drinking. Miranda's observations were fast and sharp and concise. These were men who wore dark glasses in dark rooms, who wore expensive, custom-made clothing that fit them just slightly off, as though the tailor could not quite disguise what they were. The haircuts were standardized razor-cut; even the toupées were blow-dried. They smoked cigars, long and expensive, and their pinkies glittered as the mirrored light hit the rings which seemed part of their fingers. They were men who never looked at the person to whom they spoke. Restlessly, they checked the room so as not to miss anything.

Several of them embraced Mike Stein in a standard brotherly hug of affection, but the attention went directly to Miranda. She didn't have to hear them. The words whispered into his ear would be: Who's the broad?

He introduced her and she was greeted with greatly exaggerated and somewhat clumsy courtesy. She drew back, wary and tense.

"Hey," Stein told her, gently pushing her along to the next room, "we're just passing through. They're part of the atmosphere."

The greetings here, in the last room, which had a half-wall revealing the busy kitchen, were far more enthusiastic. The embraces were of long-lost friends, survivors of wars and battles who had given up hope of finding each other.

It was a weekly ritual.

He seated her at the end of a long wooden table filled with people she couldn't quite make out: cop faces; a huddling of loud, explosive storytellers who apparently were accustomed to audiences and resented anyone not leaning forward to listen; a couple of guys on the make talking rapidly to a couple of women who were deciding if they were worthwhile.

And then, scattered throughout the crowded room, a suddenly familiar face: a genuine movie star, eating enthusiastically from a heaping plate of pasta, nodding, accepting the shoulder pat, the whispered words. She took Mike at his word: "We don't have to order, the food will arrive and it will be wonderful and I'll be right back."

Miranda realized that she was in a special room with special people. From time to time, others, tourists out for the night, birthday celebrants who were noisily serenaded in the outer rooms, peeked in and watched, pointed, waved, took a couple of flashsnaps until a guy with dark glasses told them not to. There were faces she recognized and was surprised by: a State Supreme Court judge, handsome and glamorous, stopping his fork midway between his plate and his mouth, politely listening to something being put to him by a man hovering at his shoulder. A cop—no, an actor who played a cop on TV—standing, arm around a beautiful woman but giving his fullest attention to another woman, whose eyes stayed on his mouth as they spoke. Coming toward her, Mike, leading the way for a tall, thin angry woman in her forties, wild hair, dressed in rock-star chic that didn't do a thing for her that was flattering. She was digging her fingers into the arm of her husband, who was trying to hug another man he hadn't seen since they'd parted in L.A. two days ago.

Large platters of food were placed family style down the center of the long table, and Miranda took a sampling of everything, but mostly she watched the action and the exchanges all around her.

People approached the table, identified quickly by Mike as to their occupation. She exchanged handshakes with a nightclub comic, a prosecutor in the U.S. Attorney's Office, a vice-president of a major motion picture producing corporation, a master thief turned lecturer—his topic: how to protect your home from thieves.

An incredibly handsome older man, tall, erect, with a dramatic mane of yellowish-gray hair and glitteringly bright dark eyes, approached, exchanged hugs with Mike, then took Miranda's hand. In a casual, for him natural, courtly, flattering gesture, he brushed his lips over the back of her hand. Miranda was stunned by her own reaction: she felt thrilled, intensely feminine. And then he pressed the back of his large, slightly shaking hand to the side of her face, slid it down along her cheek to her chin.

"Ah," he whispered with obvious pleasure. "This is a face. This has bones and character and mystery. You are a beautiful woman, my dear. That rarity of nature: the true beauty. Enjoy your life, my child."

He brushed his dry lips again, across the back of her hand, saluted Mike with a nod and left.

"He was so beautiful, that old gentleman," Miranda said.

He was among the most famous of all international film producer-directors, and Miranda, who had not heard his name in all the noise of the dynamic high-level conversations around them and the rattling plates and shouting from the kitchen, was stunned.

"Oh, but, Mr. Stein. He is a very eminent—oh, he is so gifted. I know his work, I admire . . . Oh, and I did not say anything to him. I did not realize."

"It's okay," Mike told her. "He's practically deaf and he disconnects his hearing aid in noisy places. I think he got a message from you, Miranda. The look on your face. Are you enjoying this? Are you having fun?"

"This is all . . . somewhat overwhelming. All these beautiful people. I've never seen such people in real life—just on the television or movie screens." She shrugged. "For a girl from the Bronx, it is a bit much."

Mike took her hand and pressed it hard against his mouth. "I'll tell you a secret, kid. All of the people here are from the Bronx. Or Flatbush. Or the Lower East Side. We all started from the same place. That's why we all get along together. That's why we all need to touch base with each other. No matter where they live or work now, when these guys are in New York on Friday night they touch base here. It's a trip back to the old neighborhood. It gives them a touch of stability. And reassurance."

"Reassurance? These people are all so very far from where they began. They are so successful and important. What reassurance do they need?"

"Hey, Miranda," Stein said softly, glancing around at the smiling, loud-talking, back slapping, hugging successful leaders of various industries. "Remember you said to me, 'It's all East Harlem.' Well, let me tell you, kid: we're all from the Bronx."

13

Miranda ate her yogurt right from the container, being careful not to drip any on the collection of reports spread out on her couch. She had intended to spend a quiet evening at home, trying to put into some semblance of order all the information that was being collected.

There were two separate categories in the case: the victim; the culprit. The background information on Anna Grace, from her birth in Brooklyn through her education in Brooklyn, Queens and Manhattan, her marriage in Queens and her employment record, was a collection of officially available information that told nothing about the personality of the murdered woman.

Miranda noted the list of people to be interviewed in a search for the actual Anna Grace. It was not to be accepted at face value that the victim was a wonderful, perfect, blemish-free angel without an enemy in the world. Very few people have an unkind word to say about a young and vibrant woman who was brutally murdered. But Miranda knew that many people had secrets, even from those closest and dearest to them. Anna Grace was now a public figure, having been publicly murdered. It was valid to violate the deepest privacy she had maintained in her life. The possibility had to be faced and encountered and clarified one way or another: was there any connection between Anna Grace and her murderer?

The search for the culprit, rightly or not, had to begin with his act of violence against Anna Grace. From what the witnesses had stated—almost without exception—the man had yelled and berated Anna as he stabbed and struck her. This was puzzling. It was unusual, and possibly revealing, that her murderer had called her names, thief-cheat-liar-whore-cunt, that among the words he had called out to his victim seemed to be a message, an indication of retaliation of some sort: There! You see! Cheat! You see!

Had the words been intended, specifically, for Anna Grace? Had they been intended for some other woman, specifically, for whom Anna had been mistaken? Or had the murderer's words been directed toward any female, any woman substituting for the particular or fulfilling the general target of hostility seething within this man?

Quickly and efficiently, Miranda sorted the growing pile of reports: copy for herself, copy for the squad, copy for Mike Stein. In the time they had spent together, at his house and at Pisani's, they hadn't discussed the case or exchanged information. It had been a time off, and yet it had had a specific purpose. He had been sizing her up, and she realized he was anxious that she be impressed with him. He was surprised and, she thought, delighted that she was familiar with his work.

His novel was strong and bitter and impressive, written with great drive and energy. His book based on his articles about the murder in Vietnam was blunt and brutal, written at a time when it took great courage to reveal such controversial events. But his columns on crime in New York lacked the passion and drive of his other work. His twice-weekly articles reflected his cynicism, his matter-of-fact

114

capitulation to the inevitability of the downward slide of city life.

She was aware, from the first moment he had encountered her at the crime scene, that this man was taken by the case in a very dynamic way. His interest was far from the pedestrian, monotone repetition of familiar crime-scene facts. He seemed to care nothing about the victim or about the murderer, nor, as Captain O'Connor might have feared, about the police.

Mike Stein was turned on in some strange but very evident way by the witnesses to the death of Anna Grace.

Miranda did not give him copies of everything she had, only those reports to which he had been declared officially entitled. She kept her own notes, comments, private data which she would not share with him or with anyone else. Not at this point.

She was surprised when he called, as if by thinking of him she had willed him to think of her. But it was business.

"I know it's Saturday night," Stein said, "and I hope I'm not interrupting anything, but I just managed to pin down this Mrs. Rolland and her husband. I know your people got a statement from her, but I'd like to talk to them myself. She agreed if we're there by eight—something to do with a TV movie they want to see."

"Mr. Stein," she said, "I am not a teenager. Saturday night is not by definition my big night. I have worked more Saturdays, Sundays, holidays than I care to remember. I'll meet you on Barclay Street. There are some reports I have and—"

"I'll pick you up in twenty minutes. That way you can listen to the tape of my interview with this bus driver, Palermo."

He speeded up the tape until the part where the two men had gotten down to business: Mike Stein's voice soft, easy, good guy, trust me, and Palermo relaxing and telling Stein whatever he wanted to know. Stein and Miranda sat in his car on Barclay Street and let the tape run out.

"So. What do you think of this guy—finishing his route while the girl sat there and bled to death. What the hell do you make of a guy like that?"

Miranda shrugged. "What would you have me say, Mr. Stein?"

"How about what you feel? Tell me what you feel when you hear this guy, picture him swinging that bus right past the girl and—"

"I think that if we don't go up to the Rollands' apartment, we might cause them to miss their TV program. Yes?"

The door opened so abruptly after their first touch on the doorbell that it seemed the woman, Mrs. Rolland, had been standing just inside, waiting for them.

"Well. Right on time. Practically," she said. "Come on in, then."

Miranda tripped over a pair of shiny brown men's shoes which had been set next to a pair of freshly whitened women's shoes, on one side of the long narrow hallway.

"Not to worry," Mrs. Rolland said in an annoyed tone. She indicated that they should continue to the living room while she just stopped for a moment and lined up the shoes the way they were supposed to be lined up.

They stepped carefully on the heavy plastic path that had been laid out over the immaculate light-gray wall-to-wall carpet. Follow the yellow brick road.

The room had the unlived-in coldness of a photograph in a moderate-priced supermarket-sold magazine: proof that you could live nicely on a tight budget; it might be inexpensive, but it could be shiny and well preserved, clean and protected. In the dim haze from the lamps in the room, all surfaces glowed from vigorous application of furniture polish. There were little handmade doilies under the lamps. All the lampshades were just as fresh and clean inside their cellophane wrappings as on the day they were bought. There were heavy custom-made clear plastic slipcovers over most of the upholstered furniture. The recliner chair was slipcovered with a floral fabric, and extra material was set at places of greatest anticipated wear. There was a neatly crocheted rectangle where the head might rest should anyone be daring enough to touch head to chair. It seemed unlikely.

A TV magazine from the *Sunday News* had been slipped under a spotless glass ashtray on the cocktail table. There were no books, newspapers or magazines anywhere.

Mike sat on the fabric-covered chair that was offered to him. It was too damn hot to even think about sitting on heavy plastic, custom-made or not. The humming of an air conditioner came from the bedroom. The two living-room windows, fronting on Barclay Street, were hidden behind heavyweight drapery. The air was oppressively stale, with lingering whiffs of lemony cleaning oils and spray-ones and paste-up room deodorizers.

Mrs. Rolland jerked her thumb at Miranda, her eyes on Mike Stein. "Who's she?"

"I'm sorry. This is Detective Miranda Torres."

Mr. Rolland murmured something; Mrs. Rolland blinked, then turned her attention back to Mike.

Miranda regained the blank, polite expression that in some strange way rendered her nearly invisible.

"As I told you on the telephone," Mrs. Rolland told him, "you're lucky we're here at all. We're still on vacation, both of us, from our jobs. Had to cut the vacation short by three days." She jutted her chin at her husband but didn't look at him. "His father. Heart attack. Third one."

"I'm sorry," Mike offered. Mrs. Rolland shrugged. She seemed to be waiting for an obvious question. He guessed right. "Where did you go for your vacation?"

"Disney World. Down to Florida." Her expression changed. She was beaming.

"Second time we've been there," Mr. Rolland added. His wife shot him a quick look and Mr. Rolland didn't say another word.

"Well, would you like something cool to drink?" She poked her husband with her elbow. "Get them some of that lemonade I made."

"No, thank you," Mike said. Miranda echoed him.

Mr. Rolland didn't know what to do. He looked from Mike to his wife, started to rise, sank back, tried again.

"Oh, for Pete's sake, sit down. You heard him say no, didn't you?"

Mr. Rolland sat down.

Mrs. Rolland was tall, long-boned and thin with the look of a woman who had once been tremendously fat. She sat in a certain way, held her arms across her body as though expecting to find more flesh to hide than was there. She had a haggard face with empty folds of skin at the neck, surprisingly fine clear skin, and eyes magnified by the thick lenses of her rimless glasses. Perhaps she would look kinder with a few more pounds of flesh; being thin gave her a mean, pinched look. She pursed her lips a few times and checked her husband to make sure he wasn't out of line in any way.

Mr. Rolland looked like a man who had been skinny all his life. He had the gawky look of a schoolboy, the kind who stayed on the edges of the playing field, trying not to get in anyone's way, praying the action didn't reach the backfield. When his wife shifted slightly, he turned to her apologetically, then pulled himself away to make more room. Under her breath, in a low, harsh voice which carried, Mrs. Rolland said to her husband, "Oh, for Pete's sake, you dummy, sit still."

Mike set up his tape recorder, asking permission to place it on the cocktail table. "This okay here?"

"Yes, yes." She watched with worried eyes.

"Thank you very much for this cooperation." He spoke quickly and softly into the microphone, naming the persons present, time, place, date. "Just ignore this thing. It's very sensitive and can pick up from anywhere in the room. Now. Your living-room windows face on Barclay Street?"

Mrs. Rolland got up from the couch the way a severely obese person would.

"Come see for yourself." She moved the heavy light-colored drapes to one side, yanked up the venetian blind and showed him her spotless, shining view onto Barclay Street. The windows were directly above the lamppost where Anna Grace had sat dying. The Rollands had second-story center seats to the event.

"You really had a good view of what went on."

"Oh yes. Oh yes. Better than some of those down the block, who claim to have seen so much, I'll tell you. And I'll tell you this too. This kind of thing—" she waved her hand toward the window, dropped the blind back into place, adjusted the drapes—"well, back home, where I come from, well, there just aren't any of these . . . these street kinds of people lurking around waiting to just pounce on people. Never used to be in good old Forest Hills either, right, Fred?"

"Well, no, really. But . . ."

Mrs. Rolland glared at him. "Fred is *from* Forest Hills. Born and bred. And his mother and father before him. Regular natives, that's all I ever heard, Forest Hills, Forest Hills. Of course, *they* live in the Gardens, which *is* another world." She jutted her chin toward the windows. "A few blocks, but another world. And they'll leave their house to his younger

119

brother. Because his brother has four children. *That* qualifies *him* for the house. Well, never mind all that," she said, as though someone else had brought up the subject. "That's water under the bridge, isn't it? But where *I* come from, those people, street muggers and such . . . Well, enough said."

"Where *are* you from, Mrs. Rolland?"

She turned to Miranda and considered carefully, then, as though admitting some deep and wonderful truth, something that would give her, among them, status, "I was born and raised in Kansas City, Kansas. That's where *my* people still are. Fred had his job here, you see, all set when he got out of the Army. And *his* roots were here and that house in the Gardens. He *is* the oldest son. For all the good that ever did us."

She resettled herself on the couch, and Fred moved away carefully.

"You had a clear view of everything that happened Wednesday night?" Miranda asked.

Mrs. Rolland leaned forward. She began to speak rapidly, and now and then, as she slowed down, Mr. Rolland tentatively interjected bits and pieces of information and observation.

They had been watching a movie on their VHS recorder. They heard a loud sound, like a scream, but they weren't too sure. They turned the movie off for a minute; it was time for some lemonade anyway. They heard the sound again, so Fred went to the window, pushed the drapes aside, pulled up the blinds and opened the window.

"Lets out the cool air, you know, so we keep it closed tight. It's amazing how cool the whole apartment is, with just the bedroom air conditioner."

"For Pete's sake, Fred, they're not interested in any of

120

that. Well, Fred couldn't make sense at all of what was going on down there. 'I'm not sure what it is I'm looking at.' That's *exactly* what he said." She shot her husband a scornful look. "Now, how can you look at something and not be sure what it is you're looking at, I'd like to know. So I looked, and I can tell you, it looked pretty clear-cut to me."

"Well, yes, I guess so," Fred said.

"Oh, you guess so." She leaned over and pinched her husband's arm. Not hard, not meanly, just a pinch, something between them. Something was going on: some signals; something personal. Miranda was as still and calm as a statue, but there was an awareness in her lack of motion. She sensed an elusive something between Mr. and Mrs. Rolland.

"What did you see, Mrs. Rolland?" Miranda asked.

"Well, there they were. This girl. Small thing in a light-colored dress, sleeveless, and this man, seemed to be wearing a white suit or light colored suit, maybe seersucker or something, or silk maybe. I don't know. At first, it looked like . . . they were . . . now, I know this will sound funny." She smiled, put her hand over her mouth, then, "Like they were *dancing.*"

"Funny sort of dancing, I said to Flora," Mr. Rolland volunteered. "Seemed to me the girl was trying to pull away."

"Oh, sure, *now* it seems that she was trying to pull away, but that wasn't what you thought then, and you *know* it."

Mr. Rolland made a strange sound. Deep in his throat, he was either coughing or laughing. It was hard to tell. "Well, it looked like she was pulling away from him and then it looked like, at one point, she . . . grabbed hold of him. You know."

"Grabbed hold of him?"

"Well, it seemed that way," Mrs. Rolland said. "In a very personal way, if you take my meaning. She sort of reached down and . . ." The woman covered her mouth with a long red hand and shrugged. "Funny what it looked like from up here. When you realize what it really was. I guess she was trying to fight him off, to hurt him, of course, but it sure seemed like the those two were sort of, well . . ."

"Playing some sort of game. That's what it seemed like," Mr. Rolland said with conviction.

There was an abrupt silence. The Rollands glanced at each other and then at Mike and then at Miranda.

"You mean," Miranda asked, "it seemed to you that this was some kind of mutual sexual encounter? That the woman was taking part, willingly, in some sort of game?"

Mrs. Rolland reached over and pinched her husband's arm and he smiled.

"Well," he said, "it was a little hard to tell from up here."

"But . . . did you hear the woman scream? Did you hear what the man was saying?" Miranda asked.

Mrs. Rolland shrugged and smiled. "Oh, well, it sounded like a whole lot of gibberish to us, of course. I guess you'd know, being it was *your* language, but we only understand English. Been good enough for us up to now, so I guess we just aren't going to bother to learn Spanish in order to read directions in the subway and voter information and such. They're printing it all up in Spanish, you know. I guess that makes it easier for you people," she said to Miranda.

"Yes. *Gracias.* It makes it easier for my people. Your people are very kind to my people."

Her voice was so flat, her face so expressionless, that Mrs. Rolland was at a loss. She nodded a few times, then smiled, not sure of herself.

"At what point, Mrs. Rolland," Mike said, getting her attention before Miranda might say anything else, "at what point did you think something *was wrong?* At what point did it seem that the young woman was crying out for help? Or that she was in trouble? Surely, her screaming must have told you that something was wrong?"

The Rollands exchanged glances. Mr. Rolland shrugged and deferred to his wife.

"Well, we just didn't watch anymore. I mean, it just seemed that these two people were . . . well, it didn't seem our business, you know. We didn't know, of course, that the girl was in trouble. Who knows nowadays? Look, these people, those people Wednesday night, maybe it was what we thought at first and then something went wrong. It could have been, you know. People nowadays . . ."

Miranda stood up and crossed the room to the cabinet containing their video collection.

"Did you switch the movie back on your VHS? What picture were you watching?" She read aloud, in a singsong voice, *"Chains of Conquest; Whips of Night; Boys Will Be Boys; Prince of the Torture Palace; Boys on Ice; Schoolboys and Their Chums; Girls and Girls Together; Girls at Play . . ."* Miranda shook her head. "I don't get it. What are you people into? Looks like you just enjoy the hell out of everything and anything."

She reached for a tape, shook her head, dropped her hand. "I'm glad I don't see a dog around here. Please, lady and mister, don't try *any* of *that* with a *small* dog. Promise!"

There was an intense silence when Miranda finally stopped speaking. Mike Stein was more interested in Miranda than in the Rollands' reaction. She had come slightly unglued.

The Rollands stared at her.

"Tell me something," Miranda whispered, leaning toward them, a confidante asking for information, to be enlightened. "Was it better when it was for real? Did it have more . . . more *punch* to it? Did it make it better for you, more exciting, when you knew, for sure, that what was going on out there was the *real* thing?"

123

No one said a word; they all stared at Miranda, who finally turned and walked to the window. She shoved the heavy drapes aside, and kept her back to the room.

And then, in a calm voice, speaking as though Miranda had never spoken, Mike Stein asked, "What did you do after you left the window?"

The Rollands followed Mike's lead. They ignored Miranda. "Oh, we just went to bed," Mr. Rolland said.

Mrs. Rolland pinched his arm very hard this time. "It was very hot and we'd let all that hot air into the apartment, so we closed the window down, and the blind. And the drapery. And we went to bed because the bedroom is kept nice and cool. What with the air conditioner and all."

"And you never thought to call the police—to dial 911?"

Mrs. Rolland widened her magnified eyes. "About what, Mr. Stein? Far as we could tell, what those people were doing down there was a private matter."

"What they were 'doing down there'? *He was stabbing her, Mrs. Rolland! She was bleeding to death! Down there. Under your window.*"

Mrs. Rolland shrugged her shoulders and crossed her arms over her body. "We're not mindreaders, you know."

A while later, maybe a half hour or so, they had heard all the commotion: police cars and ambulances and sirens and whatever. They got dressed and went downstairs, just like anyone else, to see what was going on.

"How did you feel about what had happened to that young woman, Mrs. Rolland? Mr. Rolland?"

Mrs. Rolland answered for both of them, and her voice was loud and clear. "I felt that it was their own business and we were right not to interfere."

14

Miranda invited him into her apartment this time. "I don't make good coffee," she told him. "I'm a tea drinker, so if you're interested, you're on your own."

"Fair enough. Would you like me to make a cup of tea for you? You look like you could use it."

"Oh? No. Look, I'll be right back. I want to change into something else. I feel clammy and . . . I'll be right back."

The pullman kitchen was in a recessed section of the living room, easy to conceal when the blind was let down. The living room was small, neat, cool, carefully composed. It reflected Miranda: precise and crisp and yet there was a quality of serenity, shadows and softness, an air of comfort, a good place to be. He studied her collection of books; the shelves lined the long wall of the room, from floor to ceiling. Heavy on nonfiction and textbooks: Miranda the student. It caught his eye, the bright garish color his publisher insisted would make his book a standout, *A Murder in Vietnam,* by Mike Stein. It was lying flat on top of some current books.

She was wearing an extra-large knee-length man-tailored light-blue shirt. It had an effect: a slender young female body lost inside a strong masculine garment. It conjured innocence

125

and vulnerability. And a certain calculation. Or so Mike Stein read into it. She was barefoot, and he was aware of her long slender legs. She combed her fingers through her short thick dark hair, waved him toward the couch. She brought a plate of cheese and crackers and a bowl of fruit to the cocktail table. She seemed very tense.

"Mr. Stein, I want you to know something. I do not usually react to what people tell me during an interview. It was very stupid of me and very unprofessional."

It was really bothering her.

"Miranda, what the hell. No big deal. These were very unpleasant people and—"

"No. No, you do *not* understand. I am ashamed of the way I behaved. It wasn't really directed at them. What they do in the privacy of their own home, that is their business. But you see, I *am* bothered by what is happening, what always happens when a woman is murdered. The focus is so strongly on her, as a woman. Her behavior, her actions, her very presence at a certain location, at a certain time, become questionable. Suspicious. We start with the woman and we rob her of all privacy, all dignity. We go into areas of her life that have nothing to do with her murder. We are trying to connect her with her murderer—not just to find him. But to blame her, in some way, in any way we can, for her own murder."

"We're in pretty much the same business, Miranda. We both gather information. You use it one way, I use it another."

"I am curious about something, Mr. Stein." She gestured toward his book. "If this man, this son of Chief Cordovan, *was* involved in the drug trade, and all the other things going on, if you found it out, would you have written about it? Would you have been able to do that?"

Mike Stein picked up the copy of his book, gazed at it, then

126

at her. "Miranda, I did not go to Vietnam to prove that the death of Art Cordovan's son was murder. We had an understanding, Art and I. *Whatever* we uncovered as truth, that was what I would write. No matter what."

"And would you have done that, written the truth, if his son had been involved? Could you have done that?"

Firmly, holding her by his intensity, he said, "I would write the truth. It was the whole point, Miranda. A search for the truth."

"Yes. I believe that. I believe you would have written whatever you found. As you did."

The mood changed; they relaxed, he enjoyed looking at her on her own ground. His voice went low and easy, his eyes moved slowly, taking pleasure in her. "So, Miranda. Tell me about yourself. Tell me about Miranda. I love to say your name. Miranda."

"Here I am. As you see me. At my best. At my worst. Just here I am. Miranda."

"Who do you love, Miranda? Right now, who?"

"Right now? Romantically?" She shook her head. "Right now, no one. And, no discussion, please. Of romantic matters."

He picked up a framed photograph of a young boy. The resemblance was very strong. "This is your son? Handsome boy. But so serious. How old is he?"

"He is ten years old. Mannie. Very serious." She pulled a mock-severe expression, then smiled.

"Where is he?"

"In Florida. Fort Lauderdale, with his father. And a whole big family. Even my mother is there. In Florida. Part of this whole big family."

"Now, that is intriguing. Tell me, how old were you when you were married? How old when you had this little boy?"

Miranda settled down on a comfortable overstuffed chair

that faced the couch. She swallowed some iced tea and told him, "I was married at sixteen. I had Mannie—Emmanuel Hernandez, Jr.—when I was seventeen. We divorced when I was nineteen."

Miranda and her mother had lived together in a small South Bronx apartment inside the borders, not yet burned out, but considered a danger zone. Just the two of them; her father had died in a mugging; her two sisters had married and moved away; her brother had died of an overdose. There was a grandfather, who Miranda had only recently realized was not more than fifty-five at the time of his death.

It was the second big occasion of a poor family's life, the occasion worth going into debt for: a decent funeral. A big wedding was the other end of the scale, and a big funeral, nicely done, was a sign not only of respect but of stability. There wasn't too much of that in the South Bronx. Miranda's grandfather had a fine send-off.

A week after her grandfather's funeral, her mother sat down with her in their small kitchen and told her about a date she had arranged for Miranda. Miranda was very angry but very curious: her mother had never before done such a thing.

Emmanuel Hernandez was the handsomest man Miranda had ever seen. He was tall and clean and so well groomed and soft-spoken and polite, like a prince from a storybook, and treated Miranda like a princess and her mother like a queen. They went to dinner and he drove a limousine: it was part of his family's business, he said, an automobile service. He didn't say much more. Emmanuel was ten years older than Miranda and he really didn't have too much to say about anything, but he was a polite listener, dinner after dinner. And then he told her about Florida: the sunshine, the pleasant lifestyle.

"It all happened so quickly. One day, the South Bronx,

Mama and me, and then, boom! Florida. A big house, a large family. Oh, many brothers and sisters and aunts and uncles and cousins. And children. So many, all so perfect. Nice clothes, nice manners, such quiet, well-educated, grown-up little children. And everybody, somehow or other, involved in this . . . this family 'business.' "

Mike covered his eyes with his hand for a moment and shook his head. "You mean you married into a family of undertakers?"

Miranda stood up and shook her head. Her voice changed: she was good at imitations. " 'Oh, no, no. Not that ugly unprofessional word. Please. *Funeral directors.*' " Again in her own voice, "My husband's father explained the whole thing. There are not many avenues open to bright Puerto Rican entrepreneurs in the States. Besides a bodega, a *farmacia,* a tourist office for cheap flight arrangements, bail bondsmen. So, what is left?" She drew back, let her voice go low again. *"Death.* 'Death, Miranda, dear child. Just a fact of life. Which provides us all, and will for all our generations, with all the good things we all deserve.' "

"You mean, you didn't *know?* That Emmanuel was an under—funeral director?"

"I was a *very* young sixteen. Not a street girl. Parochial school; very careful girl. I thought he was a chauffeur for some wonderful, rich family who allowed him to use their beautiful car. Then I thought his whole family were in some sort of limousine business. It wasn't until I was pregnant that I *really* started asking questions; about a month after our wedding. Specific questions, after his father told me what they all did. 'But what, *exactly,* is it that *you* do, Mannie, besides drive the cars, and wear the handsome dark suits, and help the old ladies so they do not collapse? What do you *do* besides these things?' " Miranda sighed, shrugged, held her hands out. "So he told me. Specifically. And then I could not stop looking at his hands. I could not free myself from the chemical smell of his body. I could not bear to have him . . . It was unfair to him. This I know. Mannie was, is, a very nice man. Very beautiful and gentle and kind. But this is his destiny and it pleases him."

"So you were sixteen and pregnant. What about your mother? Why is she still in Florida? With them?"

"Ah. Mama is a wonderful woman. She knows how to adjust, how to accept what life—or death—has to offer. She stayed with me, it was to be until the baby was born. But she fell in love with the last remaining bachelor uncle and they got married. And Mama works in the receiving room, greets the mourners, and she is wonderful at it. Her voice is low and soothing; she says all kind things. And she wears good dark dresses and looks so beautiful. And when I said to her, 'But, Mama, how can you *bear* to be around all this? And when your husband touches you and . . .' "

Miranda shook her head, shrugged, then looked directly into Mike's eyes, surprised by the sympathy and concern that confronted her. "My mother said, 'This sure beats the hell out of working in the garment center on that cheap polyester garbage they make specifically for Puerto Ricans, Miranda.' "

Miranda started to laugh. The sound was hard and gasping, as though she hadn't expected it. The effect was a sudden loss of control, and she hugged her body, hands on opposite elbows. "That's my mother and I love and respect her. But I had to leave that place. Even she realized that. Mannie was very generous. He helped me to get started, until I got a job. He helped so I could get my degree. But I paid. My son. They were right, of course—alone I could not raise him with the advantages of family and place, the security of a strong sense of belonging." She shrugged. "They were right. I suppose they were right."

130

It seemed as though she was talking to herself, rearguing old battles, looking for confirmation, for some sense that she had done the right thing.

Mike studied the photograph of her son. "And so this very serious young man of ten years old, he is being groomed . . ."

Miranda narrowed her eyes and leaned forward, her voice shifting again, imitating. " 'Someday, all of this, everything' "—her arm swept the room—" 'will belong to Mannie and his cousins.' Just think, a whole family of little boys being made ready to carry on a family tradition of . . ." Again, the strange laughter, stopped abruptly by a gagging sound as she turned away.

His impulse was to go to her, to embrace her, comfort her, tell her to let it out. Go with it. Instinct told him not to try to control her timing. He had a sense that this, to Miranda, this act of confiding, was a loss of self-control, a falling down of her mask. He realized she was trying to stop herself and he felt an ache of sympathy, but let her go her own way. Within moments, he knew he had been right and stored away some new knowledge of Miranda. The timing, in everything, should be hers.

She sat down across from him, and her voice was soft and calm. "I want to tell you something. I love my son. I see him often, every month at least, and at vacation time and special school occasions. But he has become so . . . so *old*. Last month I was down to Lauderdale and we were alone in the garden, Mannie and I, and he studied my face, very gravely studied me, and I said, 'What? What is it, my darling? Why are you looking at me so hard?' My heart stopped. I waited, something inside of me swelled, maybe he'd say, 'Mommy, I want to come home with you, Mommy, get me out of here.' "

Mike leaned forward and quietly asked her, "What did your son say to you?"

Miranda's head went down, and when she faced him again

it was with a serene, unknowable expression. "He said, 'Mama, you are so beautiful, why don't you wear a little more makeup? Just a little, here, on the lids, and to highlight the cheeks and then' . . . He was . . . he was . . . my ten-year-old son was talking about makeup he was learning to apply to faces of corpses!"

"Oh, Christ."

"I haven't told anyone about that. Not anyone, not even . . . Not anyone. God, it is terrible. What I've let them do to my own child. It was my fault, wasn't it, this sad little boy with the old face and the terrible seriousness of his life and . . ."

Finally she cried, and finally it was time for him to go to her, put his arms around her, assure her that she was human, it was all right to let go.

At one point, she pulled back and looked at him. "I'm not sure why, Mr. Stein, but I feel somehow that it *is* all right. With you, I mean. I do not usually, you see. But tonight, first at that apartment with those people . . . I'm not usually like this. I am usually strong, and I don't like this . . . this kind of thing."

"Miranda, let's have a drink. What would you like?"

She shrugged, embarrassed. "I'm sorry. I have nothing here. I just don't particularly like alcohol, and since I am alone now it was used up and I didn't replace it."

He shook his head. "Okay. Want to turn on? No. You don't do that. Coffee? You drink tea. Miranda, what the hell do you do when you need to relax a little?"

"I relax. I do a form of meditation. Very deep."

He grabbed her shoulders and shook her. "Do that later. Don't you disappear on me, lady. Okay, now tell me: how did a Bronx–Fort Lauderdale girl end up here, in Astoria, Queens?"

"Another long story. About a Long Island commuting

132

husband who found it convenient to stop off en route from his job in Manhattan to his family home on the Island. It was *convenient* for him. And I liked it here. So, later, I stayed." She smiled at him. "You'd make a good cop. You know exactly when to ask for certain information. I want to show you something."

She reached behind her for a silver-framed photograph, which she handed to him.

Mike studied the photograph. It was of a tall thin young man, elegant, sensuous, mysterious, with something dangerous and glamorous in his stance. There was something known and yet intriguing, familiar and yet disturbing, about him.

"You have a twin brother, Miranda? He is so like you. And yet . . ."

"No. No twin brother. No brother. Do you like the picture? Do you not recognize the beautiful young man? Is he not interesting? Do you find yourself, maybe, attracted to him in some way?" She moved closer to him and laughed. It was an entirely different sound from earlier: this was a deep throaty sound of pleasure, teasing, mocking. "Do you never play games, Mr. Stein?"

He leaned back and smiled. He ran his long fingers through his thick white hair, his eyes sparked ice blue, he licked his lips quickly in anticipation. In enjoyment of Miranda.

"Oh. Sometimes. Tell me this game—of the beautiful young man."

"Ah. Once, one weekend, about a year ago, a friend—"

"Not the Long Island commuter?"

Miranda shook her head. "No. Just a friend. He had an idea. For reasons I won't go into, I'll just tell you the game. I dressed as you see me in the picture. With just a touch of careful makeup, just for definition, to make me into the beautiful young man you see. He was quite beautiful, too, my friend, in a very masculine way. He took me to a place where young men meet other young men. And we played the game. It was a contest between us, to see who would be the more popular. Who would attract more potential lovers."

"And who won?"

"Oh, I did. You see, he was absolutely straight. As straight as anyone ever is. He did not know exactly *how* to attract other men to him. I do. I did. Of course, they never knew I was a woman. Otherwise, he would have won. It was just a game. Harmless. Interesting."

"Did you play other games with your friend?"

"This is the only one I care to tell you about. For now. Don't you think I was a pretty boy?"

"Sitting here, in this room with you, I don't see you as androgynous. Not at all. I guess the real test would be if you were able to attract women as well."

Miranda shrugged and smiled and said softly, "Ah, Mr. Stein. Only one secret at a time, yes?"

She offered her hands and he stood up, aware of the fragrance and aura of the young woman, aware of her slender body beneath the overlarge, expensive man's shirt.

Miranda led him into her bedroom. She took his hands away as he started to unbutton her shirt.

"Miranda, let me do that."

She shook her head. "No. That would make me feel like a child, to have you undress me now. As though you were still offering me comfort. This—this is a thing apart, separate and for itself, this, between you and me. *This time,* I will undress myself first, and then I will undress you. There is no child in this room."

"Miranda, there is nothing, at all, in the world, childish about you," he said, his voice deep with admiration and a certain unexpected sense of awe.

134

15

Miranda was at her desk for no more than fifteen minutes before a woman who refused to identify herself telephoned to tell her that Maria Vidales, "the Spanish girl," had returned to her apartment at 10-43 Barclay Street.

The girl was reluctant to open the door.

"No, no," she said, eying Miranda through the peephole. "Whatever it is, I don't want it. Please. Go away."

Miranda leaned on the doorbell. It was a loud, startling sound. Finally the girl opened the door the few inches the chain lock allowed.

"You do not want to talk to me through the door, Ms. Vidales," Miranda told her. "This is a matter for you and not for your neighbors."

The girl studied the gold shield for a moment, closed the door, slid the chain free and allowed Miranda to come into her small apartment. The tiny living room was filled with overlarge pieces of upholstered furniture, littered with magazines, newspapers, a collection of records, tapes, clothing, shoes, boxes filled with makeup. The walls were adorned with posters advertising rock concerts and rock stars.

Maria swept an armful of magazines onto the floor to make

135

room for Miranda. She didn't apologize or try to explain the clutter. It was a fact of her life.

"So, all right, you are a police detective. What do you want to talk to me about?"

Her resemblance to the murdered Anna Grace was stunning: same size and build; a bit younger, a bit heavier, but the same long dark hair, swept back from her face and hanging straight and loose down her back. The girl was tense under Miranda's scrutiny.

"I am sorry to stare, it's just that . . . Were you away, Ms. Vidales? I've been trying to reach you since Wednesday night. When the young woman, Anna Grace, was murdered right downstairs, practically in front of this building."

Miranda stood up and went to the window. "I think you'd be able to see at least part of what happened from here. Yes. One could see the lamppost where the girl slumped down. Where she sat and bled to death. Yes. You could see that clearly from here."

"I wasn't home," the girl said. "I was with a friend. At the beach. This week is my vacation."

She worked at a local burger franchise for the summer, until classes started again at St. John's.

"But you heard about the murder?"

"I saw it on the TV. And in the newspapers. It was a bad thing. But so many things happen every day, no?"

"And you know nothing about it?"

Maria Vidales could not meet her eyes. She grew nervous and agitated at Miranda's direct confrontation. Her face was drawn and stiff, as though she'd been very ill.

"Maria, are you in some kind of trouble?"

"Trouble? No. I'm not in trouble. Please. I don't know anything about what happened. I wasn't here. So there it is."

"Have you spoken to any of your neighbors about the murder of this young woman?"

"No. No, I don't talk to my neighbors. I work or I go to school. I don't see them."

Slowly, carefully, softly, Miranda said, "Ah. Then no one has told you yet. I see."

The girl froze. The cigarette remained unlit in her mouth, the match unstruck in her hand.

"Told me? Told me what?"

There was something here that was not right. Miranda decided to let Maria come to her.

"Nothing. Nothing, I'm sorry. Never mind."

"No. Wait. Why did you want to see me? I wasn't home. You say you came here and I wasn't home. So why bother me now? Listen. *Told me what?*"

Miranda Torres had learned a long time ago that the best way to say something terrible, unbearable, was in a quiet, soft, matter-of-fact way.

"That when your neighbors came to the street, when they were asked to look at the murdered girl, when they were asked if anyone knew her, some of them said, yes, they thought they knew this girl."

"Yes? Yes, and so . . ."

"They said, She looks like the Spanish girl. The girl who lives on the top floor, at 10-43. They didn't know your name. But they meant you. They thought the girl who was murdered was you. She looked very much like you. They were right. I can see that now."

Maria Vidales tried to light the cigarette, but her hand shook so badly that she gave it up.

"Are you in some kind of trouble, Maria? Is there someone, somewhere, who would want to hurt you?"

"Oh. No. No, nothing like that. No one wants to hurt me. You mean—to kill me? You mean does someone want to *kill* me? That is a terrible thing to ask me. It is not my fault that some girl who looks like me got killed. What does that have to do with me? Many people look like me. I can't help that. Please . . . I . . . feel sick."

She rushed from the room, and while she was in the bathroom being sick, running water, trying to pull herself together, Miranda stared after her. What had she walked into?

"Well, do you feel better now? You look very pale. Would you like anything?"

"Thank you. Thank you, no. Listen, I've got a virus, is all. My friend, he has been sick all week, so maybe . . ." The girl stopped speaking, put her hand over her mouth.

Miranda shrugged. "That's a shame. It couldn't have been much fun, to be at the beach and to be sick. What is your friend's name? Where does he live?"

Maria shook her head. "I do not have to tell you. Not anything."

"Are you here on a student visa, Maria? From Colombia?"

"Yes. It is all in order."

"Good. Then there's nothing for you to worry about, is there? Is that what's been worrying you?"

"No. I just . . ."

"Maria, where is Arabella? When was the last time you saw her?"

The girl went dead white. "Ara? What do you have to do with my sister? I don't understand. Please."

"You are worried about her, yes?"

"No, no. She's working. She's a stewardess and . . ."

"No. She's not at work. She was supposed to report for an assignment at nine A.M. Saturday morning. She didn't show up. Neither did her friend, Christine Valapo. And now it's Monday. And her boss has not heard from her or from her partner. Maria, don't turn away. Look up at me. Please."

Miranda sat down next to the girl, ignored the magazines that fell to the floor, the clothing wadded beneath her.

138

"Maria, you need to talk to someone. Maybe I can help. Is Ara in some kind of trouble? Tell me."

"No. I don't know. I don't know. She'll be all right."

"When was the last time you spoke to her? Maria. Talk to me. Look at me. It's safe, I promise you."

The girl was so frightened; so vulnerable. Miranda spoke easily, softly, familiarly: good friend, trust me, trust me.

"I think that she was . . . here . . . Wednesday night. Yes. She comes sometimes when I'm not here. Sometimes, you know, she brings a boyfriend, you know."

"Of course. So she had a boyfriend here Wednesday night? That's no big deal. And you spoke to her then, Wednesday night?"

"No. No. No." Maria gasped a huge amount of air, then began to choke.

"What did she say, Maria, when you spoke to her Wednesday night? Did she tell you about what happened? About the girl who was murdered?"

"She just said—a bad thing happened, some girl got hurt and she was afraid for me, that I might come home alone and maybe get hurt, you know? We thought it was a safe neighborhood, and this happened, so she said I should stay with my friend for a few days, let things settle and then come home and . . ."

"And where did she go?"

"I don't know. To work. She's working now, flying back to Bogotá. That's where she is."

"No. She isn't Maria. *Arabella is missing.* No one knows where she is: not her friends at Parker Towers, not her supervisor, and now not her younger sister. Is that what has you so worried: you don't know where Arabella is?"

"Yes," Maria said, speaking too quickly. "Yes. I worry about her because I don't know this boyfriend and maybe he took her somewhere and she didn't want to go there, or something like that."

Miranda stood up, walked to the window and looked down again at the lamppost where Anna Grace had died.

Her voice went hard and clear as she turned to face the girl. "No. That's not why you're worried. Why did your sister tell you not to come back to the apartment for a few days? There was no danger here anymore. The police were here, the murderer was gone. It was as safe as it could ever be. She told you something else. She said to stay away for another reason."

Maria Vidales shook her head and remained silent, but her eyes could not maintain contact with Miranda.

"What else is it, Maria? Why are you so worried? Are you worried about Arabella, or are you worried about yourself?"

"No. Nothing. I just am sick, is all, I told you that. Please, I need to go to bed and—"

"Maria, let us agree on something, you and I. It is the only way I can help you. Tell me the *truth* or say nothing, yes? Do not lie to me. It gets in the way of trust. Something bad has happened to you—or to your sister. Or you are afraid of something bad. Does it have anything to do with what happened down there, to that girl, out on the street? The girl who looked so much like you?"

Maria shook her head and spoke firmly. "No. No, it is just something with this boyfriend she was with and . . ."

Miranda cut her off abruptly. "I asked you not to lie. It is worthless. It makes no sense. You are very troubled about something and it is not your sister's boyfriend."

Maria bowed her head and nodded. Miranda softened, became the friend who was needed, who could be trusted, the person to confide in. Trust me, trust me.

"Then what? Are you worried about Arabella? Did she tell

you she would be in touch with you and you haven't heard from her?"

"She told me not to come back to the apartment that she would call me and tell me when I could come back and I don't know why she told me that and I don't know where she is and I don't know what to do I love my sister Arabella is so good to me she takes care of me and pays for this, the rent and everything and my tuition and she tells me to keep whatever money I earn for my personal things for makeup and concerts and she takes good care of me and I am frightened I don't know where she is she said she'd call and she didn't and—"

"If she was in trouble, who else would she call? Maybe a relative or a good friend to help her?"

"Maybe Carlos Galvez. He lives down there on Inverness Street. Maybe he—" Suddenly, Maria clamped a hand over her mouth and shook her head. She grabbed Miranda's arm. She blinked rapidly. "Our cousin. That's why I said him. It was stupid. She wouldn't go to him. That was stupid, about Carlos. She would *never* go to him. I don't know why I said—"

"Carlos Galvez. Your cousin. On Inverness Street."

"We do not see him. Look, he only helped us the one time, he got this apartment for me, so I'd have a nice place not too far from St. John's, that's all, we haven't even seen him in more than a year and—"

"And he lives so near, and is family?"

Maria bent forward, arms wrapped across her stomach, then pulled herself away from Miranda and rushed to the bathroom to be sick again. She stayed in there for a long time.

Maria had washed her face and combed her hair and, if Miranda was any judge, had taken something to steady and control herself. She stood straight and expressionless, her voice more steady, more angry than frightened now.

"I want for you to leave, Detective Torres. I have nothing more to say to you, and you cannot stay here if I ask you to leave. I wasn't here Wednesday night, and that is all I can tell you which is of any concern to you. Leave now. Please."

Miranda nodded. She took a card from her pocket and extended it to Maria Vidales. "Take it, Maria." When the girl didn't move, Miranda reached for her hand. "Here. Take it. The number is my office, and on the other side is my home phone number. I want you to have both numbers."

"I do not want—"

"Maria. Listen to me. I know something is wrong. Yes, it has nothing to do with this thing of the other night, all right. And probably it is something personal and private in your life between you and your sister and nothing at all to do with any police matter. But still, take this card and if you want to talk to someone, to me, as an older friend, as someone just to listen, as someone who might be able to offer you some help somehow—"

"Yes. Yes. All right, thank you. I'll keep your card."

She closed the door behind Miranda, and the locks clicked into place, but suddenly the door opened the few inches allowed by the chain.

"Detective Torres," Maria called. Her voice sounded ragged and as frightened as a small child's voice calling out in the darkness, afraid of the very sound of her own words.

Miranda came back from the elevator door and went as close to Maria as she could, straining to hear the nearly whispered words.

"Listen, just one thing. Forget what I said about our cousin Carlos. It was stupid. Neither Ara nor I would *ever* ask him for anything. Please. Please. Forget I even said his name."

142

"Yes. All right. Yes. Maria, all right. Is there anything that you—"

The door slammed shut and there was no sound at all from inside Maria Vidales' apartment.

The elevator was noisy, rattling and clanging, as it left the sixth floor. Miranda noticed how clean it was, spotless, tended by a careful, caring staff of maintenance people. The tenants on Barclay Street were lucky.

So, who the hell was Carlos Galvez?

16

While waiting for Mike, Miranda flipped through a Queens telephone directory in the cramped old-fashioned neighborhood candy store on the corner of Barclay and Sixty-eighth Avenue. Carlos Galvez was not listed. Yes, Directory Assistance did have an unlisted number in that name on Inverness Street, but, sorry . . .

Miranda thought for a moment, consulted the list of special numbers in her notebook, then dialed the squad's special contact at the phone company. After promising a covering letter from her squad commander, she jotted down both the phone number and the house number. She let the phone ring a number of times before hanging up and putting the information into a small pocket on the inside cover of her notebook. She probably wouldn't even mention anything at all about a Carlos Galvez at this time: it was just another name to be checked out.

Mike pulled up in his car, smiling as he spotted her. She was wearing a fine lightweight linen shirtwaist, pale green with a wide bright orange-and-yellow paisley sash around her narrow waist. Her long honey-brown legs were bare and smooth. She wore flat orange sandals and she smelled of oranges and lemons. Citrusy Miranda: clean and delicious.

"You are a cool lady on a hot day," he told her, slipping the lock on the lobby door while Miranda punched the bell marked "G. Randall, Apt. 2A."

The furniture in George Randall's apartment was in good taste. He had taken a few chances, mixing stripes with plaids, but the colors balanced and the whole effect was pleasant and light. He apparently knew what he was doing.

When Mike set his tape recorder on the coffee table, Randall shook his head.

"Uh-uh. I don't think that's necessary."

Mike shrugged. "Your choice. I use it for accuracy. Actually, I have a pretty good ear, but in case a question arises, I like to be able to refer to the tape. However, no problem."

"How come he's here with you, Detective Torres? I agreed to talk to you. Mr. Stein's a columnist, not a cop."

"That is also your choice, Mr. Randall," Miranda said quietly. "However, Mr. Stein prefers to get his information firsthand. My report will be my version. I try to be accurate, but . . ."

"Well, all right. It doesn't really matter. I have nothing at all to tell you about what happened Wednesday night. I didn't know a thing about it until I left for work Thursday morning."

"But you were here in your apartment Wednesday night? And you *are* on the second floor fronting on Barclay Street. And the victim, Anna Grace, was stabbed directly across the street from here."

"So a neighbor told me. I will say this. I didn't see nothin'. I didn't hear nothin'. I didn't know nothin'. And if I did see and did hear and did know, I still wouldn't have seen, heard or known. You dig that?"

"What kind of work do you do, Mr. Randall?"

"That's none of your business, Detective Torres. Incidentally, anything I say here and now is off the record. Or we are through talking?"

Miranda stood up so quickly that even Mike Stein was surprised. "Then we'd better make other arrangements, Mr. Randall. What you care to say in Mr. Stein's presence is one thing. But what you say in response to my questions is another thing. I'm a police officer and I am here in my official capacity to take a statement from you. Here are your choices. You answer my questions here and now with Mr. Stein present. Or he leaves now, and we proceed and he gets *my* version of the interview. Or, if you prefer, I'll set a time and you meet me at the 112th Precinct. Maybe in an official atmosphere you'll feel more comfortable. Up to you."

George Randall stood up to his six-foot height. He shook his head and laughed in surprise. He rubbed his hand over his eyes, walked to the window, then came back.

"Wow. Oh, baby, they really have got you good, haven't they? You are a real tight representative of the Man. Wow, you haven't looked in the mirror lately, have you, in a good strong light? You're beautiful, lady, you got the right tension and timing. So, you are the law and pow-wham-bam-don't-hit-me-ma'am! You hard and you tough, all right."

Mike held back and watched the confrontation.

"Listen, you," Miranda said. "Don't you pull black-jive-shit with me, mister. Don't you switch gears and start snapping your fingers, because you are a goddamn high-school teacher. You're a history teacher at Forest Hills High, and you're going for your master's at Columbia and you damn well don't jive to your professors and I've got a good idea you don't in front of your pupils."

He laughed in awe. "Wow, you are good, baby."

"You don't call me 'baby,' Mr. Randall. *Detective Torres,*

that's how you address me. And don't you talk 'they' and 'us' shit to me. I'm as black as I'll ever be and I was born female and Puerto Rican besides, so you want to compare notes with me, now is not the time and this is not the place. You got a statement to make: make it. Otherwise, answer my questions as I ask them."

"My God," Randall said, to Mike, "this lady is rough, isn't she?"

"That's been my experience."

"Okay, Detective Torres. I am sorry. I do apologize. All right?"

Yes, he had heard the commotion, *after* the event. He had not seen or heard anything to do with the attack. He heard someone yelling, "Call 911, what's the matter with you people, what kind of people are you?"

When he looked out the window, he saw the bus pulled up, he saw the bus driver, he saw people at windows across the street. He surmised that the girl—he could see her slumped against the lamppost—had been hurt. At first he thought she'd been hit by the bus. Then he saw all the police arrive, and then the ambulance, and all the people on the street.

"You didn't come downstairs? You didn't go to the street?"

"Now, don't go getting mad at me, Detective Torres, but come on. I am the one and only black person, of either sex, who lives on Barclay Street. I am subletting this apartment from a friend who relocated on the Coast. There was a great deal of interest in my arrival, and I imagine there'll be a great deal of relief at my departure, but I come and I go and I mind my own business."

"Weren't you even curious about what had happened?" Stein asked him.

147

"Curious, yes. Overwhelmingly curious, no. Not enough to want to go down the street and mingle with the neighbors. Come on, give me a break. With all those policemen—and policewomen—in uniform and in plainclothes. I just have a very strong feeling that my presence down there on that lily-white street, my *presence* would have elicited an inappropriate response. Valuable time would have been wasted in checking me out. You see how considerate I am."

"Then why the hard time when we first got here, Mr. Randall? If you have nothing to contribute? No information of any kind?"

George Randall was a very dark man with large, expressive black eyes. He barely smiled, yet his entire expression was warm and amused, even tolerant. He spread his arms, turned his hands palms up.

"When anyone comes to my door with a police officer's badge and a well-known journalist with a tape recorder, come on, Mr. Stein. I read your column regularly. I would not relish seeing myself, in any way, shape or form, transposed into your version." Then to Miranda, "I learned what happened from an elderly neighbor, who I met in the hall, Thursday morning. His name is Mr. Klein, first floor. He's a Jewish man, *but* very nice." Randall laughed. "Mr. Stein, that was meant as a joke. You see, when I first moved here, he was the only one who spoke to me. The other people were uneasy, they felt maybe if they ignored me I'd go away. But Mr. Klein was very kind. He told me that he talked to his wife about me, and what he said was, 'I told her, Mr. Randall, that you're a black man, *but very nice.*' "

They took a coffee break, and for the first time Mike asked her, "Miranda, how the hell did you get all that background information on Randall? How'd you know he was going for his master's and that he teaches at Forest Hills High?"

Miranda smiled. "Why, Mr. Stein. Before you arrived, I met a neighbor of Mr. Randall's. A little old man, named Mr. Klein. Jewish, *but really, very nice.*"

17

After a long day, before heading home, just a what-the-hell
shot, Miranda drove over to Inverness Street. There was a
collection of large cars parked in front of the house of Carlos
Galvez. She drove past the house, found a parking spot,
thought for a moment, then doubled back on foot and went
to his door.

From the moment the door opened, Miranda knew there
was something wrong. Carlos Galvez was too large, in every
way, for his surroundings. Carefully, he examined her credentials, glanced at her ID photo, then flicked a measuring
eye quickly and efficiently over her, head to toe. He missed
nothing. Reluctantly, he permitted Miranda to enter his
home: his domain.

The air of well-ordered opulence overwhelmed the small
dimensions of the attached pseudo-Tudor six-room house.
The Persian carpet was genuine; there was a definite feel not
only of well-spent money but of menace. It emanated from
the man.

He was tall and heavyset without the slightest trace of fat.
His large balding head was well tended, carefully styled, as
was the thick black mustache that would have dominated the

face of a lesser man. His eyes, black and large and steady, fastened on Miranda, took her measure, gave lie to his expressed courtesy.

"And how may I help you, Detective Torres?"

She began to speak, but he interrupted her. Two children, a boy and a girl, school age, had come from the dining room beyond. They were beautiful children, radiant, with strong yet delicate faces. They had their father's black eyes and fine manners.

"Yes?" he asked them softly.

The girl spoke. The boy stared without expression at Miranda.

"Papa, Mama excused us from the table. Will you hear the music with us now? We have the records all arranged."

He reached out with a well-manicured hand. His fingers glittered with diamonds: the only vulgarity about him.

"Later. Soon. Go. Papa will join you soon, yes?"

He stroked the child's head, and then her brother's. His expression was tender and loving, and they responded politely. They were accustomed to being well treated, well loved, well behaved. There was a quiet authority present in the room.

"Now." He turned to Miranda. Generously, he offered her a chair. "Coffee? Would you care for something, perhaps an apéritif?"

"Thank you, señor, no. I regret that I seem to have interrupted your dinner."

It was of no importance; it was all right. A beautiful tall, thin, elegantly groomed woman hesitated, did not enter the room until he nodded permission.

"This is of no consequence," he told the woman softly. "Join the little ones. They are preparing the music. I will be with them shortly."

She glided away with a slight nod, leaving behind an exotic

151

fragrance, subtle, barely discernible, definitely expensive.

A small dark woman, dressed in a silver-gray maid's uniform, quickly and efficiently, without raising her face or her eyes, slid lightweight doors across the archway that separated the small living room from the even smaller dining room.

None of these people, not this expensively dressed man or the woman or the children or the maid belonged in this setting. It seemed as though they had all been placed here in error.

"So, you are asking about my cousin, Arabella Vidales. And why is that?"

"A routine part of my investigation, sir. A young woman was killed on Barclay Street last Wednesday night. Your cousin's apartment faces the street. She was on a layover from her job. I am assigned to question everyone—every person—whose apartment faces that street."

"And you have not questioned my cousin? You have not been able to reach her? So, you try again. Isn't that the way it is done?"

"Yes. Exactly. But you see, Arabella Vidales seems to be—unavailable."

"Explain that." His tone was commanding; a man accustomed to making demands. The dark liquid eyes never left her face, did not miss the slightest movement of her mouth, the slightest flicker of her lashes. Miranda felt as though *he* were *her* interrogator.

She explained, briefly, about checking with the other stewardesses in the Parker Towers building. She told him she had spoken with Maria Vidales.

"And why would that be of interest to you, Detective Torres? That Maria is concerned about her sister. What does that have to do with your investigation?"

He emphasized the last two words: gave them a special

meaning which she could not immediately identify. All that Miranda knew was that she was immensely uncomfortable, and that her host was aware of this. And seemed to expect it.

Miranda shrugged. She slowed herself down. She turned the pages of her notebook. She used the moment to steady herself. She could not let him know how intimidated she felt.

But of course he knew exactly how intimidated she felt.

"Arabella Vidales was supposed to report for a flight Saturday morning at nine A.M. She didn't show up or call. Neither did her partner. This is really none of my concern, but because her younger sister expressed a certain anxiety, and since I am assigned to speak with her anyway, I told the younger girl that I would continue my effort to locate Arabella. If you know nothing of her whereabouts, then I apologize for taking up your time." As she stood, Miranda felt a sudden wave of dizziness, lightheadedness: a sense of fear.

Carlos Galvez stood up quickly, the gentleman not remaining seated while a woman stood. He seemed to close in on her, his physical presence seemed to encompass her. Miranda felt his closeness although he had not moved an inch toward her. There was a definite aura emanating from this man, part sexuality and part something else which she could not immediately identify. It went beyond menace.

Power. That was the element that dominated the room. Carlos Galvez could not be contained in this small room filled with rare and genuine treasures. He was here temporarily, carefully smoothing the lapels of his six-hundred-dollar suit, secure in the knowledge that his wife and children were under his roof and domain.

The initial feeling of something terribly wrong was compounded by the expression on Galvez' face. His mouth smiled, but those large unblinking, knowing eyes never smiled. Miranda felt as though he were physically holding her with his large strong hands, preventing her from moving. Of course he never touched her. He controlled her with his eyes and voice.

"It is kind of you to worry about the well-being of my cousin, Arabella. I am sure she is all right and will turn up for another assignment. It was thoughtless of her to cause her younger sister concern."

His words were innocent. Nothing threatening or suggestive of even annoyance or anger. The real meaning was conveyed by tone and inflection, by emphasis and timing. There was a controlled fury enveloping Miranda.

As he spoke, he moved toward the door, leading Miranda out of his home, skillfully, politely.

"Yes. Thank you so much for your courtesy. Again, I regret disturbing you at your dinner table."

Her manner, her words, her voice, betrayed deference. He seemed not only to demand it, but to expect it. It came automatically, thoughtlessly, from Miranda.

She knew he watched her walk across the tiny patio, down the narrow cement walk to the sidewalk. Without realizing she was doing it, Miranda took note of the black Mercedes parked directly in front of the house, and the black Lincoln Continental behind that, and the black Cadillac behind that. She knew that they belonged to Galvez and not to his neighbors, even though she had no idea how she knew this.

She knew he had stopped watching her as she got behind the wheel of her small blue Honda. He was no longer interested in her. She no longer mattered in his life.

Miranda held her hands up briefly, fingers extended. She was not surprised at the trembling. She took a few deep breaths and brought herself under control. Her mouth was dry and she still felt slightly dizzy. She had no idea what she had walked into, what was contained within the small, in-

154

nocuous façade of the attached house on Inverness Street.

She jotted down the license numbers of the three cars in front of the house.

She hoped Carlos Galvez had not seen her do it.

18

Miranda had a copy of her interview with Maria Vidales neatly typed and stapled for Mike Stein. He handed her a transcript of his interview with John Rolofsky, a recent emigré from the Soviet Union, now a resident of Barclay Street.

"In my whole life," Mike said, "I never saw a skinnier man. You could cut yourself on his bones. Guy is over six feet tall and he weighs in at one-twenty."

Miranda nodded as she skimmed the report. "It seems that he was a very frightened man, from what he had to say."

"Get to the closing line," Mike said. "Poor bastard. Now, *him* I feel sorry for."

He leaned over Miranda and read the statement: "So I did what the Americans did. I sat and watched. And did nothing."

He had heard the screams and shouts on the street below his apartment. He tried to reach his cousin, who had labored through the State Department for nearly four years to get him to America, but was unable to find him. Finally he had gone down to the street, stood in the shadows, watching and waiting for someone to come and help the girl. No one did. So he went back upstairs to his apartment.

"This guy is scared to death to talk to anyone. Apparently, he was interviewed by a uniform, and his cousin—Rolofsky is a mechanic and he works at a service station owned by his cousin on Metropolitan Avenue—his cousin says the guy almost passed out. A uniform means something pretty damn scary to a guy like this."

" 'So I did what the Americans did. I sat and watched. And did nothing,' " Miranda read over the words slowly and softly, then looked up at Mike and shrugged. "Yes. This is sad. This man would have helped, I think, but for his past experience."

"Yeah, but there is one thing. He did know about 911. He told me he knew, but that he was afraid to call."

Miranda studied him for a moment. "Can you understand that reluctance, on his part?"

Mike nodded. "Understand it, yeah, maybe. Accept it as valid when a girl was sitting there, bleeding to death? No way. Okay, lady, we ready to hit on this guy Harry Lamont?"

Miranda left out of her report her impressions, which were not proper police information: that Maria Vidales was very worried about not being able to locate her sister, Arabella, who, along with her stewardess partner, Christine Valapo, seemed to have disappeared. She did not describe the trembling fingers, the paling face, the doubling-over cramps, the traces of terror. None of that was pertinent.

Miranda did not write up an official report about her visit with Carlos Galvez. This had no bearing on the case at all. She did jot down a few notes which she kept for herself.

For a moment, a fleeting moment, she had thought to talk to Mike, to tell him about her visit to Carlos. To tell him how frightened Maria was, how she called after Miranda, "Forget what I said about my cousin Carlos. Please." Intuition, either rightly or wrongly, persuaded her to keep this information to herself. Vaguely, she wished her partner were around.

There was no one else she would discuss this matter with, but Dunphy was off somewhere with Homicide, checking down stories of a few more nutty confessors. Miranda would hold up any of her impressions at this time. They were extraneous to the case. A family matter. Probably.

Harry Lamont's shop was wedged into a narrow space on Austin Street between a furniture store with a wide, flashy window and a travel agency with large brightly colored posters. The narrow entrance was deceptive. Inside, the store seemed to open up. The space had been wisely used: there were double revolving racks of blouses, skirts, slacks and jackets on one side of the shop under a printed sign: FOR YOU GALS!—illustrated by a curvy line drawing of a female figure. On the other side were similar display racks: FOR YOU GUYS!—with a distorted, muscular male torso. In the center of the store were racks of unisex clothes. The sign over these items announced: MIX IT UP, GUYS 'N GALS!

He was a man with flash in his early forties. When he ran a hand through his thick, black, styled hair, a diamond pinky ring glinted, then disappeared, momentarily lost in the healthy clean mop. His face was deeply tanned in what Mike Stein thought of as a year-round Miami. He had a gambler's eyes, quick and suspicious, narrowed and sharp.

"Like I told you on the phone, Mr. Stein, I'll give ya fifteen minutes, then I close up. What a day. I'll tell ya, my merchandise walks. Runs. Ya know, I oughtta take the gal and the guy signs and chuck them. It's all unisex now. Even underwear. Not that I carry underwear but I read the ads. It's all crazy, isn't it?" He looked Miranda over swiftly, head to toe. "For you, I got a real class outfit. Green has gotta be your color. I know, I know, you're not here to buy. But another time, you come back, I got something just for you. I'll

158

make you a deal, you'll be a walking advertisement for my place. So. Okay. What do you want to know?"

Miranda dug out a file folder from her large shoulder bag, then handed him a typed copy of his statement.

"You didn't have time the other day in the office to read this and sign it. Would you do that now, please?"

He put his hand out impatiently. "Gimme a pen, I'll sign. That's it? That's why I close a half hour early?"

"Mr. Lamont, I think you should read it over before you sign this. It *is* your statement."

"Look," he told Miranda, "I got no reason to think the cop I talked to put my statement in his own words. So, okay, I don't want to make you nervous. I'm a speed reader. Watch this."

He went through the two single-spaced pages of typing. He looked up quickly and raised his heavy brows, and smiled knowingly.

"Here's a mistake. Just a little mistake, a typo, I guess. That where you want me to make my initials? That's to prove I read this, right? Okay. There. Now I'll sign it and that's that, right?"

He looked at Mike Stein's tape recorder. "You can put that on the counter if you want. I got nothing to hide. Anything I say is on the record, for you, for the cops, for anyone."

"That's just as a safeguard for myself, Mr. Lamont. After a while, words seem to get shuffled. This way, I keep one person's statement clear from another person's."

Harry Lamont lived at 10–12 Barclay Street; the far end of the block; front living-room windows; third floor.

"So what I saw is included in my statement. I heard the girl yell, scream, I heard a man's voice yelling, like an argument. Then I heard a terrible scream, like a dog got hurt, ya know?"

"According to your statement," Miranda said, "you saw the man, the assailant, run up Barclay Street, toward the tennis courts, then you saw a large white car, possibly a Cadillac, come from around the corner, slow down alongside of where Ms. Grace was sitting against the lamppost. Do you make a connection between the assailant and the car?"

"I made a connection based on common sense. The guy ran, a few seconds later this car comes along. After he looks, the guy starts burning rubber. He nearly ran into the bus."

That was not in his statement.

"What direction was the bus going?"

The bus was on its run toward Metropolitan Avenue. No, the driver didn't stop; except at the corner stop sign, then he made his turn and was gone. Which information placed the bus driver at the scene of the crime; had him leaving the screaming victim and pursuing his route, on schedule.

Mike Stein said, "Tell me something, Mr. Lamont . . ."

Harry Lamont leaned back against a shelf of colorful tee shirts and cotton sweaters. His pink shirt and pale-yellow pants looked cool and pleasant. He looked like a cup of rainbow ices.

"No, no, Mr. Stein, I'll tell you nothing. Nothing more than what I've said. Now, here, and in my statement yesterday morning. I have nothing else to say. That's it, complete. You're holding it in your hand."

"There is one question I'd like you to answer. Out of curiosity."

Lamont pulled away from the shelf and placed his hands on his hips. He leaned forward slightly; his stance was aggressive and angry.

"What you been asking everybody? What you been ringing doorbells for all up and down Barclay Street? 'Why didn't you call 911? Why didn't you call 911?' You really got a bone in your throat, Mr. Stein. Concentrate on the bum who did

160

this girl. Don't try to switch things around. You've been coming on to people, my neighbors and friends, like *they* committed some kind of crime. Yeah, a terrible crime was committed. In fact, we've had four murders of women in Queens so far this year, right, Detective Torres? You've been talking to these people like they're responsible for what happened. Why don't you get on the cops' asses? Why don't you write a couple of articles on where the hell are the police, how come they let a thing like this happen?"

"But you haven't answered the question, have you, Mr. Lamont? Why *didn't* you call 911 and get this girl the help that would have saved her life?"

"I didn't. Okay? That's it. No deep dark terrible reason; no criminal act involved. I just didn't. I'm not saying that I should have. I'm not saying I shouldn't have. I'm just saying I *didn't* call 911." He paused, let a beat go by, lowered his voice and said, *"And neither did anyone else."*

"Does that make it okay, Mr. Lamont?"

"Look, Stein. I read your column and I agree with you about a hundred percent when you write about all the punks and bastards loose all over the city. And how the politicians don't want to know nothing about nothing, except in an election year. And the way you ride shotgun on the judges and write them up when they pull some of these unbelievable plea bargain deals. The way you name the names and put it right out there. I wish more news people had your guts. But I get a feeling you're going in another direction with this thing. I get a real bad feeling in my stomach that you're off on some kind of a side trip, that you're bouncing some things on the people who live on Barclay Street. And I'll tell you, I lived for twenty-four years on Barclay Street and you couldn't find a better, harder-working, more decent bunch of people, so why don't you think it over a little, Mr. Stein, before you go off the track and start finger-pointing at innocent people."

161

"Are you aware of the fact that the victim, Anna Grace, bled to death? That she was slashed and bleeding and sitting against the lamppost bleeding to death? The EMS unit could have gotten to her within three to five minutes; that would have given her time to spare. But because no one called 911, she sat right there in front of all of you and bled to death and all of you people watched. And you have no answer? No reason, no excuse? No justification?"

Lamont dropped his hands and lowered his head, a bull getting ready to charge. He rotated his meaty shoulders and leaned toward Mike.

"Hey, listen, I don't have to justify myself, to you, to her, to anybody. I'm a respected merchant in Forest Hills, I pay my taxes, I employ minority people as salesclerks, I live a decent life. And so do all my neighbors. You go somewhere else and dig up trouble. Jeez, I would think there are enough punks and bums for you to write about for the next thousand years. What the hell are you thinking about, trying to hurt decent people with this crap?"

"No guilt, Mr. Lamont? No regret? No second thoughts?"

"Get outa my store, Stein. I got nothin' to say to you." To Miranda, "You got my official statement. You got anything else you want to say to me?"

"Nothing at all, Mr. Lamont," Miranda said.

"Good. Get lost. Both of you." As they reached the door, which was locked, he activated the buzzer. He called after them, "Listen, Stein. And you remember this. Nobody who lives on Barclay Street got one single thing to feel guilty about. And don't you forget it."

19

Elliot Wasserman's shaky voice was the second call on Mike Stein's answering machine. He played it back twice:

"I have to be assured, Mr. Stein, that this will be a confidential meeting, between just you and me and off the record."

The kid was a student at N.Y.U., and he claimed to have something of great value not only to Mike Stein but to other people in the media. He was going to Mike Stein first for reasons he would be willing to discuss at their meeting.

Mike picked the time and location: 10 P.M., his office. Official enough to appear slightly awesome to someone who was a little nervous to begin with, and private enough, once he closed his office door, so that he could control whatever followed. This sounded like a very nervous guy.

He was not, physically, what Mike had expected. He had pictured a runty little nerd of a kid with all kinds of tics and mannerisms. A good-looking, well-developed, muscled body-builder presented himself. The kind of guy who would casually admit, Yeah, I work out a little, when what he meant was he spent x number of hours every day, including weekends and holidays, doing a preset number of routines on machines and devices that to Mike resembled medieval torture equipment.

There was something missing between the physical specimen and the actuality of this kid: his handshake was as damp and loose as when he was probably a ninety-pound neighborhood punching bag.

"I'm very appreciative of your time, Mr. Stein. I know how busy you are and all."

His name was Elliot Wasserman and he was a twenty-three-year-old graduate student at N.Y.U. He was majoring in photojournalism.

"Okay, Elliot. What's this all about?"

"You said you had a VHS? When we talked on the phone? Oh, yeah, I see it. Good. Okay. So first I guess we talk, right?"

"So talk."

Mike was deliberately playing cop. In the presence of a nervous witness, nothing more than an occasional prod is necessary.

"Well, okay, let me set up the background first, right? Okay. So I'm a grad student. And I have a room down in the Village. But for the last week or so I've been on field trips, throughout the city, you know. Shooting this and that and the other thing."

As he spoke, Elliot kept flexing his shoulder and arm muscles. He didn't seem to be aware that he was doing it. If he kept it up much longer, his massive shoulders would begin to sink his somewhat short-legged body into his ankles. Elliot was all out of proportion.

Elliot Wasserman's family lived on Barclay Street in Forest Hills. A nice front apartment; two bedrooms faced the courtyard toward the street. His parents were on a trip and Elliot was staying home to feed his mother's two cats. And water the plants. The plants the two cats hadn't already eaten, that is.

"All right, Elliot. Is this it? You got shots of cats eating plants you want to show me? What?"

Elliot had a baby face, a smooth, frightened, damp blank face set on his thick neck. He had baby-blue eyes, and his mouth hung open between sentences, but he pulled himself together finally.

"Okay. What I have is a complete, beginning to end, or almost—*almost* beginning. Not the very, because, well, I didn't realize . . . Anyway, can I put it on the machine and you'll see for yourself, okay?"

"Okay."

"You want me to set it up?"

"You mean like they do on the Johnny Carson show? All right, Elliot, set it up."

As he put his cassette into the machine and clicked the buttons, as the dim picture flashed without definition for the first few seconds, Elliot narrated.

"Okay. So this is the angle from the second-floor window, facing the courtyard, but angled to the street, actually, a clear-cut view. Here we go. The sound isn't too bad, it gets better. But the picture is good, here. Here. Watch, now watch. I really got it, Mr. Stein."

He had it, indeed. It was a fairly good tape. Elliot Wasserman had caught most of it.

His first shot was of a struggle: in the middle of the street, the young woman was pushing and pulling away. Her long dark hair whirled around as she spun free, and a low soft voice was saying, "No no no."

The man was somewhat taller; he was dressed, as had been described, in a light-colored suit. The flashing of a blade could be seen as his right hand slashed through the air. He grabbed the woman with his left hand, and they pulled and lurched almost in a dance, but he was calling out to her in a loud voice, the words, in Spanish. The woman was pleading, "No! No! Please! God! Help! Help me!"

"He's saying to her, 'Cheat! Whore! I'll show you! I'll show you! Thieves!' Like that." Elliot's voice was thin and shaking as he translated.

Mike never took his eyes off the TV screen. The scenario was played out exactly as he had heard it described. It seemed familiar; a scene from a rather bad play, done by amateurs, not very convincing.

Mike watched in fascination as the young woman, abandoned now by her assailant, staggered down the middle of the street, her voice rising, then falling, a sound of despair, desperation, and, finally, a puzzled, sad cry. Unanswered. Then she seemed to take hold: she let her arms fall to her sides and she headed in the direction of the building where, they knew now, her mother lived. She made it as far as the sidewalk. She stopped, both of her hands went up to her forehead, she seemed to press her hands hard against her head, and then her knees buckled and she slid down to a sitting position, leaning against the lamppost. Her head tilted forward and the woman was motionless and silent. She just sat there. A large white car, probably a Cadillac, came from around the corner, came alongside the girl, nearly stopped, then accelerated. Quick shot of bus; spinning shot. The tape ended.

"I didn't know how much further to go. I wanted to see what I had gotten, if I had gotten anything. Jeez, I thought it was a blank, you know, God, that would just be my luck, but I nearly died when I saw what I had.

"Well, Mr. Stein? So? What do you think?" His voice was stretched thin and high-pitched, it was ludicrous, coming from such a sturdy, well-muscled man.

"Tell me what *you* think, Elliot. What do you think you've got here?"

"Well. Well, it's obvious, isn't it? I've got the actual event. Right here. There it is. As it happened. The crucial part: the heart of the encounter. The actual assault. This runs about six minutes. There was yelling, screaming, a few minutes before I filmed. That's what attracted me to the window. And then she just sat there for a while. I didn't watch anymore."

"Why did you bring it to me? Why didn't you bring it to the police? They'd be very happy to have it."

Elliot Wasserman held his cassette in his large hand. He didn't even realize that he was kneading it, exercising his hand, as he spoke.

He tried for a lower-pitched sound; a shrewder sound. "Mr. Stein. I think what I have here is a very valuable property."

"Really? In what way, valuable?"

"Well, I would imagine any of the networks would be very happy to get their hands on it. I would imagine they would be willing to bid for it?"

Mike Stein stood up, shrugged his suit jacket on and nodded toward the door. "Fine. Good night, Mr. Wasserman."

Elliot leaned back in his chair and took a deep breath. He was determined not to get up, not to run, which was exactly what he felt like doing. Having put on forty pounds of muscle changed nothing inside him. He was the same old scared little Elliot.

"Well, then. How do *you* see this, Mr. Stein?"

Mike turned, closed the door with a hard slam and leaned over Elliot.

"Okay, cameraman. After you checked out your shot, after you made certain you got what you hoped to get, after all that, Mr. Wasserman, what did you do then?"

"Do?"

"Did you go down to the street and see what you could do to help this girl?" Mike waved his hand toward the TV set. "Our last view of her, she looked like a girl in a lot of trouble. You didn't go downstairs? Okay, Mr. Wasserman. What *did* you do? Call the police? *Did you dial 911?*"

Elliot poked his lower lip out; it quivered. He looked crumpled; his face collapsed.

"Hey, look, Mr. Stein, I don't need this, really. *I'm* doing *you* a favor by coming to you."

"Is that a fact? Tell me about that, since I don't seem to follow your line of thinking."

"Look, Mr. Stein. I *know* what you've been doing. I've talked around the neighborhood. They all know me, the people on Barclay Street. You got them pretty uptight, Mr. Stein. They're beginning to close up: the witnesses. They're talking to each other and they're getting a little scared about what they've said to you, to the cops. They tell me things."

"Okay. So?"

"Well, I thought with my videotape of what happened, and your know-how and all, we—you—could probably put the finger on the guy. Get an exclusive, and *then* we—I—could sell my tape to the highest bidder. I mean, I get this feeling you're going to make a big megillah out of all this. It's been real low-key, no press, nothing. So you're planning a big exclusive on the neighborhood, right? On the 'good people' of Barclay Street. So, okay, I got it on video, what they all stood and watched—the actual killing of the girl. Gives your story a lotta impact, no?"

"The impact of my story, Mr. Wasserman, comes from two things: the content, and the way *I tell* the story. That's what I'm paid for—*my way of telling a story.* They pay for my name because my name leads to certain expectations. I don't need a videotape to clarify what I'm telling my audience. My words create the pictures, Mr. Wasserman. So, If

I were you, I'd leave that cassette on my desk and walk out and try to forget about it."

"That's very strange advice and—"

"Because you've gotten off to a rotten start. Granted, you followed a cameraman's instinct: you got the shot; you got the moment, the sound and the action. Pretty good too. Okay. What did you do afterwards? That becomes a vital question, Mr. Wasserman. *You did nothing.* Nothing was at risk as far as you were concerned. But you didn't do a goddamn thing to help this dying woman. You watched her die."

Mike stopped speaking. There was a slow rush of blood coloring Elliot's cheeks; at the same time, there was a circle of grayish white around his mouth. He began to blink very quickly and swipe at his damp brow with the back of his large, well-muscled forearm.

"Listen, Mr. Stein."

"No. You listen, Mr. Wasserman. You are very young and at the start of your career. Your action—your inaction—could close out your future. *It can be seen to.* You got that?"

Elliot roused himself, pulled himself up. "Well, look, I know about newsmen who didn't stop filming when some nut set himself on fire. Hell, they weren't firemen, they were cameramen and—"

"And they did their profession irrevocable harm. Elliot, listen to what I'm saying. Carefully. Yes, you might be able to get a couple of bucks from some network. And that'll be the end of it. You will also be nationally known, coast to coast, not for shooting the film, but for failing to take any action when you had every opportunity and no excuse. You read me, kid?"

Elliot was twitching; his shoulders were jumping in some kind of isometric rhythm. He was making Mike Stein very nervous. His large blue eyes were swimming and he was having a little trouble breathing.

"Elliot. You did a good job. As far as you went. I'm telling you what I would tell my own kid. You will destroy your future if you try to peddle that tape. Hand it over to me. This is a police matter and I'll keep you out of it entirely."

"But . . . then it's *evidence*. And it wouldn't be legally binding without me—the person who filmed it." Elliot had once been a law student.

"I wouldn't worry about it, Elliot." Mike softened, shifted gears. "Look, I'll tell you what. Give me a day or two. I'll have a little talk with one or two people I know, contacts at the networks. They are always interested in young, talented photojournalists. I'll put in a word for you. They *do* take my word, in the business."

Elliot swallowed once, twice, breathed carefully and deeply. "Listen, Mr. Stein. I can do something more for you. I mean, I'm in the neighborhood. I hear what people are talking about. *Everyone* is talking. And they're starting to get, like, defensive, you know? They know this thing is going to break, sooner or later, and they are getting nervous. There's been some talk of a meeting of the neighbors. You know, to talk about how to protect themselves. From—you."

"And you are in their confidence?"

Elliot smiled. It was the mean smile of a bratty ten-year-old spy. "Everyone knows me, Mr. Stein. They talk, I listen."

"What you want is to undertake a surreptitious assignment for me? No commitments of any kind, right? And we'll see what works out. That the deal, Elliot?"

"Except, of course, you'll talk to some people at one of the networks on my behalf. Right?"

"One other thing, Elliot." Stein said it casually. As though it weren't important. "If you can, shoot some stills for me,

170

candids of your neighbors. We can definitely do business on that."

Elliot Wasserman stood still. He had the first professional assignment in his life. Photographer for a Pulitzer Prize winner. God!

Elliot Wasserman was hardly out the door when the phone rang. It was Miranda.

"I'm at my office, Mr. Stein. Tomorrow morning my partner and I are flying down to Miami. A man named Paul Mera has confessed to killing Anna Grace."

"Just like that? Just walked into the cops and confessed?"

"No. It's a little more complicated. He was arrested as part of a large-scale round-up of cocaine smugglers. He might be trying to stall for time or just feel like traveling around a little, but who knows? So Detective Dunphy and I will leave for Miami tomorrow, eight-A.M. flight."

"Miranda, do you have a VCR? A Beta or VHS?"

There was a moment of silence. Then, "No."

It irritated him, the fact that she was always willing to wait him out. If he didn't pursue the subject, it would be dropped.

"Okay. Are you heading for your apartment now?"

"Yes. I have to pack and—"

"I'll be there in about an hour. I have a tape to show you. I'll bring my video recorder."

"All right."

"Miranda, aren't you curious? Don't you want to know what this is all about?"

"Mr. Stein, I am tired. I have had a very long day. I have a long day planned for tomorrow. I think you know this, so if you feel it is important that I see your tape, then it must be important. Yes?"

"It is important. Very. Very important. And I'm going to make a gift to you."

A silence, then, "All right. I will see you when you arrive."

She hung up. Stein shook his head and felt: annoyed? amused? Annoyed. Very annoyed. He was about to hand this girl the murderer in action. He disconnected his video machine, wound up the cord. Damn. He'd never even asked Miranda if she owned a television set. He just assumed she did. Everyone did.

Of course, Miranda wasn't everyone.

20

Detective Dunphy was accustomed to using silence deliberately. Usually, it provoked whoever was with him to talk too much. To fill the silence. But Miranda Torres was comfortable in silence. It was one of the things that unnerved him when he first worked with her. To him, silence was a weapon, and it took him a while to realize that she was not engaging him in a contest of wills: it was her nature to sit and listen and to speak only when she had something to say.

He had been surprised at her phone call just after midnight.

"Mr. Mike Stein has just brought me a videotape of the murder on Barclay Street," she said. "He will not tell me who shot it. He claims confidential privilege under the First Amendment and I think that is his right. It looks authentic." And then, after a moment, "It would not be terribly hard to figure, from the angle of the video, where it was shot from. It would be a matter of questioning a few people; probably a little background would reveal a student or a person with an amateur's interest in videotaping."

"It looks good?"

"Oh. Yes. I would say authentic. Shall I bring it with me to Miami?"

Dunphy thought for a moment. Anyone else would be filling the time with suggestions, but Miranda waited.

"If I came by your apartment tomorrow morning, could I take a look at it?"

"Yes. Mr. Stein left his video machine here. What time tomorrow, Jim?"

Dunphy stopped by at 6 A.M. He swallowed the orange juice she gave him, sipped the hot coffee and watched the tape twice.

"Jesus," he said.

"Yes."

"Christ."

"Yes."

"A murder on videotape. There are a coupla good shots of this guy."

"Yes."

"Tell you what, Miranda. You got a safe place to leave this tape? We don't want to take it to Miami with us. Let's leave it here, pick it up after we get a look at this guy Mera."

"All right."

They both recognized Paul Mera the moment they saw him.

They listened to his taped confession, read along with the typed transcription. Everything the man described they had seen happen. His statement could be played as narrative to the video of the murder of Anna Grace.

It took a few hours to go through the legalities. The criminal-justice system of Miami, Florida, was not thrilled at turning Paul Mera over to representatives of the New York City Police Department, but the suspect had waived extradition. He insisted to the Miami police that he had been in the wrong place at the wrong time and knew nothing at all, could tell nothing at all, about any cocaine operation. He had been visiting a friend when wham, bam, *policía* all over the place.

"They scare me plenty, these drug people." Mera said. "I don't wanna be around with them, no way, because I don't know nothing about drugs, I don't use, I don't deal. I don't mix with these people, not with any drug people. I like to be alone with my own thoughts. With my own things."

"Why did you kill Anna Grace?"

"My own reasons. Plenty of my own reasons."

"Did you know her? Was she a friend of yours? A woman friend, a lover? Did she do anything to you, to make you angry?"

Mera, in the square interrogation room, glanced from Miranda to Jim Dunphy, shook his head, made a growling sound, whispered something in a hoarse, angry tone.

Miranda looked at the court-appointed lawyer, a young Hispanic legal aide.

"Mr. Alvarez, kindly tell your client to speak in English. If he is not comfortable in English, please request a court-appointed interpreter."

"But, Detective Torres, you understand Spanish and if he is more comfortable . . ."

"My partner, Detective Dunphy, does not understand Spanish. Talk to your client. We'll break for coffee. If you or Mr. Mera want anything, let me know."

She glanced at Dunphy and he nodded slightly.

Mera called out, loudly, in English, "Hey, you see, man? You let her talk that way, and you sit there and you say nothing, huh? They cut your balls off and you sit there—and you want to know *why?* Why I kill this woman—Anna Grace, whatever the hell? Because she was a *woman,* man. *All of them—all the others, because they were women.*"

175

Miranda and Dunphy froze; they stared at Mera.

"Mr. Mera, please. You are tired and overexcited." Alvarez turned to the detectives. "He is tired and overexcited. He has been without proper rest, without proper food, he would like a warm shower, a change of clothes, he does not know what he is saying and . . ."

Miranda sat down. "What others? What other women did you kill because they were women?"

Mera lapsed into Spanish: a long, bitter, incoherent tirade against women. All women; all females. He described how he would fix them, what he would do to them, how he would deal with them. His attorney, looking suddenly older and smaller than he actually was, raised his hands, grabbed Mera's sleeve, tried to stop him.

Mr. Alvarez spoke a combination of Spanish and English, ending up yelling at his client, "For the love of God, shut up. *Shut up!* Say no more."

Dunphy pressed her shoulder, and Miranda left the room with her partner.

"What do you think?" she asked him.

"Who the hell knows? I tell ya, if we didn't have that videotape, I'm not sure I'd believe this guy. He's a little nuts about being picked up with cocaine dealers. He's trying too hard to distance himself from drugs."

"Maybe he'd rather take his chances in New York on murder charges. Of course, he doesn't know we have the tape. He might think we'd take him for crazy, but take him to New York just to be sure."

She was telling Dunphy the best way to handle it: let Mera think he was putting one over on them. Let him think he was playing for time, that *he* was using *them.*

Dunphy didn't realize how closely he was watching Miranda until she looked up, waiting.

"So?"

Dunphy shook his head. No. Nothing. Just thinking.

What he was thinking was that for the first time since they had started working together, he had just now realized how good Miranda Torres was.

21

Paul Severo Mera was booked at the 112th Precinct in Forest Hills for the murder of Anna Grace. He was a thirty-two-year-old illegal immigrant from Colombia. He claimed to be a chef. He could not give a list of where he had worked either in New York City or in the other cities he claimed to have lived in: Miami, Chicago, Los Angeles and Atlantic City. Wherever he went, he could and did get a short-term job. Yes, always as a chef.

There was a feeling of highly energized activity at the 112th. The arrival of a self-confessed murderer was not usual. In fact, it had never before happened at the 112th. It seemed to the desk officer that every ten or fifteen minutes another heavy gun showed up: representatives from the Queens District Attorney's Office; homicide detectives; a representative from the office of the Chief of Detectives.

Stein left the press conference on the main floor before any of his media colleagues could corner him. He waved to the lieutenant at the desk and went directly upstairs to the second floor. The squadroom door was open and there was a great deal of activity. Miranda Torres was talking on the telephone. She nodded at Mike and continued taking notes.

Mike stared into the interrogation room through the two-way mirror. The suspect had his back to Mike, but there was a certain set to his shoulders, a familiar waving of his hands. Mera stood up suddenly, agitated, walked briskly around the room. It was, definitely, the same man Mike had watched on videotape. This was the murderer of Anna Grace.

Two uniformed policemen, young, smooth-cheeked, excited at being a part of something real, something big, practically burst into the room. One of them, carrying a package, went directly to Miranda and started to unpack the knife he had just found in a search of Mera's apartment.

"Don't take it out, Officer," Miranda told him. "Give it to me, please. Were you careful how you handled this? This is very important evidence, you did realize, yes?"

The police officer nodded, he had touched it, just like she said to do, with plastic gloves; he had inserted the knife into the heavy plastic wrapping.

"Hey, that the guy that did the deed, huh?" The blond cop asked. He was so tall that he had to bend a little for a good view into the interrogation room.

"The little guy, right? The guy with the mustache, right?"

Gently, Miranda pulled at his sleeve. "No. That is a representative from the Queens D.A. The murderer is the one sitting at the table, eating."

"*Eating?* Boy. How about that. *Eating.* The guy slashed a young girl to death and there he is—*eating.* Just like anyone else."

He was overwhelmed at the reality. He had seen plenty of murderers in his lifetime, at least one in each cop-show episode on TV, but this was real. The guy in there was the real thing.

"Yes, he eats like anyone else, Officer," Miranda said softly. "So, okay, you did a good job, you and your partner.

What I would like you to do is to write a report about your search and what you found, okay?"

The second uniform was a little older, a lot tougher. He slipped his hands into his trouser pockets, took a quick look at the suspect, then turned to Miranda. His chin went up and he looked wise. He knew the score.

"Yes, well, okay, but I'd like to ask you something, Detective Torres. How come—why should Frankie here and me be working for you? I mean, what it comes down to, you're not our C.O. Or anything."

Mike admired her control. He knew that she'd been going long hours without a break; that she'd had to deal with a great deal of departmental brass and interference.

Miranda said, "That's just the way it is, Officer."

"Yeah? Well maybe and maybe not. Like, I'd like to talk to a—a sergeant, at least. I mean, I'm not sure what the hell authority *you* have."

"All right, fine. Go and knock on the door to the interrogation room. Look in there now. You see that man, in the dark suit, with the striped tie? You ask him. He is Inspector Williams of the Queens Homicide Squad. Technically, we are all assigned to him. So, go ahead, be my guest. Talk to the boss-of-us-all."

The patrolman looked into the room, then looked at his partner. "Hey, no hard feelings, you know? I'm just asking what the score is. I mean, I don't know you or nothing, so I'm not sure how come you get to tell us . . ."

"Because it is my case. My partner and I caught the case Wednesday night. So everything passes through our hands. Including your report. Yes?"

"Many of these guys give you a hard time?" Stein asked her.

"This? This is not a hard time. It's no big deal. They did a good job. They brought back the murder weapon. This one

180

policeman, he's just stretching and flexing a little. This does not bother me a little bit."

She smiled: a what-the-hell's-the-difference–boys-will-be-boys, and that's what these two are, a pair of boys. They were no more than three or four years younger than Miranda. With her smooth, miraculously glowing skin and tall lithe body, her grace and quiet presence, she seemed, to Stein, to be as untouched by what she had experienced as a child. Except, sometimes, fleetingly, there was a dark, flat deadness at the center of her eyes, compounded of sadness, the experience of terrible things seen and understood and accepted. He had caught that emptiness once or twice, had caught her off guard. Thought he had seen into the heart of Miranda, but could not be sure. Not yet. She was still, to him, a mystery.

"That A.D.A. wants to talk with you, Mr. Stein. He has a different view of your rights to confidentiality. He wants you to present him with your videotape."

Stein glanced into the interrogation room and smiled. "That little guy with the mustache? What happened, he was absent when they gave the lecture about the sanctity of the journalistic world?"

"This is his very first case. He's been with the D.A.'s office for nearly two years. Failed his boards the first time, so he's been working as a law clerk. Up until last week. Now he's for really and truly a prosecutor."

"You think *he's* gonna see this case through? Looks like it's kinda heavy. You got everybody here but the Mayor."

"The Mayor is in Italy, but he's on top of everything."

"As always."

The door to the interrogation room burst open and Mr. "Sonny" Waters, twenty-nine years old, five foot five inches tall, overwhelmed by a heavy head of thick curly black hair, weighed down by a huge dark mustache which dropped over his mouth and chin, stormed into the squad room. He glanced around, then motioned with a jerk of his head to Miranda.

"Sir?"

"Listen, that guy in there is jerking me off or something," he said. "I studied Spanish not only in high school and college, but I took an intensive conversational course at Berlitz. And, I spent three weeks in Spain with no trouble at all being understood. And—" he did something with his mouth, it was hard to tell what, maybe a smile, maybe a grimace, the mustache hid whatever it was—"and I had a Spanish-speaking lady, and we had no trouble at all understanding each other. You know what I'm saying?"

"Oh, yes. I understand English almost perfectly," Miranda said.

The short district attorney glared at her for a moment, then relaxed. "Okay, okay. So what's the story with this guy in there? I ask him questions he stares at me and says 'Huh?' Like he doesn't understand. He giving me a hard time, is that it?"

"Yes. That is it. There is nothing *personal* involved, Mr. Waters. You know, he's been under a great deal of pressure. In Miami he's been in custody for several days, and he's exhausted. The Miami authorities didn't want to give him up and—"

"They thought their bullshit cocaine bust was heavier than our quad murder? That the way they thought? Goddamn redneck cracker jerk-offs." He glanced at Stein. "Hey. Wait a minute. I know you. You're Mike Stein. The columnist, journalist, right?"

Stein played Miranda's game. He smiled and spoke in a pleasantly neutral tone. "Writer. Journalist, columnist, novelist, reporter—whatever. As long as they put my name on the check and the check doesn't bounce, I don't care what they call me. And you are Mr. Waters, of the Queens District Attorney's Office? Mr. Sonny Waters?"

Waters took Stein's offered hand for a quick shake, squinted his round beige eyes and pointed an index finger at Mike.

"You got some information we need. That is crucial to the prosecution of that little jerk-off in there. It would be much easier on you if you would just give us the name of your cameraman—whatever you call a guy who shoots video, your videoman?—and let us get him before the grand jury. Otherwise, we can't present the tape of the murder of Anna Grace. So? So? We're all in this together. And remember, one hand helps the other, right? Right?"

Mike Stein started to laugh. His head fell back and then down to his chest and he turned his back on the district attorney, waved him off, didn't watch as the furious man stormed across the office, stopped and issued some sort of dire warning in his general direction.

"You shouldn't have done that," Miranda said softly. "Little man, large ego."

Mike wrapped his arm around Miranda's shoulders and squeezed. His face was flushed and his eyes were tearing.

"I know. I know. But, Jesus. A grown man answering to the name 'Sonny.' This little . . . jerk-off. Oh, God!"

"You seem very happy, Mr. Stein. Didn't you run into your colleagues at the press briefing downstairs? I think they are all very angry with you. They have had no luck at all in trying to interview witnesses. No one will open a door. They want to know why you had early access *and* what you did to the good people of Barclay Street to make them so hostile to the press."

"Not what I've *done,* Miranda. What I am *going to do.* My first article of the series will be published Monday: 'The

Girl Who Was Murdered Twice.' Photos of all the good folk—with their own tag line under each picture. Right from their own mouths. Their own hearts. You want to know what I'm high on? A deal, kiddo. My agent called me this morning. Jesus, I haven't heard this kind of money in ten years. A book contract, magazine and film tie-in. There's still a lot of big money out there; I haven't had a crack at in a long time. Hey. Why the stare? Don't shake your head, you're making a judgment, right now. What?"

"No. No judgment. I am curious, do you want to know anything about our suspect in there? Our confessed murderer? Or are you really not interested in him?"

"I got all I need to know about him at the briefing. I told you at the very beginning, *he* isn't what interests me. He's what he is: a bum, a killer for whatever reason. He knows what he is. The good people of Barclay Street—now, that's different, They don't know what they are."

"And you are going to tell them."

"You got it, kid. I'm going to let them, and the rest of the world, get a good look at them. And for my book—I've got a fast six months to put it together—I'm going to get all the 'experts' in on it. The shrinks, the criminologists, the urbanologists, the specialists—gonna give them all a chance to explain why the good people of Barclay Street let Anna Grace bleed to death. Why not one of them lifted a finger to help."

Miranda turned away.

"Hey, listen. You know what they're doing, these good people? They're getting together and forming a committee. They've hired a lawyer. To try and stop publication of my articles. To try and sue my publishers. They've had a few meetings. Guess who's the organizer."

"Mr. Harry Lamont?" she asked.

"You got it. What are you, a detective or something? How

come you're so smart? Hey, listen, Miranda, whadda ya think Mr. Mera in there was doing with Sonny, the Spanish-speaking district attorney from Berlitz?"

Miranda smiled. "Jerking him off, of course. You heard Mr. Waters. He was absolutely right."

She answered the phone. "Detective Torres. Yes. All right, send him up. Wait, spell his name please. Enrique *Firenze*— no, I don't know him. Okay, thank you, Lieutenant." And then to Mike Stein, "Will you excuse me, please. I have to take care of this."

He waited, then smiled. "Okay, I'll call you later today, Miranda. We'll exchange information."

A well-dressed, handsome middle-aged man stood in the doorway to the squad room.

Miranda went over and extended her hand.

"Mr. Firenze? I am Detective Miranda Torres. How do you do?"

"Señorita." He began to speak Spanish, and Miranda held up her hand.

"English, please." She indicated the uniformed patrolmen, the captain and her partner, who had just come from the interrogation room.

He had an Old World elegance, a courtly, careful manner of speaking. "I am here to represent Mr. Mera. I understand that he had Legal Aid representation down in Miami and that in the presence of this assigned attorney he made certain statements. I would like to meet with Mr. Mera, to have an opportunity to speak with him, to go over any statements he has made regarding—" he spread his hands widely— "anything."

A.D.A. Waters returned and, upon being introduced to Mr. Firenze, began to speak in Spanish.

"Ah, Mr. Waters, in deference to your colleagues, I think it would be best if we converse strictly in English, yes?"

Waters glared around the room suspiciously. "Whatever. You got quite a client in there. Anybody tell you about the tape we got? Plead the guy, Counselor. Plead him and save the city money."

"Tape? What tape do you mean?"

Captain O'Connor, Detective Dunphy and Torres all began to speak at once. They surrounded the fiery district attorney and swept him into the captain's office for a briefing. Information he needed to have—updating. They were all talking at once when the commotion burst in on them. One of the patrolmen, the older one, the wiser one, the tougher one, had gone pale.

"Hey, Torres. You better come quick. Your killer is going nuts! He attacked his attorney."

By the time Miranda was able to enter the interrogation room, Mera was handcuffed and being held by the younger patrolman with assistance from two homicide detectives. Mr. Firenze was being helped to his feet and escorted from the room by Captain O'Connor and Detective Dunphy. She caught a quick glimpse of the blood that was streaming down the side of his flushed, well-shaven face. He seemed concerned about the rip in the trousers of his expensive suit. He shouted, his voice high-pitched with emotion, "Scum. You should not have done that! You should not have done that!"

It was all in Spanish now.

Mera said, "Who sent him here? Don't let them come near me. You people are supposed to protect me. What the hell is wrong with you? You want me to make this easy on you? You want me to cooperate, take a guilty plea? You want me to tell you about *all* of the murders, then you take care of me. You got that? Take care of me."

One of the homicide detectives understood enough Spanish to catch the words "all of the murders." For the rest, he depended on Miranda Torres, who said, "Okay, let me talk to him. Tape it, I'll translate from the tape later.

"You want to talk quietly with me, Mr. Mera? I'll have the cuffs taken off, if you want to talk quietly. Otherwise, well, you sit here and quiet down by yourself. Your choice."

"Yeah, I'll talk. Good, get them off. Listen, that was his own fault. Who sent him? You got any idea who sent him here? You know who he is?"

"No. I have no idea."

"Yeah? You know. He gets plenty, that bum. He makes a lot of money. I don't want him or any of them near me, you got that?"

"Yes. But I don't understand. Who is Firenze? He looks like a lot of money to me. You don't know who sent him?"

"I didn't say that, I . . ." Mera leaned over his folded hands, rubbed his forehead. "Listen, I didn't say nothing about nothing. He is a stranger who came in from the street, okay? I could tell he costs a lot the same way you can tell. Money shows, no? His clothes, his . . . The haircut, the cologne, the shoes. You see his shoes? Two hundred, three hundred bucks."

"I don't know shoes. But I know briefcases. Attaché cases, you know, like lawyers carry? His was a good one. A very good one."

"Yeah?" Mera was interested in how much things cost. "How much a very good one runs? How much money?"

"A good one, a custom-made, one of a kind—maybe a thousand dollars. The best kind, I'm talking about."

"What the hell are they talking about—shoes and attaché cases?" Assistant District Attorney Waters wanted to know. He could follow the conversation from the intercom on Captain O'Connor's desk, but it didn't make any sense to him.

Captain O'Connor and Detective Dunphy couldn't under-

187

stand any Spanish, but they did realize that Miranda was calming things down, getting things in order, settling Mera, priming him, setting him up. Playing with him. Firenze, the attorney, left without a word of explanation. He did not have to nor did he intend to tell them who had hired him or why Mera had reacted so violently.

"That's a lot of money," Mera said. "But a bum like that—money is nothing to him. The kind of money that runs through their hands—shit, they have trouble spending it, you know. Custom everything, suits, cars, whores. Custom whores. That's funny, no? A whore to order: size, color, shape, special tricks, special smell, special clothes, special special special. Oh, what the hell, a whore has a right to make money, no? I say good that they get to share some of it. They do okay because these guys, they play with the money there is so much."

He stared at Miranda. Their eyes locked. His face contorted and a shudder ran through his tense muscular body. His mouth moved and his lips pulled back and his teeth were revealed: large and white, slightly parted.

"*Bitch.* What are you trying to pull here? You see, you ask, you all ask, 'Why you kill this nice young woman?' Nice young woman. You a nice young woman, huh, you sit here and you talk to me like I am some kind of fool, you so very smart as to make a fool of a man, huh, is that it?"

The connection had been broken. With nothing to lose, she went straight to it.

"What are we talking about now, Mr. Mera? All that money. So much money. From what, Mr. Mera? Who does Mr. Firenze work for that he gets so much money? Why did someone send him to represent you? Did he have a message of some kind to deliver to you?"

"I don't want to talk to you anymore, bitch."

He stood up and banged on the door.

"Get her out of here," he yelled to Dunphy. "Get her out of here before I cannot help myself. You want to know why I killed that woman on Barclay Street? And the others?" He leaned into the squad office and yelled directly at the homicide detectives. "You want to know about the others? The three others? Okay. But you keep this bitch—or any other woman, you understand?—away from me. Fucking bitches, all of them should get it. You let me alone with her—I show her!"

Miranda sat in Captain O'Connor's office and translated the tape for him, Dunphy, a homicide detective named Teitel, and A.D.A. Waters. The tape came to a halt at the point where the detectives had taken over and Mera reverted to English.

"Well," Captain O'Connor said. He lit a cigarette and took off his old glasses, rubbed his eyes. "Well, what the hell do we have here?"

Waters started to speak, but O'Connor held up his hand. "Let's think about it for a moment, okay, Mr. Waters?" Then, to Dunphy, "Get someone on Firenze. Who the hell *is* he? Who sent him?"

"I placed a coupla calls, Captain. It's in the works."

Which was no less than O'Connor had expected.

Waters looked around the room, puzzled. "He probably comes from some Hispanic organization. Established attorneys give a certain amount of their time to cases that—"

O'Connor cut right through and spoke to Miranda. "Detective Torres, what do you think?"

Miranda studied her hands, locked together in her lap. Slowly, she looked up, directly at O'Connor. The slight shrug, the less-than-certain tone that really didn't convey doubt. "Drugs?"

"What do you mean?" Waters asked. "What drugs? The man is a murderer. You heard him. You've seen him. That man, in that room, is confessing to four separate murders of females. Here, you, Detective—" he indicated the homicide detective with his chin—"you've heard him. You're working on these homicides, aren't you? That man is the Beast of Queens. And he looks it. Doesn't he?"

The detective shrugged and remained silent.

"What are you talking about, Torres? *Drugs? What drugs?* We got us a murderer in there. You've *seen* him in action. You've *seen* the videotape, haven't you?"

"Mr. Waters, Detective Torres *gave* us the tape. And I wish you wouldn't refer to it quite so freely when—"

"Oh? *You* wish? I see. Listen, I represent the Queens District Attorney's Office and as of right now—well, with maybe a little more cooperation from the homicide squad—I think I'm nearly ready to hit up the grand jury for four separate indictments." Waters spread his arms wide, then smacked his hands together. "Clean sweep. Doesn't that please you? Why are you all so goddamn gloomy? Maybe you all need a little time off, that the problem? Heat got you down? Well, I'm putting my case—my four cases—together. You people seem to doubt his confession to the other killings. What did you expect, a videotape of every one of them? Well, life ain't that easy, is it? Listen, if you people come up with anything that might be important, call my office and leave a message. I have work to do."

The departure of the assistant district attorney left an abrupt silence in the room. The captain rubbed at his scratched lenses and set them in place.

"What the hell is this guy Mera saying about the other murders?" he asked the homicide cop.

Slowly, carefully, Teitel said, "I haven't been in on the others, Captain. We'll be questioning him in teams. I'm assigned to the Anna Grace killing. This case is the strongest."

"What do you *think*—off the top of your head—about the

possibility that he's telling the truth? That he did in fact kill the other women?"

The homicide cop, a thick, heavyset, sweaty man with small eyes set close together on either side of a small, piggy nose, pursed his lips and sucked in air before he answered. His voice was surprisingly light for such a rough, grungy-looking man.

"I don't think about nothin', Captain, but what I'm assigned to think about. I can only talk about my own particular assignment, and like I said, I think we got him real good. For Anna Grace."

"All right, pal, no one is trying to—Listen, don't you people have anything better to do than hang around here all night? Dunphy, Torres, how much overtime you putting in? Pick up in the morning, if you haven't anything special to do. You both look tired." Dunphy looked like hell; Torres looked cool—and smart. That was the word. She had a smart, sharp, cool, unruffled look. O'Connor realized he had been staring, taking stock, though she did not seem to have noticed.

"Hey, you two put in your expense sheets yet for Florida? You got that done yet?"

"We got the papers in, Cap," Dunphy said. Then, low key, taking advantage of friendship, always knowing when it was safe, "So whadda ya think? Don't you think Torres and I deserve a coupla days away from all this? A chance to breathe and reflect?"

O'Connor stood alongside Dunphy, and they watched Miranda Torres leave. He looped his arm around Dunphy's shoulder and said softly, "So tell me, kid, what the hell are we dealing with here? This guy the creeping raper-murderer Beast of Queens, or what the hell have we got here?"

"We got something not right, is what we got."

"Homicide and the D.A.'s Office are very hot to stuff what-

191

ever open crime we got in Queens into this guy's bag. And he seems not only available but eager to admit to everything and anything. This gent playing tricks or what?"

"Someone's playing something, Bill. Tell ya, these are the days when I'm glad I never passed the promotion exams. Too much responsibility for me. You tell me what to do, I'm the kinda soldier does it."

"What kinda soldier is Torres?"

Dunphy pulled back, reached up and removed O'Connor's glasses. He held them to the light and shook his head.

"No wonder you have headaches, for Christ's sake. Why don't you wear your new ones? These would make anyone blind."

"Oh? Am I blind? Am I missing something?"

The two men, old friends, years and secrets and plans and schemes between them, held a deep long unspoken communication, questions asked and answered.

Finally, Dunphy said, "Bill, the day hasn't come when you'd miss anything like that. Not a damn thing."

"Ya not interested or what?"

"Hey, this is a very interesting girl. But I'll tell ya, you forget all that when you work together. Jeez, Billy, this kid is one helluva cop. And . . . well, she's a . . . she's *nice,* ya know? She knows how to be a partner."

"Anything doing with her and Stein?"

"I doubt it. I doubt it very much."

O'Connor looked over the top of his glasses.

"But on the other hand," Dunphy said quickly, "who the hell ever really knows?"

22

They'd made a tentative date for dinner. Mike wanted to show off a little: a good French restaurant, the best food and wine and then his apartment. But a phone call from Forest Hills changed his plans. He had to visit someone on Barclay Street.

It was one of the things—among many things—that he liked about Miranda Torres. He knew there'd be no hurt feelings, no long pauses, no injured tone, no prying questions. He was surprised, however, at her response.

"That is good," she said. "I was getting ready to call you. I've been called back to work on a homicide."

"In Forest Hills? Not another—"

"No, no. Something quite different."

He knew it was all she would say. "Well, all right, then. We'll be in touch. Soon."

Stein's telephone call led him to the Stone apartment, fourth-floor front. There was fairly good view of where the attack had taken place: just to the left of center and straight down.

There were just the two of them, father and son. Jason Stone, the father, was a professional studio musician. He played a number of instruments, and on the night of Anna Grace's death he had been playing keyboard for an up-and-coming new group. They had played well into the morning hours, and by the time he had returned home most of the commotion on Barclay Street had come down to a few uniformed policemen standing around looking bored.

"Angelo waited up for me, Mr. Stein, and he told me, as much as he knew, what was going on."

Angelo Stone was a small boy in a wheelchair. It would be difficult to guess his age—thirteen—by his appearance. His body was distorted and misshapen and odd, but the cerebral palsy, with complications, had not affected his intelligence. If anything, Angelo's brain functioned in rarefied isolation not dissipated by any physical activity. Added to the fact that his IQ had been measured higher than the 170s, the intensity of his enormous light-brown eyes was disturbing.

It was Angelo, not his father, who explained his situation.

"You might say I've developed my innate intellectual abilities to the sharpness, say, of a blind person's sense of touch or hearing. It is a known fact that most humans function at about ten percent of their intellectual capacity. I think that probably that's what marks what is so-called genius from the average: the use of at least part of the ninety percent dormant ability. I really haven't had much choice in my life."

His voice had a peculiar, tinny sound. Mike searched his memory quickly. The boy sounded like a cartoon character, like a little animal. It was a parody of human speech, thin, piping, but understandable.

Angelo managed very well despite his physical handicaps. His room was filled with electronic equipment that he could operate with the fingertips of his right hand. Every item in his room that had to be activated—lights, telephone, TV, tape deck, computers—was designed to function especially

194

at the level of his capability. Angelo had worked with the engineers in developing most of the equipment.

"Angelo is a born engineer. He's studying at college level. He's planning to design equipment for handicapped people."

Angelo smiled at his father and shook his head. In his weird little voice he said, "Whatta guy, that Angelo! There stands a father, Mr. Stein." Followed by a thin, staccato sound: Angelo laughing.

Then the conversation came to an abrupt halt and the silence turned tense.

"Mr. Stone, this is all very impressive and I'm sure we'll all hear a great deal from Angelo one day. But you didn't ask me to come here for that reason."

For the first time, Angelo deferred to his father.

"Mr. Stein, Angelo was here, at this window, working on some problem. This is what he calls his 'thinking place,' right here. And he saw the attack on this woman, who was killed. He saw the man come from behind the parked cars, he saw him grab at the woman and attack her. He couldn't actually see him clearly enough to identify him, but he *could see exactly what he was doing.* He said the blade flashed in the light. He knew it was a knife."

Stein looked from father to son. An odd transformation had occurred. The boy, incredibly, had seemed to shrink even smaller. His body seemed more compacted. His head looked larger, more bloated, balloonlike, lolling to the right. His right hand, his only controllable instrument, began to shake. The boy stared at the jumping fingers.

"My reaction to tension," he said. His voice was even more peculiar: tinier, an imitation of a small child's. Angelo's breathing increased; his gasps were deep and loud, interrupted by a strange laughing, giggling sound.

"Are you all right, Angelo?"

Jason Stone put a large hand on his son's forehead. The

195

boy rolled his head back, and his eyes focused on his father's face. There was a gentleness between the two. The father's hands moved slowly, patiently, with years of experience, along his son's neck, shoulders, forehead. He patted his son's cheeks.

"This is what happens when I get tensed up," Angelo explained in his tinny voice, gasping, laughing, coughing. "All this—all these—sound effects—are completely—absolutely—un-con-trol-lable."

"Let me explain, Angelo," Jason Stone said softly. "You just hang in there, all right? All right, Angelo? Good. Mr. Stein, we've heard, from neighbors, from people on the block, that you've been interviewing witnesses to this terrible, terrible thing. One of our neighbors, a Mr. Lamont, the man who owns the clothing shop on Austin Street, he's been canvassing the neighbors. Asking who you've interviewed, what their impression of you has been. What it is you're after. He's planning a meeting with the people you've talked to. He's told everyone he thinks you're planning to do a number on them, the witnesses, instead of focusing on the real culprit, the murderer. And on the police. Well, you can guess what his attitude is, you've met him."

"Yes. I've met him."

"Well, he was here and he spoke to Angelo. Angelo listened carefully and what he's come up with is what you've come up with. The fact that all the people on this block watched a murder. Watched an attack that left the victim alive but bleeding. Watched the young woman die, rather than do anything, at all, to help her."

"*I called 911,*" Angelo said in a high, shrieky voice. His hands began to jump spasmodically as he indicated his telephone, hooked up to his bank of electronic equipment.

"*And I recorded it.*"

23

During the last four days, there had been a record number of impulse killings all over the city. Psychologists were blaming the unbearable stress of an unlivable atmosphere: the heavy thick polluted air pressed and weighted down human beings, the simple act of breathing became an ordeal, simple everyday emotional events became catastrophic. Simple family arguments or disagreements, over which TV program to watch, who drank the last can of beer or who wouldn't pass the salt, turned into homicides: by knife or family gun, kept illegally by the bedside for protection against interlopers.

Screaming, inconsolable infants were tossed through open windows or slammed against walls by distraught parents who only wanted a little quiet.

A person looking at another person in the wrong way—whatever way that was, sometimes merely by making eye contact—had unknowingly issued a challenge which ended in violent death.

Life was taken randomly, without thought and seemingly without motive. Not just the violence-prone, who went about satisfying their peculiar needs regardless of weather or atmospheric pressures, but the most unlikely, the quiet, the good, exploded in the most incredible acts of personal violence against people known and loved, or in a setting of strangers. New York City was a psychiatric casebook of violence during the unrelenting pollution inversion.

The biggest act of violence in the city, however, was not random, impulsive, unplanned or careless. It was an orchestrated mob hit, performed in five separate locations, on five carefully selected victims: two in Manhattan, two in Queens and one in Brooklyn. The hit on five medium-level organization wise guys had been programmed and choreographed so that all the victims were hit at precisely the same moment, while probably enjoying more or less identical entrees at favorite neighborhood Italian restaurants. It was as though the message was not so much in the killing as in the timing. It was an inarguable way of saying, Not only can we take you out, but we can take you out as you eat your evening meal in your favorite restaurant, surrounded by your favorite people.

Precinct detectives and homicide detectives were running into one another, hurrying from one location to another. Too many cops were on vacation. Emergency calls to summer homes went unanswered by men who had heard all they wanted to know on the radio. The city morgues were running to capacity. There were not enough experienced coroners to deal with professionally killed people as well as run-of-the-mill average mugging homicides and the tremendous number of spur-of-the-moment victims: people throttled by people who ordinarily would never even think of committing violence on a fellow living creature.

Bodies were shifted from borough to borough: Manhattan's house of death gave temporary refuge to Brooklyn and Queens casualties. In times of crises, borough and precinct lines had to be crossed.

Out at Kennedy Airport, in the far flat swampy reaches

beyond the runways, the air was fouled not only by the heavy thick fumes of dropped fuel and jet exhaust, but by the rotten garbage odor of an unofficial dump that had been used by private garbage collectors for years. Rather than go through the legalities required to obtain an officially designated dump area, it was easier to just pull off on a side road near Rockaway Boulevard and unload a dump truck filled with debris from restaurants, supermarkets, hospitals, industrial plants or whatever other customers hired private cartage.

Not only was the dump used for deposit, it was also carefully culled and searched by junk dealers who specialized in discarded newspapers, cartons, containers of a certain kind. There were those who waded through every other kind of litter until they found what it was they dealt in. There were parts of wrecked cars that even the professional dealers in such things didn't want. There were scavengers who, for whatever reason, collected glass in any condition: broken, shattered, smashed, whatever.

There was a new breed, since the enactment of the bottle law: kids, about thirteen or fourteen years old, who couldn't find jobs, who needed spending money, who were ready, willing and able to work and who had to invent their own source of income. They were the ones who discovered treasure troves of discarded bottles, beer cans, soda cans, tossed away by people who didn't care about the nickel they were losing.

Three boys searched through the mountains of garbage and swamp. They wore kerchiefs, cowboy style, over their noses and mouths, carried plastic garbage bags over their shoulders. Their take was pretty good; at least enough to justify their working conditions. It was time to call it a day. None of them wanted to be stuck out there in the dark. The leader, a tall rangy kid whose clothes stuck to him with a combination of sweat and slime, slipped on a large green garbage bag. His feet skidded and he went flying flat out, his own bag of treasures tossed into the air. He turned, hauling himself to his feet to check on the damage. His two friends stood staring, gaping at the ripped bag that had tripped him.

A stiff, curled-up human foot poked through the tear. There was a second garbage bag, identical in size and general shape, lying alongside the first.

The boys ran, leaving behind their day's earnings. They ran until their lungs were aching, their heads spinning, their eyes filled with tears.

A patrol car cruising along Rockaway Boulevard pulled up, a cop called them over and the boys began screaming in ragged voices, pointing back into the swamp garbage lot.

Although the policemen on the scene did not know it, the bodies of Arabella Vidales and Christine Valapo had been found.

24

Captain O'Connor pretended that the smell of the garbage, compounded by the thick heavy black taste of dropped fuel and the suffocating air inversion, didn't bother him. He pulled on his cigarette, choosing his own poison.

He told Miranda Torres, "I wouldn't have called you out on this, but I remembered something you said, about the stewardess who had rented the Barclay Street apartment for her younger sister. The one the neighbors called the 'Spanish girl.' "

Miranda breathed shallowly and she pretended that nothing bothered her: not the place, not the obscene fumes, not the murdered bodies of two young women her own age. She focused on the fact that she was surprised by O'Connor. She wasn't always sure that he listened when she spoke. She had underestimated him. She would remember this.

"Their boss at Avianca reported them as missing persons," he said. "He mentioned the fact that you'd inquired about them. So—" O'Connor turned to where the technicians were working—"looks like they're not missing anymore."

He watched her closely. They all did that when things got rough.

"Of what did they die?" she asked.

"They're in bad shape. What with the heat and all. But, apparently, strangulation. Both were probably raped. Maybe roughed up some first. So, what with your inquiry and then the guy at Avianca, what we probably got here are"—he glanced at his notebook—"Arabella Vidales and Christine Valapo. They don't look too good, but good enough for ID, I guess. Is there any other relative you know of besides the little sister who can ID Vidales?"

She flashed on Carlos Galvez, menacing, troubling, larger than life. She shook her head.

"No. I will get the girl."

"Okay." He turned to watch the activity around the bodies. "I think all these good people are just about finished with their preliminary work. The bodies will be taken to Queens General. You want anyone to go with you—to pick up the sister? Gonna be okay?"

"I will handle this by myself, Captain." Conscious that he was watching her closely, Miranda glanced at the attendants as they loaded the bodies onto carriers. "You know, Captain," she said, "it will *not* be okay. This is not an 'okay' thing, is it, this . . . this raping and beating and strangling of young women. It will *not* be okay for anyone at all, but in all of this, if you mean will *I* be okay, yes. I will do my job, if that is what you are asking."

He had never seen her anger before. Hints of it, flashing signs of it, quickly controlled. It was as he would have anticipated: cool, careful, limited and, surprisingly, very tough. He sensed immediately that this was necessary for Miranda Torres, this girding herself, this drawing on herself. He kept on her line exactly: offered her a hard, official presence.

"Fine, Detective Torres. Now that you've had your say, get going."

She nodded once, briskly, then took off in her car.

She tried to reach Carlos Galvez. She put aside her reluctance to confront the man again or even to hear his voice. His phone rang more than ten times before she hung up. It wasn't that far from her office and it wouldn't take more than a few minutes. She drove past Barclay Street after checking that there was a light on in Maria Vidales' apartment.

On Inverness Street, the two rows of attached houses on either side of the street showed signs of declining night life: dim lights on patios; bedroom lights glowing; the odd grayish flicker of television sets. The first thing she noticed was the absence of any cars in front of the Galvez house. No limo-size Lincolns or Caddies. No Mercedes. No lights on inside the house or on the terrace.

Miranda got out of her car and tried to see into the living-room windows. It was too dark, she could see nothing. She was both relieved and regretful. Now she would have to escort Maria Vidales for identification.

She listened for a moment to the music, hard rock, barely muffled by the apartment door. It was loud and somewhat out of control, devoid of humor or good feeling. Just loud noise, pierced by shouts and whoops of laughter. Someone in there was feeling very loose and very high.

Maria opened the door, then tried to close it when she saw Miranda.

"Oh. Look who it is. No. No, you cannot talk to me. I don't want to see you, get lost."

A young man, thick dark hair hanging across his forehead, pulled Maria away. "Who is this? Wadda ya want? Want some fun, baby? Hey, Maria, who is this, your sister? She is a beauty, this one."

A door across the hall opened, then shut with a resounding noise. Neighbors were annoyed.

Miranda shouldered her way into the apartment, closed

the door behind her. She spoke quietly, firmly and rapidly in Spanish.

"You, take whatever illegal substances you have on you and get lost. Very quickly, before I decide to bust you just for the hell of it. I'm a police officer, ask Maria."

"What the hell is this? Jeez, you can't just bust in here and—"

"Oh yes I can. I just did. Ask Maria. Tell him. Tell him to get lost."

Maria looked at her. They stared at each other, and, without words, she knew. *She knew.*

Maria whispered, "Peter, go home. Please. No, don't say anything, don't ask . . . just go home. This is between this lady and me."

There was something about both of them that froze the young man: two women, with something terrible, some secret, between them that he didn't want any part of.

Miranda reached out and took hold of his arm.

"How are you traveling? Do you have a car?"

"None of your business, what is this anyway?"

Maria said, "He takes the bus or he walks. He isn't driving."

Miranda let him go. She walked over to the stereo and turned the music off.

"I'm going to take you to her," she said to Maria.

"Yes. I thought that was why you are here."

The young girl's face sagged, her mouth pulled down, her eyes were glazed not just by drugs but as though a shield of some kind clouded them.

"Maria, is there anyone you'd like to call? Shall I call that boy back? To come with us."

Maria studied her, and her lips twisted into a grotesque smile. "No. He is no one. Without Arabella, I have no one to call."

"What are you on, right now? Are you speeding or floating or what?"

"Right now, police lady? Right now? I am on something so terrible it has no name. Could we go now? Could we not talk?"

She never asked and Miranda never told her. It was an assumed knowledge, that her sister was dead, that she was being taken to see her dead sister. The girl sat without touching the back of the car seat, rigid, frozen, blank, only her body present—Maria had gone to some unknown far place.

When they arrived at Queens General Hospital and were headed toward the morgue at basement level, Miranda heard Maria gasp, cough. Caught her as she leaned forward clutching her stomach; tried to help her.

Maria turned her back. "Leave me alone. I am all right. Don't touch me. Just don't touch me."

When she stood up, she seemed smaller, hunched forward by despair. Her complexion was devoid of color, devoid of blood, the pallor of a corpse. A long strand of thick black hair fell over her face, covered her mouth. Maria reached for it, pushed at it, couldn't seem to deal with it.

"This hair," she said. "I want to cut this hair. I want to cut this hair. I want to do it now. Could I do it now?"

"Later," Miranda said. "We'll do that later. Maria, I think maybe we'd better—"

Maria pulled herself free of Miranda's hand. "I told you, do not touch me. Let's get this over with. I want to see her. Take me to my sister. I want to do this, now."

Miranda nodded and they continued down the long, dark corridor, past piled-up cafeteria furniture, bulging garbage bags.

An explosion of laughter from a small office startled them. A short bald man in a dirty white uniform with rolled-up pants came toward them, smiling at the joke he'd just heard.

He shook his head at them, as though they knew, too, what was so funny.

"Wait here," Miranda instructed her at the door to the morgue. Her tone was crisp, official, impersonal, unemotional.

"They're not here," the clerk at the rubber-topped desk told Miranda. "They got detoured to Manhattan. We got a couple of those Mafia guys that got hit at dinner—man, one of them at a restaurant where I take the wife, a small place on the Boulevard. The other guy at some place on Union Turnpike. I wanna get the name—these guys always eat where the food is great." He grinned. "At least they had a good last supper, huh? One of them, the older guy, boy, he fell forward, bam, right into a plate of pasta. First I thought it was blood, but when they wiped it off, I gotta tell ya, it smelled lots better than blood, ya know?"

"Where are the bodies of the two women?"

He checked his ledger, then turned the book around so that Miranda could see for herself. He kept a stubby index finger on the appropriate line. "They're in Manhattan. We been shifting stiffs, I don't know what's goin' on. It must be the weather got people crazy, right? You know, one day last week, I'm here, minding my own business, and who do you think they brung in? *My bartender.* I mean, a guy I been drinking at his place for maybe fifteen, twenty years, a neighborhood joint in Queens Village, a nice place, like your own home, and some jerk, *a neighborhood guy,* not some nutty outsider, but one of the regulars, ya know, he gets into an argument about one thing and another and he goes home and then he comes back and points a gun, right between the eyes, blows this guy away, right? Willy, the bartender, twenty years I known him. Funny, I never knew his last name until I put him in the book. Wilson. Willy Wilson, right? Now you tell me, lady, is that crazy or is that crazy? Jeez, you just don't know when you get up in the morning, right?"

"Right," Miranda said.

She took Maria's arm and led her back along the darkened corridor.

"I made a mistake," she said, holding tightly to the girl. "We have to go to Manhattan."

Maria made the identification quickly, quietly, calmly. Yes. It was her sister, Arabella Vidales. The dull eyes glinting through the swollen lids, the strange expressionless face, distorted by death, the beautiful hair, flattened and matted to the texture of rotting vegetation—none of these things could hide the fact. This was Arabella Vidales, her sister.

Miranda led her to a waiting room, pointed to a contoured plastic chair. The room was filled with groupings of plastic furniture for grieving relatives. Maria's eyes were tremendous, black, glistening, vacant. The girl was traveling, and Miranda did not want her to go too far away.

"Do you know," she said, "that the girl, Anna Grace, looked very much like that when she was in the morgue? *Look at me, I am telling you something.*"

Maria stared through her.

Miranda leaned close, cupped Maria's chin in her hand.

"Listen to me. It would have been *you* in there, in a box, with your mouth hanging open and your eyes looking at nothing. Seeing nothing, feeling nothing, not ever again. He thought he was killing you, didn't he?"

Maria tried to pull away, but Miranda tightened her grip.

"No. Let's talk about it now. Here. While you can still talk to me. I don't want to stand over your body and look at your corpse."

The girl began to moan. "Don't say that. Don't say that. Oh, please don't say that."

"But it is true, yes? Mera thought he hit you and he was

wrong. Then Arabella and Christine got hit. Why? Tell me, Maria, who did this? It wasn't Mera. He was in custody in Florida when this happened. You know what that means, don't you? Someone is still out there. I think you are in a very bad position, and I think you know it and I think you need help."

The girl blinked, pulled back and finally confronted Miranda. "Oh, and *you* can help me? *You* can keep me safe, huh?"

"Only partially. You'll have to help yourself. I'll do my job. I'll do the best I can, but I can't do *anything* without your help. Maria, for God's sake, tell me what happened."

"You are so smart, lady policeman. You are so smart. You tell me. You know everything."

Miranda lowered her voice so that Maria had to listen closely.

"All right. Arabella and Christine were carriers. Cocaine, maybe heroin. They were carrying, for Mera. Mera, I think, is a nobody—an intermediary, in some way. That was why he was going to hit you. To teach *them* a lesson. But he made a mistake. He hit the wrong girl. And then . . ."

"Yes? Oh, and then? And then you don't know. Not anything because you are wrong about everything. My sister . . . my sister . . . Arabella met up with some wrong men. Sometimes I worried about that. Arabella . . . my sister . . . was so trusting, you'd think she'd know better . . . but I was worried. She said something about some guys they met, somewhere, I don't know. And this happened to them because she didn't have good sense. There. So much for your stories, lady policeman. Did you sit up all night and make up any more stories to tell people?"

"Maria, I worked narcotics for many years. I know a setup. I know carriers learn to skim. And to deal a little on the side."

She read Maria carefully. The girl clenched her teeth together, winced as though she was biting on a nerve.

Miranda continued, taking her cues from Maria's reactions. "So, sometimes, they skim a little too much and get caught at it. Sometimes, it's just a little bit, at first, a little bit to maybe help out. A sister, maybe, who can pick up a few extra dollars at school. A little pushing, cocaine, to keep the brain going, to get through the hard nights before an exam." She shook her head. "No big deal. Maria, I went to night school for my degree, I know the hours. I know what a help it can be. Just a little, carefully used, not abused. My God, there are times you'd pay anything you had, for just a little help, for something so nice to make all the hard work a little easier. I know, Maria. I was there. You don't think I'm totally out of your world, do you? I'm a few years older than you are. I've been deep in the middle of it. A little is okay, is good, helps. A little dealing, with friends, my God, they love you for it, it's not for the money, it's to help them. You don't hold them up, you're not looking to get rich, just expenses and a little extra. What kind of sister would Arabella be if she didn't cut you in for a little small piece of it for you and your friends? She took care of you, I'm sure she did. Why not? There's no harm in small amounts."

"Then why are you making such a big deal out of it?"

"Because of the *others*, Maria. The bigger people. The ones who make all the nice times, the cool times, the helping times, turn bad. The big guys who don't want young women like Arabella and Christine to have any action at all, not a nickel's worth for themselves. I think, maybe, Mera was doing some skimming himself, and found out they were skimming, too, and wanted to blame them for the whole thing. I think that's how it happened. He put the whole blame on them. He'd say to 'the others,' see, I took out the young sister, to teach them. But then he found out his mistake and got frightened and ran. Down to Miami. And the others—the big deals—they decided to kill Arabella and Christine just to be on the safe side. Does that sound reasonable to you?"

Maria stared at her blankly.

"But there is just one loose end still remaining, Maria. Mera took out the wrong girl. That was just her hard luck. Anna Grace died for no reason at all except that she looked like you and that Mera made a mistake. So that leaves you, still walking around. You don't think they're going to let you walk around much longer, do you?"

Maria Vidales took in a long, slow breath. She sat up straight, her spine rigid, her chin high. Her voice was scratchy, as though the words were being forced over a raggedly sore throat.

"I don't know what the fuck you are talking about, lady policeman." She made a sharp, derisive click with her tongue. "It is terrible to see what happens to one of *us* when she becomes one of *them.*" Her final words were a harsh, hissing sound, "You are worse than all of them put together. You turn on your own."

She looked away, her mouth twisted contemptuously. She did not see the sudden, passing pain on Miranda Torres' face.

25

Because she felt she had nothing to lose, Miranda decided to take a chance with the girl.

"I must stop first at my apartment, then I will take you home," she told Maria. "There is something I must check out."

When Miranda pulled up in front of her building, she studied the girl beside her. She had gone stone cold; frozen; expressionless. She heard without seeming to hear. When Miranda told her to come with her for a moment, unquestioningly Maria Vidales went along up to Miranda's apartment.

Miranda wasn't sure it was the *right* thing to do, but she was sure it was the *only* thing to do. If she was to lose Maria now, she would lose her completely without hope of reaching her again.

She watched the girl's blank face, looked for some sign of what had to be going on within. Maria had gone so far into herself that she seemed to have disappeared.

"This will take only a few minutes," Miranda said. "There is something I want you to look at."

She still had Mike's video machine to play the duplicate

of the murder tape that he had given her. "You might as well have a copy," he had said. "Jesus, there are people who would pay a fortune for a copy of this. A real, honest-to-God, genuine snuff tape. The real thing."

At first Maria glanced at the TV screen blankly, and then, hearing the scream, she leaned forward, narrowed her eyes, then turned away.

Miranda stopped the machine, afraid she might be erasing something. She did not like machines. And she did not like what she was doing.

Maria stood up, but Miranda came to her, hands on her shoulders.

"No. You sit here and you watch. If it takes all night, Maria, you will sit here and watch the whole thing. Beginning to end. Watch Mera and this girl. You know and I know what *he* did not know. He was killing the wrong girl. *He thought Anna Grace was you.*"

Maria struggled, whirled around, her face coming alive, her eyes filled with tears which spilled down her suddenly flushed cheeks.

"No. This is a trick. I do not want to see this, this filthy thing. It is a trick."

Miranda was stronger, far more in control of the situation.

"Sit down. Here. Drink this." She had prepared some iced tea. She was afraid to give the girl anything stronger. She didn't know what drugs Maria had in her system.

Maria drank without stopping, gulping, seeking something from the cold liquid that wasn't there. She grabbed Miranda's hand.

"What is this tape, this movie? What kind of trick is it?"

"No trick. It is real. Some film student on Barclay Street shot it. From the moment Mera stabbed her to the end. Exactly as it happened. *Maria, it is you he is stabbing.* You know that. You know it."

Maria folded herself back onto the chair, legs under her body, arms hugging herself, holding herself. Her mouth fell open and she gasped with each terrible flash of the knife, she moaned with each scream. She pulled her hands over her eyes. Miranda stopped the machine.

"No. Do not cover your eyes because it is so terrible. It continued. He did not stop because it became unbearable. He wanted you to die and you kept fighting back and he kept slashing and stabbing. Look at it, Maria, damn it, you look at it and you listen and don't you forget this for the rest of your life. *You* were stabbed and slashed that night. *You* were left to bleed to death while your neighbors looked out of the windows and watched you die. Now you watch this, beginning to end, you watch it as it happened. It was happening to you. As far as Mera was concerned—the girl was you."

Miranda reversed to the beginning, then pushed a button and the murder began again. Maria watched, scarcely breathing. She stared until the screen went gray, still watching, still watching.

"All right. There," Miranda said. "You've done what no one has ever done before. You've sat and witnessed your *own* murder on videotape. Every stab, every wound, every hurt was on your body. *Maria!*"

The girl seemed in a trance, beyond feeling, hypnotized by the blank TV screen. Miranda grabbed at the girl's pocketbook, dumped the contents onto her desk. There was a makeup case filled with capsules, pills, substances of different kinds for different feelings. There was a vial of cocaine. Miranda prepared two thin lines on the back of an envelope, carefully, professionally.

"Maria. Come here. Just this once, Maria. The rest of all this goes down the toilet, but you come over here now. Do this."

It took effect immediately: it brought the girl sharply,

starkly into the experience of what she had just seen. She began to shake, her teeth began to click together, not from the drug, but from the realization of what she had just seen and what it meant.

"Tell me about Carlos Galvez, your cousin. Where does he fit in?"

Maria clutched at Miranda, caught at her sleeves and pulled herself closer.

"Not him," she whispered. "He doesn't exist. I don't know who you mean. *Please.* Detective Torres, for God's sake, *please.*"

"All right, then. Maria, all right. For now. No Carlos. No cousin. Tell me about Mera. Paul Mera—where does he fit in? Why would he want to kill you?"

"What you said before. What you guessed. What you said."

Miranda thought quickly: remembering, trying to get the girl to fill in facts for guesses.

Slowly, reluctantly, Maria told a somewhat disconnected story, whispered, shuddered, cried. And then begged for more cocaine. Miranda ignored her and put together the sequence of events.

On certain trips, both Arabella and Christine carried fairly large amounts of cocaine which was picked up by Mera. Lately, he had begun skimming. He had shown the stewardesses how easy it was, but it had to be done quickly. He was on a tight, well-monitored schedule. He needed their help and he paid them a nice bonus for it.

It really was so easy. It seemed so silly to let Mera give them just a small extra amount of money when they were taking most of the risks, so they skimmed a little for themselves a few times. Claimed they'd been delayed at Kennedy, some minor problems, some briefing of the crew. Mera had caught on very quickly.

214

"When Arabella called me, she said Mera had asked about me. He said he'd been thinking, Why shouldn't your little sister have a piece of the action? She's a college girl. Plenty of customers there. He told Ara to have me come over to the apartment, and he'd set something up."

And so her sister warned Maria to stay away; that something bad was happening. That she would take care of it, but Maria was just to stay away.

"Then she called me again. Wednesday night. When he was out there, on the street. Killing . . . that girl. Killing . . . me. Ara called, she said something terrible was going on. I should stay away until I heard from her. That she would take care of it."

"What did she mean by that, that she would take care of it?"

"I don't know. I don't know," Maria said, her voice beginning to falter, the words coming slower. She sniffed, and coughed and looked up at Miranda. "Look, I need . . ."

"And did you hear from Arabella again? After that last phone call?"

Maria shook her head.

"And you were afraid for her and Christine. What did you think would happen?"

Maria looked up, angry now, drawing on her anger to overcome her fear. "What do you mean, what did I think would happen? Look what happened! Look where my sister is."

"Who put her there? Carlos? Is he the next in line, Carlos? Did Mera work for him?"

"For who?"

It was to be that way: no further information. No Carlos. A pulling back and withdrawing. The beginnings of denials.

"Maria, I'm going to ask the district attorney to put you in protective custody. You are in immediate danger and—"

215

"Custody? Are you crazy? You think I'm going to go along with that? I'm not going to jail."

"No jail. A safe place."

"A safe place?" Maria laughed. "Where is that, a safe place?"

"I promise you, I will find a safe place, where you can relax. Where you don't have to be afraid. Not a cell, Maria, someplace where . . . Let me work this out. You will have someone around at all times to protect you and—"

"Forget it. I am not in danger. Who would want to hurt me? Look, Detective Torres, some bad guys took my sister and Christine out on a date and it must have turned sour. Sometimes, Ara did not use good judgment. You can ask any of the girls who she worked with. So they ran into some really bad guys and, I don't know, maybe they were doing drugs and things got out of hand. And then these bastards panicked and dumped them out there. In that place, you said, out by Kennedy and . . . You get the idea?"

"Oh, yes. I do understand. That will be your story. Fine. Stick to it. Publicly. Let that be your statement, your theory, and the police will be looking into it, trying to find the 'bad guys' who your sister and Christine Valapo dated. That's okay. It can be your cover story. But in the meantime, you will be safely hidden away and—"

"No. Uh-uh. No. I just want out of here. Right now."

Miranda leaned back against the counter that separated her kitchen from the living room. She folded her arms and raised her chin slightly and smiled. "There's the door. Go."

Maria hesitated for a moment, found her pocketbook, tossed her belongings into a bag. "Where are my . . . things? Never mind. It's no problem. Forget it. By the way, where are we? In Queens?"

"In Astoria. If you want, I'll drive you back to your apartment. If that's where you're going. Or we can call a cab. Or there's the subway."

"Never mind what my plans are. I'll do whatever the hell I want to do. And it has nothing to do with you. Or the police or the District Attorney or . . ."

"Or Cousin Carlos?"

Maria stood absolutely still for a split second, eyes frightened and then angry.

"Forget that, Detective Torres. For your own sake and mine, forget him."

She left Miranda's apartment and found a cab.

Detective Dunphy, who had been sitting Miranda's apartment since her phone call from the morgue, followed the cab to Barclay Street, watched Maria head for her apartment, watched the lights go on. He used his car phone to tell his partner to relax and go to bed and get some rest. He'd sit Maria for the rest of the night.

He didn't ask Miranda any questions. He knew she'd tell him whatever he needed to know.

26

Assistant District Attorney Jerome call-me-Sonny Waters looked around the squad room as though calculating a jury. He did not seem too pleased by the stone-eyed detectives who watched his every move without expression.

"I do not understand the attitude of any of you people," he said. "I do not know what is bothering you people. *We have a man who is confessing to four murders.* He has been cooperative, helpful, willing, he has been giving us the information we've been looking for. Look, we have him cold, flat out, on the Anna Grace thing, right?"

No one said anything. He looked at Captain O'Connor, who seemed to be staring at something slightly over Waters' head.

"I don't understand why you people tried to question him about the murder of those two stewardesses who got themselves bumped and dumped at Kennedy. There is nothing whatever, at all, to connect him with those two women. Right? Right?"

Captain O'Connor sighed and then said quietly, "There is nothing—at all—to connect Mera with any of the other three murders in Queens this year. We have about five or six

218

confessions to each of those murders. All carry about as much weight as Mera's."

"Now, see. That's what I'm talking about," Waters said to the roomful of detectives. "Here we have an honest-to-God verifiable murderer, we got him on videotape, we got a million live eyewitnesses, and we got his confession. So, he gets shook up, say; his conscience bothers him, say. Or whatever. So he figures, What the hell, they can only put me away once, I might as well clear the decks. So he confesses to the other three murders. And you won't accept his confessions as valid. Why? Why? Because he changed his m.o.? Because the other women he grabbed in the dark and raped and then stuck a knife in their throats? So he did it different with the Grace girl. Who's to say he can't try something a little different? Listen, Captain, I'm told he has information that only the murderer could have and—"

"Someone has been feeding him information," Captain O'Connor said. "It's that simple. I don't know why or . . ."

Waters put two hands on O'Connor's desk and leaned forward. He shook his head, then looked around the room and focused on the homicide detective.

"You. *You*—you're from Homicide, right? What's your name?"

The homicide detective said, "Sergeant."

Waters went rigid. Everyone here was determined to give him a hard time. "I didn't ask your *rank*. I asked your name."

The homicide detective said, "My name is Richard Sergeant."

Waters stared, turned it over in his mind, then said, "All right. All right, you work homicide, right, er . . . Detective Sergeant? Well, he—" the D.A. pointed at O'Connor while he kept his eyes on the homicide cop—"he is accusing your co-workers of—"

Captain O'Connor's fist came down heavily on the surface of his desk. It was a loud crackling sound; like bones breaking.

Waters jumped, startled.

"Hold it, Waters. I didn't accuse anyone in Homicide or any other police officer of anything. There are a lot of ways that information can get leaked when a man is being held and some little deal might be under way. My concern is why this guy Mera is willing to confess to all these murders, but when my people tried to question him about these two murdered stewardesses he—"

"Hey, hey, Captain," Waters' voice went buddy-buddy; one of the boys. "Who the hell can account for what goes on in the mind of a nut? Now, I will say this detective . . . this lady here must have been surprised by Mera's reaction to her and her partner. I understand he got a little upset and—"

Detective Dunphy caught the signal from O'Connor. He interrupted the D.A. "Your man went completely bonkers. He banged his head on the table, then rolled all over the floor kicking his feet and et cetera. But the minute my partner mentioned calling Kings County, he got his act together."

"So? So what does that indicate to you? He's a nut—that'll probably be his defense. So what, what's your point?"

Miranda picked up the opening from Dunphy. They were on a good line. "The point is, Mr. Waters, that Mr. Mera is selectively crazy. When he doesn't want to discuss something, such as the murder of the two Avianca stewardesses, he pulls this act and—"

"Ah, oh, okay, I see now. 'This act.' And you, girlie, are also, in addition to being a lady cop, you are also a shrink? An expert in nut cases and related behavior? That will save the city a lot of money—an all-in-one lady-cop-shrink. What a very accomplished person you are." He turned to

O'Connor. "Not only she's sexy, she's multitalented. Terrific."

Captain Bill O'Connor was six feet two inches tall. There were times when he seemed smaller, more compact, but there were times, as now, when he rose slowly, deliberately, that he seemed to be a giant. He had a way of straightening his spine, pulling his head up and back and glaring down. A.D.A. Waters took an automatic step back from the captain's desk.

"Okay. That's it. This woman is Second-Grade Detective Torres, a valued member of my squad. You will not refer to her in any other manner but by her title: Detective. And if you don't like the attitude of any other member of my squad, or anyone else working for me in this investigation, you will discuss it, in private, with me. And I will tell you something, *Sonny-boy.* I don't like you or the fact that you are totally and completely incapable of dealing with the entire situation. Now, you can go before the grand jury and go for all the indictments you can get. That's your job, not mine. But that doesn't mean shit as far as reality is concerned."

Waters clenched his fists and rocked back on his feet. His voice was very shrill and thin and he was aware of it and tried to pitch it low, but it kept getting away from him.

"All right. That's it. Fine. I'll let you people stew in your own mess. I won't forget your lack of support. There are other people in the New York City Police Department, *other people* who will be more than happy to know that we can clear the books on the so-called Beast of Queens. There are citizens of this borough—women and girls—who will rest easier knowing that we have this man behind bars. And that I'm the one responsible for that. I'm not soliciting opinions from you people. Your only responsibility will be to testify before the grand jury in the Anna Grace matter."

As he spoke, he kept his head down, to help modulate his

voice. He gathered his papers, which had been spread out on the captain's desk. He was very careful not to make even passing physical contact with O'Connor, who seemed to keep getting taller and larger.

"And I won't forget what's been said here in this room, Captain O'Connor." He looked straight up, into O'Connor's icy eyes. "No. I won't forget. Remember that." He was more than slightly unhinged. He whirled around to make his exit and banged into the edge of a desk, tripped over a chair, cursed and gathered himself together for a less than great exit.

"Mother-fucking moron," O'Connor said. Then, glancing at Miranda, exercising the delicacy they all seemed to exert in her presence, he said, "Sorry. That bastard got me a little off guard." He rubbed his mouth roughly. "Jeez."

"Okay, troops. Let's settle down and wind this up for tonight. I want to get this a little clearer in my mind. Two things: Tell me again Mera's reaction when you asked him about this Maria Vidales."

"He panicked," Miranda said. "He swore he had never heard of her. And he said, 'If she claims to know me, she's lying.' "

O'Connor leaned on his desk, puzzled. "But she hasn't claimed to know him. You said she swore she'd never heard of him."

"In her formal statement, yes sir." Miranda had typed up a short report of her conversation with Maria at the mortuary.

O'Connor went through his papers, found it and nodded. "Yeah, okay, I remember. Very quickly, remind me of your theory—about Anna Grace and Maria Vidales and Paul Mera and the stewardesses."

She glanced at the homicide cop, and O'Connor nodded;

he was okay. Briefly, she told them her theory: mistaken identity; a drug connection. And, for the first time, mentioned Carlos Galvez.

"And you haven't been able to contact him, about his cousin's death?"

"No. Jim and I stopped by the house on Inverness Street before we came here, and it's dark. We're going to hit some neighbors tomorrow, see what we come up with."

Dunphy dug a scrap from his notebook and handed it across the desk to O'Connor. It was a Motor Vehicle check on the three automobiles that had been parked in front of Carlos Galvez' residence.

"All rented, Captain. Under different names. We'll know more about it tomorrow. All returned, by the way—nothing outstanding. The guy pays his bills, anyway."

"And your theory, Miranda, as to why Mera would confess to three murders he hasn't committed? And go nuts when asked about stewardesses—denies any connection whatever?"

"I think that he wants to distance himself from anything at all that would connect him with the drug trade. I think he is so terrified of his own mistakes, of the people who will want to take care of him, to deal with him for these mistakes, that he would confess to anything that would put him in a special category. The Beast of Queens is not put into the general prison population. He is kept separate, apart. He is guarded, protected. He is in a position of demanding special consideration right now—special privileges, special security. Give him what he demands, he will give you back whatever murders you want. A trade-off."

O'Connor carefully considered what she was saying. He listened with the respect of one professional for another. Then, finally, shrugging, "Well, okay. The rest of you people, you do have a job to do, you do have some work to attend to?" Then, to Miranda, "Before you leave, check with me, Torres."

She waited the ten minutes it took for the office to empty out. Only one detective was left hunched over his desk, the dim yellow light targeted on his typewriter as he squinted over notes and tried to make sense out of his work.

She tapped on the door lightly and went into Captain O'Connor's office.

"Yeah," he said, indicating a chair. He hesitated as though making a decision.

"How's it going with Stein?" he asked finally.

Miranda sat up straight on the hard wooden chair. She felt a surge of energy and alertness. It wasn't an answerable question and so she waited.

O'Connor said roughly, "I'm not asking a personal question, Detective Torres."

"I'm not sure what it is you *are* asking me, Captain O'Connor."

"All right. Here it is. Stein is not to get any further information about any other aspect of this case—or any other case—this squad is working on. He had access only to the Anna Grace killing. As far as I know, we've had a full and open exchange of information with him. He's given us some background stuff on the witnesses, which is of more value to him than to us, and we've given him access to everything we've done on the case. And that is that. Right?"

Miranda raised her head slightly. The tight line on her jaw was accented by a streak of light which bounced off the captain's desk. Her tension resulted in a great control over her voice and expression.

"Do you really think it was necessary to tell me this, Captain O'Connor?"

O'Connor reacted to the challenge. He felt that she took advantage of her position—of being a woman. None of the men, not even Dunphy, would challenge him as openly. Or as angrily.

"Apparently I do think it's necessary or I wouldn't be sitting here across the desk from you, Detective Torres."

There was a moment's silence before she spoke. Carefully. "I'm not sure what you require of me, Captain. My reassurance that I fully understand the limitations of Mr. Stein's accessibility privilege? I fully understand and have worked under the guidelines you set for me at the very beginning." She took a deep steadying breath. "I really *don't* understand what it is you are asking me, Captain."

When it got down to it, Captain William O'Connor wasn't too sure himself. He trusted Miranda, as far as he trusted any other detective in his squad: totally. With reservations. It was the nature of the job. It was based on years of experience with people in a variety of situations that average people would never encounter in several lifetimes.

Besides being beautiful in a way he could not clearly define to himself, Miranda Torres was exotic, intriguing, tempting, because of her very self-contained inaccessibility. He had never before felt such awe and respect for a woman as he felt for her. She was a puzzle to him: intelligent, better educated than most of the others in the squad, yet open and willing to learn, to absorb, to listen and to share her knowledge, without flaunting, without any indication of awareness of her superiority. She was also highly connected. And never once, in all the time she had been in the squad, had she ever, in any way, by any slightest suggestion or indication, given the impression that she was aware that it was general knowledge that she had a powerful 'rabbi' watching out for her. He had expected a certain arrogance, veiled perhaps, but not even a fleeting glimpse of power had ever shown.

He wondered about her. He wondered about himself and his interest in her.

Then he wondered about Miranda and Mike Stein, and in fairness to her, resentfully, he decided that as long as she stayed within the official guidelines, as long as she did not violate the confidence he had placed in her professionally, he had no right to question her.

Because what he was asking her was personal and he knew it.

Miranda knew it, too, and in her quiet, firm and decisive way she was telling him to mind his own business. Not with the arrogance of a power that protected her, but as one who knew and exerted her own rights.

"Miranda. Go on home. You and Dunphy pick up on this business of the girl, Maria Vidales, tomorrow. Do you know where she is right now?"

She took her cue from him. "As far as we know, sir, she is staying at Parker Towers, with some of the other stewardesses. They have gathered around her, but I think . . ."

He tapped his finger on a typed report. "This memo about protective custody for Maria Vidales. You realize that it has to go through the D.A.'s office? That would require the cooperation of Sonny-Boy Waters."

"Yes. Yes, I know."

"Well, We'll see. Keep me informed. And, Miranda . . ."

She waited. When he waved her out, she nodded. The moment passed between them as clearly as if he had spoken.

He had apologized.

27

The heat had broken, the inversion had lifted, the sky was painfully blue, the clear sunshine was welcomed by the residents of Inverness Street. People who had been imprisoned by the poison of pollution puttered about on their tiny lawns, tried to revitalize dying flowers and took advantage of their small but pleasant patios. They watched the odd couple carefully: many strange things had happened in and around that particular house. The girl seemed much younger than the man. At least, she kept a pleasant face on her. The man scowled and frowned, but, when he spoke, he seemed nice enough.

The tension broke once the couple identified themselves as police officers. Everyone seemed eager to talk about their neighbors, the Galvez family.

"Absolutely totally gone," a large gray-haired woman told them. "I don't mind telling you, we've had some strange ones in that house, but they were the strangest."

"But nice-looking people, you have to admit that," a woman from across the street said.

"Who cares, nice-looking," Mrs. Wyman, the next-door

neighbor, said. "What I want to know is what were these people up to, anyway?"

The residents of Inverness Street had been apprehensive when they saw the latest family move in. The house had been rented through the years to an unstable collection of people, from welfare mothers, their children and their boyfriends to a group running an illegal limo service from this one-family-house-zoned area. They watched, worried, as the Galvez people moved in.

It had turned out better than they could have dreamed. The family was quiet, neat, polite. The children were beautiful, well-mannered, replied shyly when greeted. The wife was gorgeous, always so well groomed, always with a smile, a nod, a good morning.

The husband?

The neighbors took turns: He was handsome, a big man, a fine, well-dressed, very what? courtly man? with manners that seemed out of an old movie.

Their furnishings had been glimpsed on the day they moved in: expensive. No one had ever been inside their home, but it was obvious these people knew how to live.

The mystery was, why were they living on Inverness Street?

"Wait, I'll get Mrs. Ferguson. Her husband works in security in Alexander's. Mrs. Ferguson knew how to get information. Wait."

Dunphy and Torres drank homemade lemonade and ate freshly baked cookies and listened to more testimonials to the Galvez family.

In the matter of automobiles: given the experience of a limousine-service operation in their quiet neighborhood, hearts turned to lead when three large black automobiles appeared in front of the Galvez residence and the attached houses on either side.

Mr. Morris, a neighbor to the left, was a man who thought well of everyone until he had proof otherwise. He approached Mr. Galvez on the street and explained the problem. There was no place for the women to pull up to unload the marketing before putting the car into the garage around back. His large automobiles, they took up so much room, could he perhaps . . .?

"Mr. Galvez apologized, oh, he was so very nice about it. He had some men working for him, they drove the cars, very quiet, never a sound from them, and he went over, said something, they nodded, very respectful, and that was that. The cars never caused a problem again. They pulled up in front of the house, the family came out, into the cars and away. Came back the same way. They only parked in front sometimes at night. And not even very often. Very cooperative. A very nice fellow."

It was indeed Mrs. Ferguson, the ex-policeman's wife, who managed to put together a story. She had spoken to the housekeeper, chatted with her as she hung laundry, in the small garden in the backyard. Mrs. Ferguson shared her tomato crop and her flowers with the woman and got information. In strictest confidence and over a period of time.

Galvez was not their real name. Their real name could not be told. They were political refugees from a South American country that had been taken over by a Communist dictatorship. Mr. "Galvez" had been a very important member of the overthrown government: if not the actual president, then the power behind the throne. He had been a general or something very high like that.

The various drivers dropped bits of information to Mr. Morris, the friendly neighbor, as he admired the automobiles. Why did the family always stay together, yet they separated into three cars whenever they went anywhere?

For safety. That was all that was said. For safety.

"They used other cars too, sometimes," Mrs. Ferguson told them. "My husband noticed that on his days off. Sometimes, just regular Chevies and Fords would pull up, the family would rush into the cars, and then the three big black cars would join up at the corner. Like an entourage. They were bodyguards, those men."

No one had ever had a conversation with the wife. The children were never seen without an adult. And then, one night a week ago, a moving truck pulled up, at night, just before darkness, and quickly, soundlessly, everything from the house, neatly boxed and wrapped, had been taken away.

Cars pulled up, the family—and this time the housekeeper too—got into the cars and disappeared. Forever.

"And God knows," Mr. Morris said sadly, "God alone knows what's going to move into the house next!"

That seemed to be the matter of gravest concern. Given the history of the house, they had every reason to worry.

28

Bloated with lemonade and cookies, both Miranda and Dunphy turned down the coffee offered to them by Captain O'Connor. They both felt a little queasy confronting the gusto with which he attacked his hot-pastrami sandwich.

"So, okay," O'Connor said, holding up his hand, chewing and gulping and swallowing. "Boy, I haven't had a pastrami for weeks. My wife keeps reading all these articles. I tell ya, if I gotta die, let it be from too much pastrami instead of too little. Okay, what the hell have we got here?"

The two detectives looked at each other. It was obvious they had a difference of opinion. Dunphy tended to believe the political-refugee story—to a point. He had set in motion inquiries through various federal agencies.

"Of course, if this story is right, I wouldn't be surprised if any knowledgeable agencies refused to confirm it. If the guy is here incognito, for asylum, and he is in danger from political enemies, they're not about to tell us too much about him."

"No more than he would have permitted anyone he employed to reveal what the people of Inverness Street believe they found out. It doesn't work that way," Miranda said firmly.

Dunphy stared straight ahead and said, "Uh-huh."

There was an edge in his voice, and the tension in the posture of both detectives caused Captain O'Connor to wrap up the rest of his sandwich for later. If he was going to eat pastrami, he was damned well going to enjoy it.

"Detective Torres, what's your feeling about this guy Galvez? All you got is the fact that the girl, Maria Vidales, mentioned that he was her cousin and that he might have heard from her sister, the stewardess, on the night that Anna Grace was killed. You went to see the guy and got what? Nothing, right?"

Miranda hesitated. She studied her fingertips and then looked up at the captain. "I went to see him. And from that meeting received nothing but an impression. Which made me feel very uncomfortable, very . . ." She shrugged, searching for the right word. It would not come. "There was a something. One could not put a name to it, but with Galvez something was not right. Something . . . very wrong."

O'Connor's voice was as deadpan as his expression. "Something very wrong. What? You can't say. And you haven't seen him since. He pulled out before his cousin's body was found, right?"

"I don't think the Vidales girls were his cousins. In fact, at the morgue, Maria made certain admissions to me—but again, what she said there and in my apartment she will not repeat. She denies. I have no proof."

"If you tell me that Maria Vidales made certain admissions to you, Miranda, I believe you. Not necessarily her admissions, but that she did make them to you. Why she was so frightened of this guy—whether he was or wasn't a cousin—I don't know, but . . ."

"He is a frightening man," Miranda said. They held it

there, midair: a statement with nowhere to go. Finally she said, "Whatever reason Maria Vidales had to be so frightened of him, I can understand her fear. More than that I would have to get Maria Vidales to verify."

"If he was a highly placed political refugee from a maybe violent-power background, wouldn't that be enough to scare a young girl? Or anyone, for that matter?"

It was a reasonable suggestion, and yet Miranda knew that Dunphy was wrong. She shook her head.

Captain O'Connor asked her, "Why do you doubt the story that went around Inverness Street?"

"Because if it *was* true, the information would never have surfaced. This information, this story, was deliberately put out. He knew the people on this street were naïve, nice, sweet, quiet people who were curious about him and his family and the cars and the trips. Inexperienced people who were curious and who thought themselves so clever to learn all this top-secret information. If he was what he allowed them to be told, he would be invisible, and his family—"

"What we have here, Captain," Dunphy said, "is not only an expert in the world of the narcotics conspiracy but in international intrigue. She knows all about how these people would live. Look, you want to explain it some more to us dumb Queens yokels so that—"

Miranda turned in her chair to face Dunphy. She spoke slowly and clearly and precisely. "That is not why I have tried to tell you about this thing. I know certain things and how they are done. I am trying to put all of this out before us so that with an exchange of information—"

O'Connor moved his hand too quickly and knocked over his container of coffee. It soaked what was left of his pastrami sandwich.

"Goddamn it, damn it." He dug out a handful of tissues and began blotting the mess. He dried off his sandwich and took a large moist bite, grimacing. Finally he said, "We will wait on this for verification, any kind of verification or information from Washington. And I want to assure you, Detective Torres, that there *are* people in Washington, D.C., in certain federal bureaus, who will give me confidential information when I need it. So I wouldn't worry too much. You let *me* worry about all this from now on, okay? You people got your reports up-to-date?"

"On your desk, Captain." Dunphy pointed to a folder, stained with the coffee. Dunphy leaned forward, extracted some typed papers, shook the coffee from them. "I'll get you a clean copy."

"Fine. Then go home. Both of you. Just go on home. And let me eat the rest of this mess in peace."

Before he left the office that night, Captain O'Connor received a telephone call from a highly placed federal official in Washington. Without any further explanation, he was told that the matter re Galvez was being handled at a high governmental level. O'Connor and his people were to back off.

A second call, from his friend in a position to know about such things, informed O'Connor that there was no information confirming or denying anything about anyone named Galvez. No one seemed to know when, where, why or how Galvez and his family had come to the United States. If, in fact, they *had* come to the United States. O'Connor's friend told him, in essence, to forget the whole thing.

Captain William O'Connor sat and stared at his telephone for a long time before he dialed Jim Dunphy's number. He spoke quietly, with little or no modulation. He gave away nothing, not his feeling, his opinion, his anger or his agreement. He then asked Dunphy if he wanted to call his partner and give her the message or should he do it?

"I'll call, Captain," Dunphy said very formally.

"All right. And—this goes for both of you. Take a few days off. You both deserve. Report back on Monday. Or Tuesday. Whatever."

"Yes, sir, Captain," Detective Jim Dunphy replied.

29

She had warned him she would not be good company. He promised that being with him for a long weekend would give her a new perspective. It wasn't that she objected to having a few days off unexpectedly, she told him, it was just that she had been *told* to take the time.

Miranda would not discuss any aspect of her current investigation. This was off limits to Mike Stein. Nor was he particularly interested. He had his own concerns. When they reached his house in Bridgehampton, he settled her on a large, formless, lush couch, surrounded her with beautiful pillows of all shapes and sizes and fabrics.

"Take off those sandals, lean back and relax while I fix us something light and fast and terrific. And give you something to read while you're waiting."

She had expected the sensational first article: he had prepared her for it. Still, it took her breath away.

THE GIRL WHO WAS MURDERED TWICE
by Mike Stein
(first of a series of six articles)

Featured was a photograph of Anna Grace, identified as the victim. Next to it, shocking to Miranda, was a photograph of Maria Vidales. They both looked vaguely dreamy, vapid, unreal. In the pictures, side by side, they might have been twins.

Under Maria Vidales' name was the statement VICTIM'S MOTHER "THOUGHT IT WAS THE SPANISH GIRL."

There was a picture of Paul Mera, identified as THE MAN WHO KILLED HER THE FIRST TIME. There was a legend instructing the readers to turn to the centerfold for pictures of the "other murderers."

Spread over the two pages of the centerfold were photographs of all of the people on Barclay Street who had been interviewed. THESE ARE THE PEOPLE WHO KILLED ANNA GRACE THE SECOND TIME.

He had gotten a great deal of background information on everyone in the story. His opening dealt with Anna Grace: traced her background, her life, her marriage, her devotion to her husband, to her mother, to her profession. "Yet she was ultimately rejected, allowed to die, not only by strangers but by the person who allowed personal vanity—and possibly prejudice—to corrupt a mother's love."

Miranda skimmed the story, amazed at how much information he had been able to gather and compress. It was well done for what it was, sensational, intriguing and leaving the reader wanting more.

"I've finished the articles," he told her. "A few days off, away from all of it, then I'm digging in for the book. I've a tight deadline and a lot of work to do."

"Will it be very different from the articles?" she asked.

"More analytical. I've been in touch with people—the 'experts' in behavior. They're working up information for me—why these people failed to act, why they are reacting so defensively now. These bastards are trying to institute a

237

lawsuit against me, the paper, my publishers. It's all to the good. More publicity."

"Do they have any grounds to sue? You have called them all murderers. You don't think that is valid for a lawsuit?"

Mike Stein smiled. "Miranda, let's not talk about any of this, okay? When you called me, remember what I said?"

"Yes. That you were planning to call me and ask if I could get a few days off. To come out here with you. To relax. To get away from everything and everyone and just to . . ."

"And just to."

"And I said that it was a very good idea, Mr. Stein. And I think it was."

He took the articles away from her. "Let's really forget all this. Now, lady, tell me. Why do you insist on calling me Mr. Stein?"

She traced a fingertip along his mouth, tickled the corners into a smile.

"Because it pleases me to do so, Mr. Stein."

"Miranda, Miranda. Saying your name pleases me. It is a gentle, sensuous experience. Miranda," he said softly.

"How easily we please each other."

"Not quite."

"That was the beginning of pleasure. Step by step into areas of pleasure, all separate and apart. Verbal, unspoken, playing lightly, gently. We set the scene for our pleasure, slowly, slowly."

Her sensuality was total. She was one of the few women he had ever known who genuinely *liked* her body, enjoyed the long, languid stretching that made her aware, section by section, of every bone, every muscle, every inch of skin in which she was encased.

He was fascinated by the color of her body: the play of light on the hollows and the sharpnesses, the mysterious darkness that glowed golden with undertones of cinnamon and bronze. From every angle, she appeared not only sensuous but maddeningly familiar: from another time and place and dimension. From some Egyptian-tomb wall painting, from some exotic, ancient place. She was Mayan, Aztec: a wary goddess, no complaisant virgin awaiting sacrifice to fire.

Miranda: her high cheekbones and fine jawline; her black brows over blacker eyes; her wide full lips, turned up at the corners into a puzzling, amused smile; her long fine nose.

He ruffled her short black hair which clung to her skull and framed her cheeks. He pushed it back, to see her broad forehead, damp and serene.

Miranda. He said her name. He enjoyed the taste of it, the feel of it in his mouth, and then the taste of her as he enjoyed her body, encompassed her flesh and felt captured by her as though they had entered into a mutually agreed-upon secret and ancient and sacred rite.

Miranda.

They exchanged secrets and dreams, carefully. He told her, as they walked hand in hand at the water's edge, what the articles, the book, the possible film, meant to him. Another chance.

"I'll be fifty in a month, Miranda, and I've been feeling a hundred. I felt as though it was all over, all in back of me. That I'd had it, used it up, blown it, wasted it. It's another chance that I hadn't expected. I'm wiser now, I think. I'll savor whatever is ahead."

They stood on the beach and looked up at the house. "My ex-wife gave me a Labor Day deadline—sell it or buy her out. Now it's mine. Really mine."

"This house, it means a great deal to you. It is an important part of you. It is . . . what would I say your 'place'? Where you feel you belong."

"You've got it. It's where I always want to return to, no matter where else I've been. I really was afraid to lose it."

"Then I am glad for you, Mr. Stein."

"Tell me your dream, Miranda. You must get sick and tired of your job. How much longer can you see yourself doing this—being with this 'underlife' of the city."

She shrugged. "For a time."

"And then?"

She studied him carefully before she spoke. "Law school."

He looped his arms over her shoulders in an easy, friendly way and smiled down at her. He shook his head. "Oh. Miranda. Are you planning to be the savior of the great unwashed? Stand up for them in court and make the deal to put them back out on the streets? With all you know about it?"

"You make certain assumptions, Mr. Stein. You make very quick surface evaluations. And sometimes you are wrong. About this, you are wrong. I want to specialize in constitutional law. Someday, I want to be admitted to practice before the Supreme Court. From the heart of the Constitution, Mr. Stein, is where all else in this country begins. Are you familiar, intimately familiar, with this document of our country?"

He let his head fall onto her shoulder, pulled her closer. When he pulled back, she was smiling at him, mocking him.

"You are right. I've made certain assumptions. With you, Miranda, I must learn to make no assumptions. You are like no one else I've ever known. You . . ."

"I am me. Just let me be who I am, not who you *think* I should be. Yes?"

"Oh, yes. Oh yes, Miranda."

She had another surprise for him. She was a powerful swimmer and she took swimming very seriously. She didn't pace herself to his less-than-athletic crawl. Swimming was a solitary thing for Miranda. Something she would not share with him. He became exhausted quickly, then sat on the beach and watched her. However she moved, he found pleasure in watching.

When she came from the water breathless, smiling, exhausted but exhilarated, her flesh cool and firm, he held her against him, his hands at the back of her head. He pulled back to study her face, her mouth opened slightly, the flash of white teeth, the slight gasping for air, the glinting amusement in her black eyes, the smile. The secrets contained behind that face: Miranda.

They had bought a selection of gourmet food from three or four fancy shops in town. Catering to the summer people, directly from the Upper East Side.

"I would rather have fresh vegetables," Miranda said, wrinkling her nose at the exotic, expensive food.

"You are too healthy already. When you want plain and simple—good. Then *you* do the cooking. When I'm the cook, we eat from expensive cartons."

They ate and made love and showered and made love and listened to music and they fell asleep in each other's arms. They awoke at about ten that night and began to clean up the modern, high-ceilinged house. Miranda looked overhead: there were skylights in nearly all the rooms. She studied the stars and felt light and serene and happy. She had consciously stopped thinking about anything that bothered her. It was something she had learned to do, a form of self-taught meditation, to free her mind, if only for short periods of time.

Miranda did not particularly like his house, but she took pleasure in his pleasure. It was a handsome house. When it had been built, it was unique for the area. Now it was only one of a hundred variations, which to Miranda all looked more or less the same. She preferred simplicity by the ocean—a cabin, a cottage. This was too much: too sharply angled and opened and calculated for effect rather than for comfort.

She had admired his body: long and lean and well muscled.
A bit too white; he'd had no sun all summer and he had to
go through shades of red before he tanned. His white hair,
which he had had since his late twenties, framed a
still-youthful face. An oddly boyish face with pale translu-
cent blue eyes. She knew that his boyishness was studied and
insincere, but it was pleasant and he was good to look at and
to touch. He enjoyed the physical things that she enjoyed.
He was as willing to follow and learn as he was to lead and
teach.

He was an interesting man, and Miranda Torres was glad
she had come with him to his house in Bridgehampton. She
felt better, more in control, less tense, ready to put her energies back into her job.

She dug into her pocketbook to check that she had not forgotten anything.

And then everything between them changed.

"I can't believe I've been so careless," she said. "I have
been carrying these around with me since last week. You see
how crazy they have made me, the people from my job. I
am usually very efficient. So maybe the captain was right. I
did need a few days away."

"And do you feel more efficient now?" he asked.

They were each of them busy with last-minute, get-
ting-ready-to-leave chores. He was checking out the refriger-
ator, making sure it was empty and clean so that he would
not be offended in the future by some terrible-smelling corruption of what had once been beautiful.

He glanced at her, saw her expression: tense and serious.

"What?" he asked. "What are those papers?"

"Death certificates," she told him. Reading softly, more
to herself then to him, she quickly mouthed the injuries inflicted on Arabella Vidales. An assortment of horrors and

humiliations ending in death by strangulation. Christine Valapo's death certificate listed nearly identical information, but Miranda read each word, quickly and efficiently. As though she had an obligation to this unknown murdered woman not to shrug off the specific facts of her death.

"I've been carrying these around all this time. And a copy of Anna Grace's death certificate. List of wounds inflicted, damage done to her and—" Miranda stopped speaking abruptly. She squinted, held the paper closer, went toward the floor lamp. She held her finger at the words and looked up at him.

"Mike," she said.

It was a peculiar sound, the sound of his name: puzzled, stunned, a turning to him for clarification.

"Well, at least she hadn't been sexually mauled and beaten the way those poor stewardesses were. And she wasn't left in a garbage dump, in a . . ."

He stopped what he was doing, stopped collecting things, packages, suitcases, bags of food.

"Miranda, what?"

She did not answer, but instead she extended the death certificate toward him. Without realizing it, she didn't release it to him, merely pointed at the words on the bottom line: *"The cause of death as determined by the autopsy on the body of Anna Hynes Grace: cerebral aneurysm."*

Her reaction confused him. She seemed to pull herself back into the tense, wary, uneasy posture that had characterized their first few hours together.

"Miranda, what the hell? It's a mistake, that's all. A miscopy from another death certificate. Jesus, over a period of what? seven days, there were something like twenty-five deaths by violence in Queens. Unheard of. You yourself said they were shifting bodies around. Didn't you tell me that the stewardesses were sent to Manhattan and no one

243

even notified you? Come on, we'll get it all straightened out."

She read through another portion of the report and she told him, "It states that none of the stab wounds was fatal. None pierced any vital organ or caused undue internal bleeding and . . ."

"Miranda. For Christ's sake. If you knew the number of mistakes that are made every day in medical examiners' offices all over the country you'd—"

"Remember my interview with the lady doctor—I forget her name—at the hospital where Anna Grace worked? I asked why Anna had gone home early that night and she told me about terrible headaches and—"

"And I happen to remember," Mike told her impatiently, "that in the same report you mentioned that the doctor who was on duty that night, the night the Grace girl was murdered—that Indian doctor—he didn't think much of the 'headache.' He thought it was just an excuse to get off early."

"But she had no reason to do that. It could have been the way Dr. Ruggiero—that was her name—said. The headache must have gotten very bad, must have frightened Anna. She was a nurse, she knew certain things about her condition."

"Jesus," he said, looking around, addressing the walls, the furniture, the books, the empty space, "Now the murdered girl has a 'condition.' Great. Terrific. What else?"

Miranda's silence was abrupt. Neither of them spoke, and she studied his reactions, his need to move about the large high-ceilinged room. He kept touching things, tables, pillows, art objects, as though trying to steady himself.

"Mike," she said, "Dr. Ruggiero felt that Anna Grace had a serious problem: possibly a brain tumor. She was trying to talk her into some tests. She believed that Anna Grace was trying to avoid finding out. The doctor said it wasn't the most unlikely thing in the world that if she hadn't been attacked

244

that night she could have had some kind of . . . seizure. I guess—" Miranda looked down at the death certificate—"I guess an aneurysm might be the right word."

He snatched the death certificate from her hand and waved it at her.

"It is a mistake. Just that simple. A goddamn clerical error that we'll just have to get corrected. A phone call will straighten it all out. Jesus Christ, Miranda. Jesus Christ. It *is* a mistake. Christ, can't you even give me a nod, a small 'Yes, Mr. Stein, it is a mistake'?"

She didn't answer him, and his voice went hollow.

"Listen, Miranda. Let's say, for the goddamn sake of discussion, no other reason, that, okay, Anna Grace died of an aneurysm. Well, she's dead, right? And we all saw the tapes of Mera stabbing her, killing her and . . ."

Slowly, she shook her head from side to side.

"What? What?" He imitated her slow head shake. "What, no? Miranda!"

"If she died of . . . this that the death certificate says, then he did *not* murder her. He can only be charged with *attempted* murder. Mike, there is a difference. And you know it."

"Do you realize, do you even *begin* to realize, what that 'difference' would mean? For my articles about those good people of Barclay Street who—"

"No, Mike, no. It in no way justifies their behavior. No matter what, they did exactly what they did. They watched, they refused to help her, they refused to summon help, they just . . ."

"They just what, Miranda? They just watched a young woman, who just happened to suffer from a few nonfatal stab wounds, sit down, lean against the lamppost and die from a cerebral aneurysm? 'The Girl Who Was Murdered Twice,' Miranda, that's the title of my future. Not 'The Girl Who

Would Have Been Murdered Twice, Had She Been Murdered Once.' But of course, she was only slashed around, and there was nothing anyone could have done from the minute she left her job with that fatal headache. Come on, Miranda. Listen, it's a mistake, this goddamn death certificate. That's all, a damn mistake."

"Then tell me why, Mike, why is it that you believe it?"

His mouth dropped open and his throat was dry with a tight burning sensation.

She put her hand out for the death certificate of Anna Grace.

"Jesus, is that what you think of me? That I would . . . ? Listen, I assume there are copies of this? And official records, et cetera. I want to hold on to this so that when I give the information needed to track down this mistake, I know what I'm talking about. Okay? You want it back? Do you really want it back? Okay. Fine. Here."

He roughly pulled at her shoulder bag, fumbled with the flap and tried to find an opening, a place to put the crumpled report. Miranda slid her pocketbook off her shoulder and held it against her body.

"No. You keep it. You are right. There are other copies. And records. And—" she offered him the words as a gift of hope, as an indication that she *did* understand his anguish—"and, yes. You are probably right, Mike. I am sure of it. It *must* be a mistake."

If she had called him Mr. Stein, he might have believed her.

246

30

Mike glanced at his watch: 7 A.M. It was time to call the old man who was living on a small horse-breeding farm in up-state New York. He lived a regimented life: up at 5 A.M., an hour's canter on his favorite horse; breakfast, newspapers, and then he accepted phone calls from 7 A.M. on. He received a rather large number of calls from all over the United States.

Dr. Aaron Toledo had been the acknowledged grand-master of pathology: former chief medical examiner for the city of New York; former chief consultant at leading hospi-tals and universities not only in the United States but throughout the world; author of six textbooks on pathology and methods.

It was Dr. Aaron Toledo who, discounted and discredited and forgotten after some political scandal more than fifteen years ago, had catapulted back into prominence some ten years ago when he conducted the methodical, remarkable au-topsy on the body of Arthur Cordovan, Jr. son of the Chief of Operations of the New York City Police Department. It was through Mike Stein's Pulitzer Prize–winning book on the entire matter that Dr. Toledo was once again accredited, remembered and, in effect, resurrected as an outstanding scholar and specialist in his field.

Dr. Toledo was, at eighty-eight, available for consultation. He answered the telephone on the first ring, and his voice was strong and sharp and authoritative. Let's get to the point; let's get to the matter at hand.

Mike Stein could picture the old man: his small bald head leaning toward his right shoulder, his thin cheeks sucking in and out as he pursed his lips over his long yellow teeth. The old man's eyes, small and beady and bright, had excellent sight, and he wore eyeglasses for close work only. He would be squinting in concentration. His body, bone thin, fleshless, would be tensed. He would flex the joints of his arms, then his legs, as he listened for the precise details. He would interrupt with a deep, hard hacking sound, ask a question, accept the answer or demand greater clarification, then give permission to continue. His mind clicked and stored and combined facts like a computer.

Mike explained it all, starting with the scene of the murder and moving to his articles, the book, the opening up of what had been a closed future. Dr. Toledo knew exactly what it was like.

He omitted nothing. Mike recited Dr. Ruggiero's statement to Miranda; told about the Indian doctor who had sent the woman home with an incredible headache. He described the death scene he had watched so many times on the videotape: the small quick jerk of the woman's head forward, the lack of further motion.

"Sure as hell is possible. And is likely," Dr. Toledo admitted. "Okay, tell me this. When she was in position, at the death scene, was there much blood? Wait, don't answer yet, I'm not finished. I don't mean the amount of blood you'd expect from a series of slash wounds. I mean a great, gushing amount of blood?"

No.

"Well, there could have been internal bleeding. Sometimes you get a person died of bleeding, they seem pretty clean on the outside, you make the first down cut and a gusher hits you in the face. Internal bleeding. She should have been filled with blood with no place to go. Average person has maybe five, maybe six quarts of blood. Can survive the loss of *maybe* two quarts if you get to him quick and start fluids. So if the person is lying on the sidewalk and there isn't all that much blood, the bleeding *could* be internal."

Dr. Toledo wasn't speculating. He was setting up how it could be made all right.

"See," the doctor told Mike, "a person who is dead does not bleed. No heart to act as a pump, get it? The bleeding stops and all the blood in the body settles toward the earth. If the victim is face down, then you got a dark, black front. Face up, you got black ass and the back of the extremities. If she was sitting there dead for that time, she'd be pretty black-bottomed."

"I don't know. I didn't see that."

"No, but the M.E. did. Okay, here's what you want to know but don't know enough to ask. First, no, an aneurysm could not be caused by the wounds inflicted. It's a fact of nature. There is this very thin piece of tissue that gets thinner and thinner as the blood pumps through. It is getting ready for overload and can burst at any time. Now, what you tell me, this girl had other symptoms. Very possibly she also had a brain tumor. A CAT scan was indicated, her doctor friend was right, but the Indian guy was right, too, in a way—it was written. That's all you can say about an aneurysm kicking off, blowing up.

"What you have, then, is that this s.o.b. was *possibly* hacking away and stabbing away at a dead woman. Possibly she was dead on her feet: a walking dead woman. The aneurysm, if there was one, was programmed to go off whenever and wherever. You covered that with me very clearly.

"So now, it seems, you have a problem. *But it can be remedied,* if that's what this phone call is all about. I already told you what findings would support your feeling that all those good people watched this girl die over a period of some fifteen or twenty minutes. When she was probably bleeding to death. Internally. As the autopsy stands now, calling in the Marines within one second couldn't have helped her. If, in fact, *the initial autopsy report is correct.*"

"And how can the initial, incorrect report be corrected?" Mike asked.

"This is really important to you, Mike, right? A whole new future for you. I know what that means. Holy mackerel, do I know what that means. Well, kid, there is one hitch here. Hang in and listen. *It can be corrected.* People get careless and mix findings from one case onto another report, get me? I can get someone in Manhattan in to do the right thing. This young fella, you might say he's a protégé of mine, related to the family by marriage and things like that. So, there he is, more than happy to do the old man a favor. No great problem, really. But—it would have to come from Chief Cordovan. The request for correction."

"From Arthur Cordovan? But why? None of this concerns Arthur. He doesn't know anything about it. This concerns me, Doc."

"Well, I'm a funny fella, like," the old man said in his sharp crackling voice. "It was Art Cordovan did me the favor, picking me to autopsy his son. Got back my credentials, my rightful place, you might say, because of him. Now, I know you wrote the book and all, but I gotta tell you, Mike, this old man owes one to Cordovan. And," he said carefully, "I want a Police Department connection for this young fella I mentioned to you. It's tough out there alone. You have Art

250

call me, just ask for a clearer autopsy report on this Anna Grace. See, if this girl's heart was punctured just the smallest, tiniest bit, boy, the blood would pour and fill up all the cavities. Like I said, the first autopsy cut would reveal a gusher. Not all blood escapes the body. So there you have it. She bled to death just like good old Mike Stein is gonna say in his articles telling about the cruel indifference of all those people in Forest Hills. Stick it to them, son, they deserve it."

"Dr. Toledo—" Mike began. The old man interrupted him immediately.

"Hope this doesn't create too big a problem for you, son, but what the hell. Arthur Cordovan owes you a big one. So use this to even up the score all around. That's how these things work. As you very well know."

31

Arthur Cordovan sat motionless on the pale linen couch as Mike Stein explained the reason for his visit. He listened with the total, complete concentration of a trained, experienced and unsurprised professional policeman. He listened with no change of expression, no flicker of emotion.

"The thrust of everything I've written and am planning to write is what I believed was the fact that Anna Grace could have been saved. She died because no one acted to save her. Take that away, Arthur, and there is no way the situation can have the impact I've been going for in my articles."

Cordovan understood the situation completely. What he hadn't yet heard was where he fit in. His voice was low and tough, the interrogator tired of waiting for the essential facts. "Okay, Mike. I'm with you. I understand. Even the possibility that the Governor's bill might lose the bipartisan momentum up in Albany that your articles have set in motion. You're not here just to bring me up to date."

For the first time since he'd come to know the journalist, he sensed Stein's uncertainty. Cordovan's narrowed eyes concentrated on him with tremendous intensity. "What's going on? You said there was a *mistake* in the autopsy report.

'Nothing that can't be corrected.' So? What's the problem?"

"It's delicate, Art. It has to be done—carefully. . . ."

From the moment Mike Stein mentioned that he'd called the "old man" upstate, Cordovan's warning systems were on full alert. He held up his hand and stopped Mike in the middle of a sentence.

"What you are suggesting is illegal, and we both know it. The charge against Mera, given the autopsy report now on file, would have to be changed to assault with intent and—"

"Art, this guy is confessing not only to the Anna Grace killing but to the other three open Queens rape-murders, claims he's the so-called Beast of Queens. They're listening to him. They're actually building cases. Enough, anyway, to close out the investigations. The guy is a killer—to all intents and purposes."

"Not good enough. 'To all intents and purposes' does not add up to *fact.* His lawyer could make his own headlines if . . ."

"*If* he ever got hold of the 'mistaken' autopsy report."

Cordovan sat very still, comfortable in the luxury of his own home. His second wife, an artist, had fine and cultured tastes and he loved his Manhattan apartment lifestyle. There was a waiting quality to his stillness. He had been a policeman for all of his adult life. He had survived one departmental purge after another. He had kept out of every scandalous situation. He had pursued his own career, carefully studying, getting college degrees, preparing himself for promotion. One of the Department's five ranking superchiefs, he was a careful, knowledgeable man.

"All right, Mike," he said flatly. "You've been holding back the main whatever, right? Your ace. You've been trying to figure out when to deal it. Now's the time. Do it."

"For the old man's own reasons—he's got a young protégé down in the M.E.'s—he wants the request for a 'corrected' autopsy report to come from you. Just a phone call to him, upstate. Just a 'Hello, Doc.' So then the young guy who does the correction will know he's got a friend."

No surprise showed, because Cordovan was not surprised. Or shocked. Quietly, softly, tensing for the worst, he asked, "And why would I make such a phone call, Mike?"

The transcript of Angelo Stone's call to 911 was devastating. As the two men listened to the tape, Arthur, puzzled, squinting, leaning forward, trying hard to catch the words that were lost in the sounds, gasps, coughs, inappropriate laugh sounds and high-pitched squeaks which became more and more urgent, turned to Stein.

Mike Stein leaned over and switched off the tape machine. He handed the folded transcript of the telephone call to Cordovan, pointed at a line of type, switched the machine back on.

The Chief's face went dead white as he read and listened.

> "No, please, you must listen to me. There is a terrible thing happening right out in the middle of the street. This man, he has a knife, oh please, lady, he's hurting her . . ."

The operator's voice, which was hard and flat and uninflected at first, became both demanding and sarcastic.

> "Is this some kind of joke you're playing, sonny?"
> "Oh, no, I'll try to speaker slower, clearer . . ."

Through his gasping, through his frantic attempt at control, Angelo Stone did, in fact, give the details of the attack on Anna Grace, as it was happening. He gave his name, his phone number, his address, the exact location of the attack that was, at the moment, taking place outside his window on Barclay Street in Forest Hills.

The 911 operator discounted his information completely. Because his voice sounded like a cross between Mickey Mouse and Donald Duck.

"Let me talk to your father. Or your mother. Right now. Or are you alone in your apartment, sonny?"

"I'm alone. What difference does that make, oh look, lady, I know it's hard to understand me. I can't help that I get . . . Lady, I have C.P. and—"

At no time was the operator's voice less than loud and clear. Her sound was deadly.

"You have C.P.? What's that stand for—Communist Party? You a Communist? This what they tell you to do for fun? Tie up emergency lines?"

"Cerebral palsy . . . palsy! For Christ's sake, lady, listen—"

Righteousness and indignation from the 911 operator.

"Don't you take the name of the Lord in vain. And listen, you little . . . maybe you think this is funny, calling 911 and pulling this stunt. I can hear your friends laughing in the background, and I'll tell you this: don't you *dare* call 911 again, don't you dare. Because you want to know something? We have ways of tracing calls and we put people in jail who . . ."

The Chief of Operations stopped reading the transcript at that point. The tape was nearly over. The boy had tried desperately to get help for the victim, who all during the conversation with the 911 operator was being slashed and stabbed and mauled by Paul Mera. And was then left to die.

"I had to play it a few times to get the kid's words down, Art. The operator—well, no problem hearing her. In print, Art, the whole conversation is devastating. Here's this kid, doing what you people have been telling people to do, what the Crime Witness Responsibility Bill is all about, and here's this kid—on the phone with 911. Jesus."

Cordovan loved the New York City Police Department with the intensity he had reserved for his dead wife, his murdered son and his present marriage. With all its weaknesses, its mistakes, its problems, he loved it. The Department had sustained him in tragedy and he loved it for its strength, its camaraderie, its cohesiveness despite the everlasting in fighting and shifting and wheeling and dealing among all the diverse departmental groups. When essential, ranks closed tight and protectively. He loved the Department in a way no outsider could ever really understand. He suffered for every mistake, because the Police Department's mistakes were exposed, examined and judged in public by forces that knew nothing, really, about the pressures, the unstated, unwritten, uncontracted-for demands upon the very soul of the policeman. As one would protect a family member from outside dangers, Cordovan's instincts were to protect his Department, whenever and however he could.

Without looking at Mike, he held out his hand. "Gimme the old man's number."

He accepted the scrap of paper without looking at it; slid it into the pocket of his cashmere cardigan.

"Here," Mike said, "here's the tape, Art. It's the only copy. Except, of course, for the official copy of 911 that you guys . . ."

Cordovan slowly raised his face, the blank, bland expression accepting his part of the conspiracy.

"What official copy are we talking about?"

They held it between them for a moment, then Mike Stein nodded.

When the journalist held out his hand at his departure, he was surprised by the tight, long-held pressure of his friend's grasp. He was held by the hard fixed stare that seemed to be looking right into his soul.

"Hey, Art, c'mon, kid. We've been through too much together, you and I. Hell, we took on the whole goddamn United States Army and we vindicated your son . . ."

Cordovan dropped his hand and took one step back, his eyes studying the effect of his words, which were hard, sharp steel bullets.

"And now we're quits, Stein," he said. "I hope it was worth it to you."

32

Captain O'Connor made sure that everyone had a corrected copy of the death certificate in the name of Anna Grace. As extra confirmation of the mistake, he also provided them with the erroneous death certificate made out in the name of one Maeve Wendell, age eighty-seven, of Queens Boulevard. She had expired, unattended by a physician, the morning after Anna Grace's death. As required by law, she had been autopsied.

"This lady, without a mark on her body," O'Connor told them, "according to the first death certificate, was full of stab wounds, slash marks, et cetera. They were shifting bodies around, autopsy notes and findings were sent to the wrong boroughs—it was some mess. More than just these two mistakes were made. So, this clears up the incorrect death certificate. Anna Grace did indeed die of massive internal bleeding due to a microscopic puncture of the left ventricle which resulted in said massive internal bleeding. All in line with the external wounds on her body, most of which were slashes. Only two of the eighteen wounds were actually of any significant depth. And this old lady, Maeve Wendell, died of a cerebral aneurysm."

He glanced around the room for reaction, questions, statements, anything. He came back to Miranda Torres. She sat with her case file on her lap, her hand holding a report.

"Detective Torres, do you have a question?"

"Captain, in reviewing the case file, I reread the statement given to me by the lady doctor, Dr. Ruggiero, where Anna Grace worked. About her concern that Ms. Grace was having a clinical problem with her brain: a possible tumor, she said. And, Ms. Grace left the hospital early that night, complaining of severe headache and—"

"And all of that is academic, isn't it, Detective Torres? What possible difference can any of that speculation have now?"

"Last night I telephoned Dr. Ruggiero. To ask her a few things about the medical condition of Anna Grace. Based on the original death certificate and on her statement to me."

O'Connor looked over the tops of his glasses at Miranda. "Why?"

"Out of curiosity."

He waited, then, "Yeah? And? So?"

"Dr. Ruggiero said that I had been mistaken. That at no time did she ever mention to me, even by implication—I am reading from my notes of last night—that Anna Grace had any such problem. She stated she did not know what I was talking about. She seemed—upset."

"Yeah? So? Wait a minute. Do you have a signed statement from Dr. Ruggiero? Did she sign anything confirming your interview with her?"

"I have no signed statement from her. I have only my report of the interview. Since she was not on duty the night of Ms. Grace's death, and since I do have the statement of the doctor who was on duty, to the effect that she left early because of a severe headache— No. I have no signed statement from Dr. Ruggiero about Anna Grace's possible brain condition."

"All right. Then none of this is pertinent, is it? None of this goes before the grand jury. I thought I made it clear that we are here to discuss the presentation of the case to the grand jury so that we will all be at our best when that nerdy Sonny-Boy Waters, Queens County's newest assistant district attorney, comes over here to bust our chops."

He scanned his notes, then looked up and said, "Miranda, what? Is there something else you want to say about this?"

"Yes, Captain. I called Dr. Ruggiero this morning. I thought maybe last night she'd had a difficult tour and it was not a good time to talk. She told me not to call her again. That I would be wasting my time. I spoke to her at her home number. She said she'd resigned from St. John's Hospital. She had a new post. *An important new post.*"

The other detectives in the room began to react: a few cigarettes were lit, lukewarm coffee was gulped from stained containers, Tic-Tacs were popped into dry mouths.

No one, including her partner, knew where this seemed to be heading or why.

O'Connor stared at her for a minute, then said, "Okay. Take a break. Fifteen minutes. Nobody leave the neighborhood, okay, gentlemen? Stretch your legs. Miranda, you want to talk privately or you want your partner here?"

Miranda looked troubled and didn't answer. Dunphy shrugged: hell, no problem.

When they had all cleared out, Miranda leaned forward on the edge of her chair and spoke quickly and earnestly.

"If they had mixed up her autopsy report with the victim of a gunshot wound, or someone who had drowned or died of natural causes or in a car crash, very well, mixups happen. But, Captain, what would the odds be, do you suppose, that Anna Grace's cause of death should be listed as something

260

that had been discussed with me, in detail, by her doctor? It was the very reason she had left early—the severe headache, a sign, given her history, of potential trouble that might lead to the very cause of death given in the first certificate."

O'Connor stared at her without expression. Then he put out his hand impatiently for her report of her interview with Dr. Ruggiero the day after Anna Grace's murder. He scanned it quickly, remembering certain passages. Finally he looked up.

"Well, it does add up to what the Indian doctor said: 'It is written.' It sure was written for Anna Grace to die that night."

"One way or the other," Miranda said, softly insistent.

O'Connor was not a man who went out of his way to look for trouble. There was enough controversy and danger on any given day to occupy all of his energies, intelligence, creativity and instinct for survival. The girl across the desk from him was probing deeply, and the further she probed, the darker and more confused things looked.

"Miranda, are you suggesting some sort of conspiracy? Are you suggesting that for some reason or other, through an act of criminal collusion, someone at the M.E.'s Office was prevailed upon to change the death certificate?"

"If Anna Grace did die of an aneurysm—"

"Detective Torres, I fully understand all the various implications. *All of them.* And there are many. More than would be normal in a more normal case. Of collusion. Or whatever."

"Captain, I went a little further. Relative to Dr. Ruggiero. I made certain inquiries. She is on a terminal leave from St. John's. As of September fifteenth, she has a new job with the United States Health Services. A high executive position at a great deal more money than she has been earning."

"You have been busy."

They let it sit there. He rubbed his lower lip and studied her wounded face: insulted sensibility. By now, with more than six years on the job, with the kind of exposure she'd had to the real world, the life below the surface, he was surprised, touched, that her feelings were very genuine.

"Exactly what is it that you suggest be done, Detective Torres? Let's say, this being the best of all possible worlds, where all good things and true can be accomplished by the pure in heart. What would you like to see done?"

Without hesitation, she told him. "Another autopsy of Anna Grace's body. Witnessed by a disinterested party."

"I see. Anything else? I mean, where would you like the investigation to go from there?"

"If the first report was correct, Paul Mera could only be charged with attempted murder. It might then change his stories about the other three murders. I feel sure he's confessing to ensure that he is accommodated with the kind of protection he wants. And then, using the leverage that he no longer is considered a special prisoner, we might be able to make some connection between him and Maria Vidales and the two stewardesses who were murdered. I think that's the direction that should be taken. And—"

"And *I* think that I have indulged you for about fifteen minutes too long." He leaned his elbows on the desk, gestured brusquely to the men in the doorway to wait until he signaled them back into the room. "Detective Torres, you've been up a lot of hours going over all of this. Making phone calls. Telling yourself a whole lot of theories and possibilities. And fairytales. You can do all the theorizing you want: on your own time. And keep it all to yourself. You've told me, now forget it. You got that? We will go with what we're here to do, which is to get you people ready for the assistant district attorney and his presentation to the grand jury. That's it. Is that clear?"

She raised her head, her chin tilted too high and her stare containing anger, cold and furious contempt, and suddenly, a certainty of knowledge. He felt accused.

He poked his index finger at her. "And listen, you, you're not the only thinking head around here. We're all in this together, so you just get back on the team line. And," he added as an afterthought, "do not discuss any of this with your friend, the journalist."

Miranda pulled herself up straight and spoke with great control. "I should think, Captain, as one 'thinking head' to another, you would realize that Mike Stein is the last person in the world who would be interested in my 'theories.' "

The other detectives filed into the office quietly, without making eye contact with either Miranda or the Captain. For the rest of the meeting, any questions that were asked were low-key and polite and procedural.

Miranda Torres remained silent and expressionless.

She had nothing more to say.

33

Mike Stein's articles were given sensational handling. In large black headlines, each featured witness was announced in his own words: "I WAS JUST PASSING THROUGH"—bus driver had schedule to keep; "IT WAS THEIR OWN BUSINESS ENTIRELY"—middle-aged couple watched with "interest"; "I DID WHAT THE AMERICANS DID. NOTHING"—Russian immigrant studies for citizenship.

Miranda flipped through the collection of articles yet to be scheduled. They would all be headlined except if some major local or national catastrophe interrupted the rhythm that the articles had established.

She had driven out to his beach house for the day because he was holed up, working on his book.

"I'm glad you came," he told her. "I was afraid you wouldn't. You look tired, Miranda."

"I am tired."

"You look sad."

"I am sad."

"Don't be sad. Wait. I'll give you something to be happy about, okay? The only nice thing to come out of all this.

There was a young boy I interviewed. I didn't tell you about him. Angelo Stone."

He described Angelo: his life, his handicap, his remarkable talents and intelligence. He changed the important details, however.

"So this kid was home alone and he was the only one—the only one who *tried* to get 911. Angelo is so limited in his movements, everything depends on a very precise timing, an exact relationship between the elements of his activating equipment."

Mike told her that Angelo, in his excitement and agitation at seeing the attack on Anna Grace, had turned in his wheelchair, headed for his special telephone equipment, but he had toppled from his chair and was unable to move until his father came home, hours later. By then, of course, Anna Grace's body had been removed.

"And that is something for me to be happy about?"

"Not yet. This part."

Mike had been impressed by the young boy's sincerity and horror at the lack of humanity on the part of his neighbors, at the handicapped youngster's need to tell Mike that he wasn't handicapped in human concern. Mike spent some time with Angelo and was impressed by his amazing capabilities. Mike just happened to have a friend at IBM.

"He visited with Angelo and his father—here's the happy part—and his division is planning to develop some of Angelo's inventions and adaptations. They've given the kid not just a scholarship but a paid job as a consultant on designs to assist the handicapped. Angelo is set for an open-ended future. Now, does that make you happy?"

"Yes," Miranda said. "That is a good thing."

"Good. So will you try not to look so sad? You didn't eat anything, you don't want to go for a walk on the beach. I would suggest a nice long, relaxing rubdown, Miranda, but I get the feeling that isn't what you want." There was a long, tense silence. He drew in his breath and then asked her, "What is it you want, Miranda? Why are you here?"

"To talk."

He dropped onto the chair opposite the sofa and studied her. The beautiful Miranda. The lovely, earnest young woman with whom he was slightly in love, slightly in awe of. He hadn't come upon such hard, certain honesty, such street-wise innocence, in a lifetime. She had a wounded, vulnerable, suffering look. She actually believed in something, in rules and doing things the right way—whatever the hell that meant. She was in great pain and he could not help her. But he tried.

"Miranda, I told you it had been a mistake. Didn't you see the corrected autopsy reports that Captain O'Connor got?"

She stared at him. "There are questions, Mike. There are questions involved here. There are . . . many things involved here."

She understood his calmness completely. He was safe. His articles were safe. His book was safe. His movie was safe. His future was safe. He could afford patience, and there was a patronizing tone in his words. He was being generous.

"Go on, Miranda. Run through your list. It's all academic. A mistake was made and corrected. Can't you accept that?"

"The odds on the mistaken cause of death being something her doctor had mentioned to me, an aneurysm—the odds are about the same as winning the lottery."

"And yet somebody *always* wins the lottery, Miranda."

"And you win this lottery, yes?"

He shook his head sadly, shrugged. "What else? Anything else that you haven't already mentioned to me, that is bothering you?"

266

"Yes. I think that Bill Grace has a right to know how his wife died. I think he should be told, privately, so that he doesn't have to go through the rest of his life thinking she might still be alive if *only* someone had called for help. Let him know: it wouldn't have mattered, her death was inevitable. And then he can get on with the rest of his life. And her mother . . ."

"And her mother? Who thought 'it was the Spanish girl,' so the hell with that yelling, crying, pleading, knifed-up girl out there? What do you want to give the mother, Miranda?"

"Truth," she said softly. "It will mitigate nothing for her. Nothing. But she should have . . . the truth."

"And the truth will make her free?"

"No. Nothing will make her free. Your article on Anna Grace's mother, it will be the last one?"

"Oh, yes. It will be the *featured* one, the ultimate one. Oh, yeah." He waited. "Anything else?"

"Yes. Something else."

She confronted him with such hard intensity he felt it was impossible to move, to blink, to glance away.

"You asked me, at the very beginning, you asked me what gets to me. You were upset that I wasn't surprised or infuriated by the behavior of the people on Barclay Street. Well, I'll tell you now what gets to me. I'll tell you what has surprised me. It's that someone like you— I've read your work for as long as I can remember. You've written constantly about the need for honesty, for exposing the liars and the cheats, for cleaning up government, for making life more livable for all of us. For having courage, for taking the hard way when it is necessary to do this. And then, when something comes along and it doesn't meet with *your* needs, when it isn't what it seemed at first, when it would change what it is that you want—then you abandon all the things you said you lived by."

As if talking to a distraught child, he reached for her hands and said, "Miranda. You are wrong. A mistake was made. And the mistake was corrected."

"That's the part of it that I cannot . . . That there were, God, how many people involved? How many people does it take, how many contracts, how many favors, to do such a thing? To change an autopsy report to fit a theory, to fit the needs of a journalist?"

Mike stood up abruptly, tired of defending himself. He paced around the large open room, flung a pillow from one chair to another, reached down and pulled her to her feet. There was no more pretense; he had reached honesty.

"Let me tell you, Miranda, about the *needs* of a journalist. Twice a week, I've been turning out the routine garbage about the throwaways of our society. Victims as well as perpetrators. They're all interchangeable, they all have small, unimportant, uninteresting little stories that all end in the same way. Sooner or later. I just switch around the names. You give me details of a crime, I'll tell you who did it, why he did it, how he did it, and who the hell cares? That's honesty. That's integrity, and I have been drowning in it for years. Nothing has touched me, impressed me, moved me, no particular victim, no special asshole who makes up for an abused childhood by committing sadistic acts on other victims."

"But you could have written other things. You have knowledge of other worlds and—"

"It's all the same, out there. It's all victims or perpetrators. You saw those guys in Pisani's? Did you take a good look? I mean a *really* good look? In their eyes, Miranda. It's all there in their eyes. The fear of being a victim, of being a loser, of even *appearing* to be a loser. A guy could be the biggest schmuck in the history of the world—some little twenty-four-year-old vice-president of some network thinks his idea of a circle of houses that talk to each other is the greatest thing since Thomas Edison—and the schmuck turns into a power. It's not just the money, Miranda. It's the power that comes *with* it."

"But your success was genuine, Mike. With your novel, with the Vietnam book."

"Genuine did not translate into big bucks. Did not translate into real—*real*—success."

"As measured by your childhood friends from the Bronx."

"As good a measurement as any other. And I'll tell you something. One of the reasons I went nuts when I turned forty—married a twenty-year-old kid I didn't even know, fathered a little boy I hardly ever see—was panic. At the realization that it was all behind me. I turned down all the crap that was offered me after my Pulitzer—all the TV-series ideas, all the wild action movies they wanted me to put my name on. I had integrity, Miranda and I walked away from millions of dollars. Instead, I lectured bored kids who wanted to be star TV news commentators, and I wrote about the scum of the earth who were bringing us all down. Nothing mattered. My baby bride divorced me and got herself a baby bridegroom. My oldest son is fathering my 'fatherless' last-born. And I just kept churning out the latest atrocity: who-what-when-where-how? And who the hell cares?"

"Until the night on Barclay Street."

"Until the night on Barclay Street. Something opened up inside of me. Some sense of indignation I didn't realize I still had. A sense of outrage. A need to write about it, to explore it, to explode with it."

"But, Mike, your outrage is proper. The actual cause of Anna Grace's death changes nothing. You could still—"

"It changes everything! Don't you get it, kid? The outrage out there"—his arm swept the room—"is more like relief. 'Hell, I'm glad it didn't happen under my window.' It's vicarious outrage, a way of exorcising their own indifference. You know what the hook was, Miranda? The title: *The Girl Who Was Murdered Twice.* Ah, Miranda. I've been offered more jobs, more assignments, more ways to make money. In two weeks I'll be fifty, and that's just another number. My future is still there. I'm taking all I can get."

"So you can walk into Pisani's and have them all look at you with their worried eyes and hug you with envy instead of with love."

"You got it, kid."

She shook her head and went out to the deck that surrounded his beach house. It was damp and sticky and the air was foggy and wet, with a mild breeze coming off the ocean. He came behind her, his arms turning her to face him. He moved his mouth along her cheek, back to her ear, he whispered and encouraged her, then met her lips. She stiffened when he tried to bring her back into the house.

"Miranda. Come with me. For as long as it lasts. Take a leave of absence. Come out to the Coast with me. Miranda, in your whole life, have you ever done anything just for the hell of it? For the fun of it?"

"I have not had the luxury."

"I'm offering it to you now. A whole new world, Miranda."

She shook her head sadly and then stood, studying him, motionless as a statue. Finally he knew why she had always seemed so mysteriously familiar. Nefertiti: the proud, beautiful, mystical, strong, innocent yet knowing and indominatable mask of the queen. Miranda.

"At the center of my world, Mr. Stein, there must be truth. I cannot exist without this center." She frowned for a moment, then smiled, raised her hand and snapped her fingers. "As for the Coast, which you offer me as a gift, I will tell you what I have told you before: it is all East Harlem."

34

Miranda went to her bureau, opened the top drawer and removed a small ceramic box with the face of a cat handpainted
on the lid. She took out the card that Senator John Collins
had given her more than a year ago. She studied the telephone number he had written in ink on the reverse side of
the simple but impressive business card. She breathed quickly
and felt the dryness inside her mouth. Well. Now she would
see how this thing worked.

Carefully, Miranda dialed the number.

He answered on the second ring.

She had caught him just right. He had arrived in New
York to attend a testimonial dinner, had stopped by his office to pick up some papers. Which was why he had answered so promptly. He would be in New York for a few
days.

She was awkward and hesitant, unsure of how to proceed.
She was about to ask if she could possibly visit his office when
he suggested he stop by her apartment.

"I have a feeling this is rather serious and best handled
face to face, right?"

He was wearing formal dinner clothes. He was taller, more vivid, handsomer than she had remembered, with the charisma of a movie star. He was gracious and charming and polite and oddly old-fashioned, courteous and concerned, giving her his total attention. From time to time, he asked her to slow down: he was taking notes.

"Remember, Miranda, you are in the middle of all of this and it is all new to me. It certainly is involved, what with the drug thing. That seems to be at the beginning and heart of everything that follows, doesn't it?"

He saw that immediately. She didn't have to sell him on anything. He was quick and sharp and bright. He made connections quickly as she explained. Finally, he snapped his notebook closed.

He spoke about what she had told him, committing it all to memory, checking that he had gotten it all.

"Then the so-called Beast of Queens is probably still out there, despite what this fellow Mera claims. Yes. And I *do* understand the attitudes involved, especially Mike Stein's. His story would fall apart if she had died of an aneurysm. No help in the world could have saved her. The whole impact of including the people of Barclay Street as this young woman's murderers would fall apart. The theory that they could have saved her with a phone call, had they cared, falls down. *If* she died of an aneurysm."

She nodded. He had listened closely, carefully, his face revealing understanding. His mind worked like a cop's: like the way his brother's mind had worked on good days.

"Isn't it ironical, about Kevin?" he said, mentioning his brother. "For all the years that his illness brought him so close to suicide, when we finally hit on the right treatment for him, when he finally was able to put it all together, to take joy in his life—we lost him. Christmas Eve was an awful time for a heart attack. Sad. Did I thank you for your letter and mass card, Miranda?"

"Yes, Senator, in your note. I am glad, though, that Kevin had at least some small time to look out at life without all the pain he had lived with because of his—illness."

The basically hard cop face softened, became gentle, remembering his brother's good days, and his brother's partner. "You were good for Kevin. He liked working with you. You were steady, Miranda, and you gave him more than you know. Truly. I mean that."

She accepted fact as fact: she and Kevin Collins had been good partners.

"Well, now," the senator said, "on to this dinner. It should be against the law to require people to dress like this in weather like this. However, it's all part of my job."

He looked down at her, his smile lopsided, like Kevin's. "Not to worry, Miranda. It will all be cleared up. I promise you. Give me a couple of days. This is a lot to handle. And it will all be done discreetly; this is between the two of us. I'll call you—let's see—Wednesday night? Around nine P.M."

He leaned down, gave her a brotherly kiss on the cheek, whispered, "Miranda. It'll be all right. God bless."

For the first time in a very long time, Miranda felt safe. She had handed a heavy burden to someone far better qualified than she to deal with it. It was a wonderful, suddenly overwhelming feeling of relief. She turned and reached for the telephone, and then the good feelings were over.

Mike Stein was the only one she really wanted to talk to, to tell him, to share it with him. Instead, she dialed Florida, spoke to her mother, who sounded annoyed, as though Miranda had interrupted something. Then to her son, who sounded formal and polite and disinterested and then relieved when she asked again for his grandmother.

"Mama, maybe I'll come for a visit soon. I'd like to see you and Mannie. I guess I'm feeling a little lonely."

Her mother sounded vague and put upon, unwilling to pick up on Miranda's feelings. "We've planned a trip, it's all set. Emmanuel and his uncle and father are looking into something on the islands, and so Mannie, all of us are going to see and—"

"Not to Puerto Rico?" Miranda felt a sudden panic. Too far away, too far. "Mommy, you're not planning to move there, all of you?"

Her mother was sharp, brisk. "Miranda, I didn't *say* that. You don't listen. Just for a visit, and the men will see to business. Ah, here is my husband now, Miranda. We have an appointment and . . ."

"Yes, I understand. I'll call another time and we'll have a long talk. I send you a kiss, Mommy, and for Mannie a hug and—"

"Yes," her mother said, "yes, yes. Me too." And she hung up.

Miranda set the receiver in place, and when the phone rang she jumped. Her mother, calling back, saying, Miranda, what? Tell me, talk to me, let me comfort you, let me reassure you.

Or it was Mike Stein, saying, Miranda, I want to see you, I need to see you, to hold you, to talk with you, to tell you that somehow we will have to work all these things out, so that everything comes out right, as it should.

It was an old friend, a man she hadn't seen in a while. He was happy, but he caught her sadness, her sense of disappointment, and he backed off. No, she could not see him for dinner, no she didn't know when would be a good time, listen, please, there was something going on right now, a problem she could not discuss. Could he just let her get back to him when things were a little better?

Friends were meant to stand by, not to probe, to just stand by. The hell with it, he would be patient or not. To hell with it.

Miranda went through the next few days on automatic. She didn't read Stein's articles. She had already seen them in typescript. They were the topic of the television news interviews at five, at six and at eleven and were set for the late-night discussion shows and for the morning talk shows and the Sunday specials. The experts were expressing various opinions. Tempers were rising as experts crossed swords. The residents of Barclay Street were letting their attorneys talk for them. They were pressing lawsuits against Mike Stein, the New York *Post,* his book publishers and the movie company which had bought an option on his yet unfinished book. When approached by members of the media, the Barclay Street residents hid their faces behind folded newspapers, or behind their hands, or a few, defiant, angry, fed up, faced the cameras and microphones and reminded their tormentors, "We didn't stab that girl. Go away. Go interview the murderers and muggers, what's the matter with you people? Leave us alone."

The Barclay Street Syndrome found its way into the vocabulary not only of the specialists of the world, but of the people on the street. Debates, discussions, panels and citizens' meetings were planned, along with opinion swapping over a sandwich at the lunch counter, from office desk to office desk, between husbands and wives. And there were even quickie books out on the stands.

The Anna Grace Bill, also known as the Witness Responsibility Bill, was set for debate up in Albany. No one doubted its swift passage. Those who had allowed this wounded young woman to die before their eyes on the sidewalk of their middle-class, so-called civilized neighborhood were to be immortalized via the bill bearing their victim's name.

Senator Collins called Miranda at one minute before nine o'clock Wednesday night, just as he had promised.

"Miranda, it's John Collins. How are you? Feeling a little less uptight than when we met?"

He sounded concerned and pleasant and easy. And yet there was a forced casualness, and to her trained ear, to her detective's analytic brain, the sound of his voice did not match the friendly inquiries into her well-being. Miranda felt a chill run down her back, so fast and unexpected that her body shuddered. She was afraid and she didn't know why.

"Well, I've had time to check out everything—and I mean *everything* that we discussed the other evening. I've had staff members running all over the place, and I can bring you up to date. And, Miranda, be absolutely assured that this was done in the most discreet manner possible. No one at all has any idea why, or for whom, the inquiries were made. Not even my staff members have any idea of the range of inquiries made."

That was good. It had been one of her concerns. That was good.

So. First: the autopsy mixup was *legitimate*. If truth be known, the M.E.'s Office was in a terrible mess and this was just the latest of many mixups and near-catastrophes that would emerge under closer investigations which would be set in motion at some time in the very near future. By various agencies, incidentally.

"It was indeed a mind-blowing coincidence that the mistaken cause of death was given as an aneurysm. Given your previous conversation with Dr. Ruggiero."

Who, by the way, had been on a longtime wait list for the appointment that had just become available to her. It seemed she had been unhappy on the staff of St. John's for a long time. If she had been brusque and abrupt with Miranda, well, that was what others on the staff she worked with had found recently also. Everyone was relieved when her new job became available.

It was just that simple.

Miranda did not answer. Senator Collins did not seem to notice. He continued running down his list.

"Now, Mera. He was caught in a cocaine raid in Miami. You might say he was the 'stranger in town' in the wrong place at the wrong time. The Miami narcs do not feel he is personally implicated in the drug trade. Nothing really connects him to it, and their feeling was that he was just too jumpy a type to be in on anything heavy. He was scared to death of the drug dealers. He's a Colombian, he knows how they operate. He was more willing to put himself into the hands of the New York cops for murder than to be involved in any area of the Colombian drug trade. And I understand," the Senator said, "that there is actually a videotape of Mera killing this poor Grace girl. Is that true?"

"Yes, that is true."

"Remarkable. But then again, we live in strange times."

"Now," he continued checking his list, "the murder of the two Avianca stewardesses is being handled by Queens Homicide. I understand there are certain leads. It seems the two young women met some 'gentlemen' on their last flight. They told one of their colleagues that they thought they had 'landed some heavy dudes.' Seems like they ran out of luck. I think the squad is pretty good, Miranda. I think they'll do the job."

"Yes. They are good men."

"Let's see. Hold on. Oh yes. Now, this is something I am a little hesitant to go into. Let's touch very lightly on this, and forget it. It is 'political,' Miranda. The cousin, on Inver-

277

ness Street, okay? The family is very deeply out of sight. Their security measures were unbelievably lax; almost a joke. All I can say is, they are 'ours' in the sense that our government is responsible for their well-being. Apparently, and for whatever reasons we can only surmise, their own people seem to have blown the cover originally provided. They are gone, Miranda. All of them. They do not exist. Follow?"

"Yes, Senator. I follow."

"Good. All right, so what do we have left? Yes. Maria Vidales. There is information that she is staying somewhere upstate, with a boyfriend. The stewardesses at Parker Towers verify this; they have heard from her. You see, Miranda," he told her, "I have covered everything that's been bothering you. Very carefully, as you can see."

Very carefully. Very smoothly.

"Ah, yes," he continued, "we are now back to Mr. Mera and the three open Queens homicides to which he has confessed. The investigating officers were as skeptical as you at first, but it seems he has come up with information that only the murderer could have known. Did you know that each murdered woman was found to have a house key pressed into the palm of her hand? Obviously, he didn't do this to the Grace girl, since she had the key to her mother's apartment in her hand already. But did you know that about the other victims, Miranda?"

"No. I did not know this."

"Well, neither did anyone else but the murderer. And the detectives on the cases, of course." He took a significant pause. "And Mera knew about it. This business of a key."

"And now you know about it. And now I know about it."

There was dead silence on the phone as her remark was being evaluated. Miranda felt numb to the soles of her feet. She felt sick and dizzy.

The Senator's voice, cheerful, reassured and reassuring, broke the silence.

"Well, then we are up to date, Miranda. Everything that has worried and concerned and bothered you has been looked into carefully, evaluated, examined and now reported to you. I can fully understand how worried you've been. It is always a worry when there are open, unanswered questions. You were right to have called me. Now, Miranda, that brings me to something else. Something very personal and I hope important to you. Something I think Kevin would have endorsed wholeheartedly. He told me about how supportive you always were, what a good, decent, fearless partner you were. Miranda, I come from a heritage of taking care of my own. I believe in looking after someone who's been good to my family. And you fit that description, Miranda. You saved Kevin's life."

"Yes," she said softly, waiting.

"Did you tell me, or was it Kevin, that you were planning on law school one day? Constitutional law?"

Or was it Mike Stein who had told him? she wondered. Was it?

"Yes. Someday."

"Miranda, surely you know about the L.E.A.A. program, federally funded higher education for outstanding police officers with the educational and intellectual qualifications? Miranda, how would you like to get going? Members of the Department, for the last fifteen or more years, have been sent on full scholarship, under the grant, while drawing full departmental pay, to places like Berkeley for Ph.D.s, to the University of Chicago—to universities and law schools all over the country. Does this sound good to you?"

In a hesitant voice, she said, "It's a little late to apply now, isn't it? I haven't taken the boards or applied or . . ."

United States Senator John Collins laughed. It was a sound of relief, of tension breaking.

"That can be handled, Miranda," he said easily. "Tell me, where would you like to go? Here, in New York—Columbia, N.Y.U., Fordham? Or Ivy League, Harvard, Yale, or the Coast or . . ." There was a moment's hesitation, to alert her, to make sure she understood that he knew all he needed to know about her. "Or, how about the University of Florida—or Miami, do they have a good law school? You'd be near your family."

Miranda held her hand over the mouthpiece of the telephone. She glanced all around her living room, her eyes moved over pictures and books and records, her furniture, articles of clothing. She tried to center herself, anchor herself into her own reality.

"Senator, I . . . What am I being paid off for? I haven't agreed on anything."

The silence now was hostile, and his voice was finally hard and menacing when he resumed speaking. "Miranda, I'm not going to respond to that. I'm going to say that you are exhausted, that you've worked very hard, that you are very diligent and dedicated. I know that about you. Kevin was very fond of you; very proud of you. Of your determination and tenacity and integrity in a field where one can be so easily corrupted. Integrity, Miranda, has its limits. When it bumps up against hard realities. When nothing will change, when there is nothing at all, in any respect, to be gained by anyone. And actually there is nothing to 'save' or reveal or work for. Look, Miranda, I'll be here for another hour or so. I know this offer has come suddenly and unexpectedly. I know you're probably stunned and confused. But there are no strings attached to this, Miranda. And I want you to know that when you finish law school, you'll have the option to return to the Department or not. If you resign, there would be any number of criminal-justice agencies, federal and private, anywhere in the country, that would be more than privileged to hire you with your background and credentials. You'd have it made, Miranda. You'd be able to work up to the highest positions in the country. To have *real* input. To make a *real* contribution. Miranda. You think all this over, all right. And you call me back within, let's see . . . within two hours. All right?"

"Yes. Yes, Senator. Thank you. In two hours."

Could they do that? Could they just reach out and move people around and switch jobs and opportunities and make careers happen and law school available, at full pay, tuition paid, all expenses? Could they just do that—put a price tag on anybody, pay the price? In return for what? What did they require of her?

Silence. Absolutely nothing more than that. And nothing less. Her corruption by silence. Mike Stein could profit from their system; and Dr. Ruggiero could profit; and the Governor could profit politically with his bill. And she didn't know who else or for what price.

What she did know was that Miranda Torres would not profit from their system. Something inside her—something, let someone else name it—would not let her do this thing.

The Senator picked up on the first ring; he had been waiting.

"Miranda?" His voice sounded tight and uncertain, and the easiness, the friendliness, was gone. She wondered how it was possible that he was afraid of her. She did not know, but she sensed his fear and it astonished her.

"Yes. It is Miranda. Senator, thank you for all the things that you have offered to me."

The silence between them settled.

"But," he said. And then, kindly, patiently, hopefully, "Miranda, think very carefully. Take what is offered to you. Just take it and make the most of it and live the best life you can, the best way you can."

"I think the best way I can live would not include taking a law degree as a payoff for my silence. I don't know exactly—as of right now—what I will do. But I will *not* be a part of this thing that you have all agreed upon. *It is wrong.*"

"Miranda. You make me feel so . . . so sad. I wanted to . . ."

"I think, Senator," she said kindly, sorry he was so upset, "that now we are even. You tried. Thank you."

The Senator's voice was devoid of the edge of anger she had heard in it earlier. It was as though he pitied her, or himself, or both of them. He was resigned to fate.

"Miranda, there is nothing I can say to you, then. If you feel this is a matter you have to handle in your own way, well, then, so be it. I think you are very foolish. But again, we each of us has to live within ourselves. Good luck, Miranda. And goodbye."

"Goodbye, Senator Collins."

35

Captain O'Connor called them into his office in the late afternoon. Miranda left an unfinished report, about a housebreak in Forest Hills Gardens, in the machine. Telephone calls were abruptly ended. The captain looked very tense, and whatever squad members were present crowded into his office silently. It was hot and sticky and smelled of sour air-conditioned air and remnants of sandwiches and junk food and old damp coffee containers.

The captain stood behind his desk. From his manner, his posture, his obvious tension, they realized that whatever it was would be short if not sweet.

"I have just received notification from the Queens House of Detention." His voice was flat and official as he read from his notes. "At approximately one-thirty P.M., this date, Paul Mera was found dead in the isolation cell where he was being kept at his own request and for his own protection." He glanced up, but no one had moved or had made a sound. The captain dropped his note pad on the cluttered surface of his desk. He wiped his mouth roughly with the back of his hand. "What seems to have happened," he said, "is that our Mr. Mera was having a late lunch. A not too bad late lunch pro-

vided for him by some league or other that has been interested in his case. Maybe they shouldn't have been so good
to him. Mr. Mera apparently choked to death on a large, un-
chewed bite of steak. Are there any questions?"

Silence.

"Now, that's interesting," the captain said. "I've got a
room full of expert investigators and not one single one of
you people has one single question." His eyes circled the
room, stopped at Miranda. "Detective Torres? Isn't there
anything you'd like to ask? Doesn't anything strange or peculiar or questionable or anything occur to you?"

Miranda did not move; did not blink; she did not respond
to him in any way. She absorbed his anger, understanding
his need to vent it in any direction.

"Well, of course," O'Connor continued, "a few things
occur to *me*. But you will understand, it is in the nature of
the policeman to question things. To be suspicious of the
most innocent of events. After all, this was apparently the
kind of thing that happens in restaurants all over the world,
every day of the week. At banquets, at family parties, at supper in the kitchen—some poor bastard bites off more than
he remembers to chew, and he chokes to death. Right before
the very loving eyes of family and friends. Most of whom are
not trained in the Heimlich technique or any other of the
well-publicized lifesaving actions available to them. Of
course, at the Queens House of Detention, one might assume
that . . ."

O'Connor turned his back on his staff. He pulled himself
up straight. He seemed to be aligning his spine, centering
himself. He faced them again.

"I am sure, gentlemen, and lady, that whatever questions
immediately occur to me have immediately occurred to you.
All possibilities will be duly gone into at the Office of the
Medical Examiner, of course. The initial cause of death so

284

far is 'accidental choking.' So be it. Now, whatever questions, comments, remarks, observations, insinuations, suspicions, wisecracks or any other damn thing you have on your minds—let's have it. Now. Here."

No one spoke. No one met his eyes straight on. It was for O'Connor to break the silence.

"Okay. Then, that is it. Once you're outside that door"—he pointed past them, to the outside world—"this is a closed and finished issue. Ya got nothing to say in here—ya got nothing to say. Period. Understood?" He refused to accept their silence. "I asked you people, *understood?*"

There was a scattering of voices, low, embarrassed, uncomfortable: "Yessir," "Understood, Captain," "Yo," "Right."

Miranda kept her head down, and he did not prod her again.

"All right, then. Get the hell outa here and finish whatever you're working on before the end of your tour. Anyone want to talk to me privately? About anything?"

Silence.

"Go on, then. Get the hell outa here."

Every member of the squad left the captain's office. There was absolutely nothing anyone wanted to discuss with him.

36

She was not really surprised by the telephone call from Maria Vidales. She knew that if Maria was alive she would call. Miranda knew it was not over. She knew she could not just pick up her next assignment, conduct her next investigation, type her next report and file it away, make her next arrest, testify in her next case. It was not over.

The girl's voice was soft and tense; her breathing was rapid and shallow and noisy. Her words were interrupted by an eerie, sighing sound.

"You said to call you when I was ready. And now I am ready."

"Where are you? Where have you been? Who have you been with?"

"I've been . . . upstate. With my boyfriend. At a place, with him. From right after the funeral. I told the stewardesses, at Parker Towers, I'd be all right. They didn't know where I was. No one did."

"Where are you calling from?"

"I'm at Kennedy Airport. I have a ticket. My passport. All arrangements. I am—I will be safe soon."

"And why are you calling me, Maria?"

Silence. Then, a deep moaning gasping sound as she struggled to breathe. It was strange, unsettling. It was frightening.

"Because I have something for you. Look, do not ask too much, all right? Because of my sister, Arabella, I cannot just walk away. And let him get away . . ."

"Who? Who are you talking about? Say his name."

A sigh; a gasp for breath.

"Carlos Galvez."

"Who is he? Tell me this, now."

"Not some small connection, someone just up a bit from that bastard Mera. Our cousin, yes. But . . . he is not what you thought—the next step. He is one of the big people. He was in Forest Hills to set up something very big, with some important people in the United States. Ara made a big mistake. She called him about Mera killing that girl. You don't call someone like Carlos—about anything. You don't *do* that."

"He had Ara and Christine Valapo killed?"

"To him, that was nothing. Look, meet me. I have certain things to give you."

"What things? Tell me."

"I have certain papers. Certain documents. I have tape recordings. Miranda, I have enough so that I must ask you to hold back until I am out of the country."

"And where did you get all these things, Maria?"

There was silence, then a long, soft release of breath. Maria's voice shook. "From my sister. Arabella was, she was, involved more than I have said. She and Carlos were—all men have their weakness, no? She needed insurance. From time to time, she saw things, she had a chance to get copies of things that— No. I will not tell you more than this now. Not now. When we meet. Look, Miranda, when you see what I am giving you, you will be . . . It is heavy. Very heavy."

"Are you alone at the airport?"

"No. My boyfriend is with me. He will stay with me until I am on the airplane. You must come alone, Miranda. If I see you bring anyone else, if you're trying to take me back into it, I will destroy what I have. I will just sit in the parked car and watch you drive around until you give up. You cannot find me. This is my show, Miranda. Take it or leave it."

Miranda hesitated. Maria had described a far corner of the airport for long-term parking. She was to drive around according to instructions, until Maria's car, a dark-blue Volvo station wagon, pulled out. Then she was to follow the Volvo, pull up in back of it and get out.

"Maria, I don't like the location. I want to be around lights and people. We can arrange a meet in one of the waiting rooms. You pick it now. Or, when I meet your car in the lot, you lead the way to a terminal. We'll both get out and sit down inside, where there are—"

Maria's voice took on strength and anger. *"Then don't come.* That's all. Forget it. It is nothing more to me now. I tried. That's it!"

"No, wait. Don't hang up." Silence. Miranda spoke quickly, softly. "Maria, you can understand my feeling that—"

"I do not care for your feeling. I do not care that you are afraid. Do you understand that? I am giving you a chance. I am doing what you asked. It is nothing to me anymore. Not one way or the other. I have nothing to gain, nothing to lose. I am out of it. Do you want Carlos Galvez or not? On my terms? Right now, you tell me."

"Yes. I want him."

"Good. Then meet me as I tell you or forget the whole thing."

"Yes. I will meet you. On your terms."

Miranda sat and stared at the telephone. She had little more than an hour. She tried not to let panic control her thoughts. She wanted to call someone, to have someone know about this. To have someone know what she was walking into.

Mike Stein? He wouldn't be interested. He had what he wanted. They hadn't spoken since the afternoon at the beach house. He no longer existed for her.

Dunphy? Her partner had no part of this. He had a family; he was set in his job. He had put in his time. This had nothing to do with him.

The captain? O'Connor knew what the score was. He had let the squad know. Any questions, comments, remarks, what? No? Good. Case closed. He wouldn't even want to *hear* about this.

The Senator.

Miranda turned his card over and over on the flat of the telephone table.

Yes, he had "looked into" things. Given her his version of where everything stood. Based on information given to him. He could have been misled, misinformed. He had tried to answer all her questions.

And he had been right about Maria Vidales. Miranda felt a surge of excitement. She had thought Maria was dead, if not in terrible danger. The Senator had said she was upstate with a friend, and he had been right.

Miranda was reaching. Maybe she had been wrong about him; too tensed up, too quick to judge. Maybe she had read him wrong.

She hadn't actually asked him for a real favor yet. Not the life-or-death, one-time-only favor that is meant by the word "contract." She had asked him to look into something; that hadn't been all that heavy. Not in the way they seemed to define a favor.

Now she would ask him for the favor he said he owed her: the "taking care of one's own" favor. She would tell him about Maria's call. She would ask him to stand by her when she returned with this unspeakable evidence of corruption, hard evidence. If she returned with what Maria said she was prepared to deliver. If she returned.

Miranda glanced at her watch. Time was short.

She dialed the number on the back of the Senator's card, the exclusive, unlisted telephone number to which, since his brother's death, Miranda was the only one in the world with access.

She listened to the dropping sounds, the clicking, grinding shifting of gears, the split second of silence before a lifeless, automatic, metallic voice delivered the message.

"The number you have reached has been disconnected. It is no longer a working number."

37

Two thoughts flashed through Miranda's consciousness with the rapidity and crackle of electricity:

This is not happening to me.

This is happening to me.

At the dead center of her awareness, deep below the surface terror, removed from her physical reactions, beneath the shortness of breath, the pounding of her heart, the pumping of the adrenal system, the fight or flight reaction and the automatic mindless need to hold them off, Miranda checked off what was happening to her from a calm, rational, almost curious and impersonal distance. And she admired, with controlled insanity, their quick, certain professionalism.

She had done whatever she could to insure her safety, given the circumstances. She had surveyed the area, checked out the cars in the immediate vicinity. Maria was in the back seat of the Volvo station wagon; a driver, her "boyfriend," was at the wheel. Miranda parked her car in a freestanding position, at least two car widths from the Volvo. She held her revolver in her hand. She glanced around at the yellowish damp pools of light which hit the hoods and roofs and trunks of the long-term parked vehicles. She got out of her car on the passenger side, walked directly to Maria's driver. Maria called to her: "Yes. Here. Please. I am here. Come into the car with me."

"Come out of the car. Both of you." Miranda held her .38 Detective Special loosely in her right hand.

Quietly, without protest, they got out and submitted to her quick, fairly thorough frisk, standing, arms up on the roof of the car, as though they were all playing a game.

"Please," Maria begged. "Come into the car with me, Miranda. There are things I want to show you that . . ."

Miranda looked around, shook her head. "No. You come to my car. Your boyfriend stays here, in clear sight."

Maria reached for the rear door of her own car. "I have tapes to give you, photostats, evidence. I will not go with you. I do not trust you. I do not know who is in your car, what police you have hidden there."

Reluctantly, instinctively aware of the fact that she should not consent to being in a confined place, Miranda got into the back seat of the car with Maria, and as the girl spoke she kept her eyes on the boyfriend, standing where she had told him, in front of the car, in full view.

Where they had come from, how many of them, from what direction: none of that mattered. What mattered was that within minutes, just long enough for her to draw a few steadying breaths, it all happened.

A series of cars pulled up, three? four? Dark, silent cars alongside the Volvo, across the front of it, behind it. Miranda dropped the notebook Maria had given her, let the tape cartridges fall to her feet. Her right hand tightened on her revolver, and she reached out for Maria's arm, but there was so much commotion on all sides. She felt a rush of warm air as the car door was pulled open. She tried to pull free of the weight of Maria's body, suddenly fallen against her, for a split second covering her face. Hands were on her wrist, pressing a sensitive nerve, preventing her from pulling the trigger to get off a shot, forcing her hand to fly open. She didn't hear her gun hit the ground: it had been taken from her.

For a split second, she saw Maria's face, then it disappeared as Miranda was pushed down to the floor. She heard Maria's voice, a thick sob, "I'm sorry, I . . . ." There were two men, one on either side, hands holding her arms, a heavy wool-smelling hood of some kind was yanked over her head, pulled down. Her head was pushed down until she felt a crackling at the nape of her neck. There were men in the front seat. She heard Maria, outside somewhere, crying, "Don't hurt me. I did what he said. Please . . ."

Not one single word was spoken in the car; just heavy forced breathing sounds, grunts, a deep sob from her own throat. There was a series of noises, car doors slamming, motors churning, racing, cars lurching. Miranda felt her body jerk and roll on the floor of the car. She was steadied by rough hands and held in place by a booted foot.

This is not happening to me.

This is happening to me.

When the car stopped with an abrupt slamming on of brakes, again the foot held her, to keep her from rolling.

They were taking care not to hurt her. That was good. She held on to that thought.

She listened but did not hear any of the other cars. Doors flew open and hands reached down and dragged her up and out. She knew she should be experiencing pain. She had been battered and dragged and slammed around, and yet she felt none of it, not even discomfort. Her body was numb, responding on automatic, removed from the control of her brain. That was good. Her brain could function, and the hell with the rest of her. She would control her thoughts, then she could control her own actions, if not theirs.

It is a damp, sewery location, garbage, rot, decay: smell of abandonment. Rough hands on her shoulders, on her bound-together hands, behind her, steered her, pulled her, yanked her up when she stumbled, blind inside the woolen bag; up a step, a small distance and then another step, her shoulder hitting first one side and then another—through a doorway.

The familiar deep voice, startling but not really unexpected.

"Take that off her head. And take the ropes off her hands. That is not necessary," Carlos Galvez instructed the others.

A hand reached up and grabbed the woolen hood at the top, pulled it up, her hair crackling and standing up with electricity. When her hands were freed, automatically she reached and stroked her hair, pressed it firmly to her head, held her hand there, feeling the familiar contour of her own skull.

He said something in a deep angry voice, not to her, to the others. He snapped his fingers, an imperious command, an emperor issuing orders. There was a moment filled with noise as the other men left, the door, metallic, heavy—steel? a storage shed of some kind?—slammed, flew open from the force and then was closed again more carefully.

She began to control her breathing, to consciously make contact again with her body, to experience the physical signs of pure terror without allowing herself to be totally incapacitated by the sensation.

He held her with the force of his personality, and it was easy and comforting to drift into his orbit. At the center of his huge, magnetic eyes, however, Miranda caught a flash of the cruelty of the mesmerist. She was in his power and she must not allow herself to slide away.

His hands went to her shoulders and he pulled her gently toward him, then stepped back until they were in the center of the small dark, ill-defined room. A shed of some kind, a storeroom, dank, dark, smelling of discarded things.

"Miranda," Galvez said. His voice was soft and sad. Truly sad. He shook his head. "Such a beautiful young woman. Truly beautiful. What a terrible world that has not a place for such a singular person. You're too good for this not-perfect world, Miranda. The world is not a good place and one must bend and twist and look off into the distance. You look people directly in the eye. You look the world in the heart, and then you tell what you see. Has no one taught you how to survive, *niña?*"

A numbness spread down from her shoulders to her elbows. Her hands turned cold and useless. He was pressing his thumbs in some expert manner that rendered her powerless. Her knees buckled. Her body was betraying her. She blinked hard to get the shimmering tears out of her eyes so that she could see him clearly.

He reached up gently and wiped a tear from her cheek. "Tell me how you feel, Miranda. Tell me. Right now, tell me how you feel."

"I feel frightened," she said.

It was her forgotten voice, her child voice, her first-day-of-school voice when the tall, hollow-cheeked mother superior asked her what was the problem.

"Are you frightened that you might not be able to do the work here, Miranda? That you are in a school where only the brightest girls belong and you are the first black girl here? Are you frightened that you do not belong here, cannot do the work here, is that what you are frightened of?"

"Yes," the child Miranda had said. No, her inner heart said. I am frightened of *you.*

For the first time in all those years, the strong mask slipped and fell away. The child had been there, all those years, waiting. And always afraid.

"I feel frightened," she said to Carlos Galvez.

She could hear the others outside, talking, moving around. There was no one in this room but the two of them. He had pulled two chairs up to an old, scuffed enamel-topped kitchen table. He gestured toward it.

He shook his head at her as she sat, and studied her with concern and sorrow.

"Let me ask you, Miranda Torres. Do you know what a million dollars is?"

"A lot of money," she whispered.

"No. Not yet. Ten million dollars. A hundred million dollars. That's a lot of money." And then, slowly pulling back his lips as he shaped the words, leaning forward, forearms on the table, face ferociously intent on hers, he said, "A thousand, million dollars. *A thousand million dollars.* That is a *billion dollars,* Miranda. No one, no one can imagine what that is. And thirty, forty billion dollars, every year, untaxed, unaccounted for to anyone. There is no competition to this kind of money, this kind of power, anywhere in the world. And that is what you are up against. You, Miranda."

They continued to stare at each other. His voice was very low, soft, almost comforting.

"Do you know what can be purchased with just *one* of these billion dollars?"

She shook her head, confused, wondering why he felt the need to tell her these things. Good. Good. Keep talking to me. Good.

"One can buy a man." He snapped his fingers. This was nothing. "A community, a town, a city, a state, a government. With all the billions, a country. The whole world can be bought. Owned. Controlled. Has been bought. Will continue to be bought." He studied her intently, then leaned back in his chair, his eyes never leaving hers.

"This is hard to visualize. To understand. Then, how much money do you think it would take to buy a journalist renowned for his integrity? Ah, no answer. Then I will tell you. Five hundred thousand dollars."

Slowly, she shook her head. "I don't understand. Buy him? For what reason? To what end?"

"To keep him out of areas that we do not want him to investigate. To keep to the point that took his interest initially: the indifference of the 'good people' of Forest Hills to the dying of an innocent young woman."

Carlos Galvez knew everything. She didn't know how, but she accepted as fact that he did know: that Mike Stein had learned the truth about Anna Grace's death and somehow covered it up because he would not risk his last chance to achieve what he wanted in this world.

"It was all carefully done, Miranda. We are a careful people. Particularly when dealing with people of 'well-known integrity,' such as your Mr. Stein."

His smile was bitter and hard. "Before he is tempted to go with your truth, Mr. Stein is approached by a young independent producer with impeccable credentials and available funding. For the rights to his book, and for his services as scriptwriter, Mike Stein is bought for five hundred thousand dollars. Of course, his script must reflect the fury his book will show, at the indecency of so-called good people who allowed this girl to bleed to death while they watched. The truth, of course, would have ruined Mr. Stein's big comeback. So he was bought. Done for half a million. To him, a very good start back to whatever position it is he seeks in his life."

Carlos shook his head and smiled contemptuously. He snapped his fingers. "A half million dollars, and *done!*"

His voice changed as it did whenever he spoke to her about herself. "And you, Miranda. A beautiful young woman, with your eyes so clear, your head held so high, your heart so pure. So sure of yourself, of what you believe. Did you really think you, *you,* could change anything?"

She did not answer. There was no answer to give.

"Not so smart, little one. Not so smart. It would have been better if you had accepted the chance offered to you. You should have gone to the law school. There was a good future offered to you. It was a fair offer."

Miranda felt shock, as sharp as the point of a nail, pull down the back of her skull, along her neck, down her spine. Her body jerked, her mouth fell open. She shook her head.

"There is no way you could know this."

"Do not look so stunned. So unbelieving. I know everything. Do you not, even now, realize this?"

"You could not know this."

"There would be just one way, yes? Just one person to tell me about this offer, and that you turned it down, and that there were no alternatives for you. Just one man."

"I don't believe you."

"Oh, yes you do. You believe it. You're here because you turned down what he offered to you. Because *he* turned to me at this point."

"No."

Carlos stood up and turned away from her, exasperated. It was important to him that she believe him. Perhaps in the telling, she would realize that he was not a heartless man. It was only that she had used up her choices. Surely, she could understand his position. Miranda did not know why, but in some strange way she realized he wanted her to accept and understand his position.

He spread his large hands on the table and leaned toward her. His mustache, large and black, vibrated as he spoke.

"You worked with his brother, Kevin. From time to time, he made certain that his brother had some good drug arrests. Not great arrests, not important arrests, but good arrests. So you two built up a good record. That was his gift to his brother." He raised his hand, anticipating her. "Oh, no, the policeman brother knew nothing. Nothing at all, truly. Kevin Collins was very much like you, Miranda. A true believer. Law and order and justice, and do the very best you can. And because you were good and kind and loyal, because you helped and protected his brother when he was ill, because of your loyalty, you were rewarded. A man truly appreciates these things. He took care of you. He had you promoted and transferred to a safe place, where you'd be out of it all: the drugs, the filth. And look what happened! Here you are, in the middle of it. And then he gave you a wonderful opportunity to get what you want in life, and you turned it down. So here you are, with me, in this room. Innocence, Miranda, regardless of what the good sisters taught you, does not protect you in the real world."

"The sisters." She clenched her fists. "They taught me many things."

She felt him behind her, his hands on her shoulders, gently, rhythmically, pressing. Softly, she asked him, "Where is Maria?"

His hands tightened on her; her muscles felt suddenly cramped and injured. He released her immediately, then leaned and whispered into her ear. "No. Not a word. Not a tear for this Maria. Not from you, Miranda."

She turned her head, confronted him. "But she is a young girl. She is . . ."

He walked away from her, quickly, as though it took great control to tell her, carefully, what he knew. His voice was hard and flat.

"She is *scum!* As was her sister. And that other one, the

other airline girl. *Scum.* My cousin's daughters, and I took them in and took care of them. They knew, *exactly,* what they were involved in. They loved the money and the fun and the excitement and then, fatally, the drug itself. This girl. This Maria. She lied to you every time you spoke to her. *Every time.* She and the others and that . . . Paul Mera. A man who pretends to be a rapist." He spat the word in disgust, shook the thought from his head. "Lowest of the low. He drew them in until they turned on him. They feed on each other, these . . . these people. She set you up, this beautiful girl, this young girl. She brought you here, for what she thought was an exchange. Your life for hers." The bitter sound, almost incredulous, was scornful laughter. "Sewage for purity."

"But she is a young girl," Miranda said softly.

Galvez shook his head. "These scum have no age, Miranda. The drug becomes their years, and the true character surfaces. They lie and cheat and betray and steal for the moment's high. They burn everything they touch until they burn out. Or are extinguished."

"But you are the major supplier of—"

He stopped her cold by merely raising his arm, pointing his index finger at her. His posture, his stance, the narrowing of his eyes, the concentration and intensity he focused on her, caused her breath to catch in her throat. Miranda felt hollowed out and empty and fragile. Very breakable.

The moment passed and he seemed to resettle, to relax, to focus on her with a different kind of interest. His voice went soft again, a lover's voice. There was that also: his sexuality, a constant, surfacing now and then, stronger at certain times. She could feel herself responding to it as though her body was separate and apart from her mind's control. It was as if he was surrounded by a magnetic field that seemed to

300

draw her closer and closer, arousing not just her fear but, to some large extent, her curiosity.

"But you, Miranda. Ah, you. Miranda Torres. Who are you? How do you come to be in this corrupt world? You've been out there, for years, in the filthiest part of the world, out on the street, in all of the garbage, and you've come through it all uncorrupted, with a strange pureness intact. How did this happen? Are you some special reminder, of what once was, of what might still be, somewhere? Some innocent time and place? Some place of rest and peace and beauty and surety and certainty?" He gently tilted her face so that she had to confront him directly. "Tell me, Miranda. Who are you? *I need to know.*"

"I am just myself. I am the only person I can ever be." She shrugged and said quietly, "I am what you see me to be."

"There is a mystery about you. All the others, anyone I've ever known, the women especially—each has so many faces, so many lies, so many deceits, so much deception. From moment to moment, the lies to please, to win favors, to cheat, to distort. To win. Whatever the individual sees as the prize. What prize would tempt you, Miranda?"

"No prize, señor. A prize is something given: a lottery. A chance thing."

"Would you not accept a chance thing? A thing given? Your life as a prize? Would you accept that?"

She froze. His face revealed nothing but deadly intent. She had no clue as to what her answer should be, what it was he wanted of her. He gently brushed the back of his hand against her cheek, just once, then insisted, "Tell me. Answer me. I want to know. From your heart, Miranda. Exactly as your heart tells you to answer. It is important." And then, ominously, "To you as well as to me."

It didn't matter. It was a game he was playing to amuse

himself. She had seen him glance at his watch: he was using up time in a way that pleased him. So be it.

She answered him directly, without calculation. It did not matter.

"My life is not a prize to be given. *It is mine.* "

Carlos Galvez laughed. It was a sound of honest enjoyment, of unexpected pleasure. His smile was wide, his large mustache spread, his strong white teeth gave an unexpected innocence to his face. The smile made him, for no more than a split second, look younger, uncorrupted. But then his face fell back into place and he shook his head.

"Oh, you will make problems for me, little one. Right now, at this exact moment, could you not at least let go a little? Must you be, at this moment, who you have been all your life, Miranda? Even great trees have been known to—"

From outside, or from another room, there came a muffled scream, a young woman's voice, anguished, frightened, pleading. And then the clear hard unmistakable sound of a revolver shot. Another. Then silence.

Miranda drew in her breath, twisted toward the sounds, and he surrounded her, turned her around to him. He began to talk to her, quietly, soothingly. He was comforting her. She heard some of the words, caught the drift of what he was saying. It was peculiar, strange, removed from where they were, from what was happening, from what and who each of them was. It was totally unreal and yet it was all encompassing: the sound of his voice as his hands held her against his body. She felt his touch move from her shoulders to her throat, then, gently, to some location behind her neck, and all the time his touch was gentle and, in some strange and terrible way, was welcome as though she had been waiting for him for a very long time. It was a loving touch and in no way did she feel frightened: she felt herself giving in, gliding, with his touch and his words. His loving voice filled her with strange peace and calmness. Now pressed against him, she could feel the fabric of his shirt, a fine, expensive linen, smell the sweat that had come through from his body, the light exotic masculine fragrance of his cologne. In her mouth, she swallowed hard over the metallic taste of fear and horror, ignored the last warnings of her brain and listened only to her body's euphoria. And to his words.

There was a peculiar exchange going on between them, but before she could begin to figure it out she felt herself sliding away. The last thing she consciously felt and consciously heard was Carlos Galvez as he bent over her and gently kissed the back of her neck and then whispered into her ear, "Remember me, Miranda. Remember this."

And then she slid all the way into soundless, sightless, tasteless darkness. Nothing.

Nada.

38

Nada. Nothing.

Layers of silence; shades of darkness. And then a weightless rising sensation, strange and gentle, an easy floating upward toward the surface of a far-off and ill-defined reality.

With a slow beginning panic, Miranda became more and more aware. The silence was no longer profound. There was an occasional muffled humming sound, low and sporadic and unfamiliar, growing stronger, clearer and finally recognizable. People were standing nearby, whispering, focusing on her.

She visualized the scene: she lying there, still and cold. They, their faces sad, regretful, sorrowful, watching her and their memories.

Oh God. Is this what it's like? All those times, did *they* know, as she now knew? Had they been aware, her father, her brother, her grandfather, friends, all those others? Those people Mannie and his family fuss over? Is this what it's like: I hear and know but cannot reach out. No matter how hard I try, how determined I am to let them know I am still aware. Is this my last awareness? Is this the way it is supposed to be?

"Easy, Miranda. Easy. It's all right."

She felt a strong pressure on her wrist, a human touch, connecting with her, acknowledging her awareness. She had, then, really made that slight sighing that inside herself was a roar of despair. Using tremendous will and concentration, Miranda forced her eyes open, fractionally, just enough to see the blurred outline of a face leaning toward her.

"I am Dr. O'Brien," he said. "You are in a hospital. It's going to be all right. You are safe and you are going to be all right."

She slid away again, safe now: down and back, an easy progressive slide into some formless safe dark place.

They came to her, over a period of time, when the doctors approved that she was ready for them. To talk, to reassure and to question. They told her their end of it, the captain explaining, the other squad people nodding and waiting for her.

There had been a telephone call to Police Headquarters with the words that guaranteed immediate response: *police officer needs help*. Squad cars responded to the location: an unused maintenance shack not one hundred feet from where the bodies of the two murdered stewardesses had been found.

They walked into a scene of carnage, and as they sorted it out, describing the bodies, Miranda helped them make some sense of what they had found.

Maria Vidales, dead of two bullets in her head. Her "young man," strangled; the two thugs who had abducted Miranda, shot twice each behind the ear.

And Miranda, unconscious, presumably left for dead.

Carefully, Miranda explained what had happened, how she had come to be there, at that shack with Maria Vidales. She did not relate any of her conversation with Carlos Galvez: she did not discuss billions of dollars and a United States senator or governments owned and the all-inclusive control, the ultimate power achieved through the accumulation of such money. She just said that inside the shack she was alone with Carlos Galvez and then she was in a deep sleep. She thought she had died. Apparently, she was still very much alive.

"As far as anyone outside this hospital knows, Miranda, you just don't exist. He thinks he killed you." Captain O'Connor spoke very softly, leaned close to her, actually took her hand and squeezed it for reassurance. "The news story was that three unidentified men and two unidentified women were found murdered in the maintenance shack. You're under wraps. Don't worry about anything. We'll take care of you."

She nodded and felt the loosening of his reassuring grasp on her hand.

"You know, Miranda," he said, slightly puzzled, slightly worried, his face creasing, "you're the only cop who's ever seen this man, this Carlos Galvez."

It was not an accusation; it was a statement of fact. And yet it seemed like an accusation.

"Yes. That is true."

O'Connor's eyes slid away, no longer able to meet her steady stare. "He's been treated as nonexistent, political, all the way to the federal level. It's as though he just doesn't exist. I mean, the man just . . . vanished."

"Yes. I understand."

O'Connor put a cigarette into the corner of his mouth, but changed his mind. He leaned over her, and she wondered if he had been this old all along. She'd thought of him as a man in his prime. He seemed smaller and tired and used up. He returned to a more personal ground with her. It was where he was more comfortable.

"Tell you something, kid. Seeing you unconscious, knowing he'd tried to strangle you, scared the holy hell out of me.

I mean, you were alive and in some kind of coma, and all everyone kept saying was the possibility of brain damage. Jesus. That would have been . . . I just want to tell you, Miranda. I am glad you're going to be all right."

His caress, his hand on her face, was clumsy, a large rough man's tenderness. Miranda nodded and felt her eyes closing over the exhaustion. Over the sorrow she felt when seeing Captain O'Connor's face. He was a good man who was accustomed to finding things out; to getting answers to questions. To getting to the truth at the center of events. With this, all of this matter, he was to have no questions and did not seek any answers she might want to volunteer. It was a matter that had nowhere to go.

"We'll all be in seeing you, Miranda. We don't want to bother you right now. You just get the rest you need, kid. Sorry we can't let anyone in your family, or any friends, know about this. We have to keep you under wraps for now."

"I understand," she said. "I understand."

"Good. Rest now, Miranda," the captain said and left the room.

And don't make waves, Miranda.

This is how it is done, she thought. This is the other side of Galvez' operation: silence. Official silence. There was nowhere to go with information or testimony or an eyewitness account. There was nothing to bring to a district attorney. The most pure, totally uncorrupted, eager, anxious D.A. would stare and say, "What? What do I take to the grand jury? Hand me something; show me something! Documentation, tape recordings of pertinent conversations. Give me some proof, some evidence, something in my hand to hold up and say, Here, this connects with that and leads to this and it all begins and ends with the power of unimaginable sums of drug money."

She had nothing but her knowledge, and it was totally worthless.

Mike Stein had made his deal: was satisfied with the future he had accepted.

Captain O'Connor, with his sad, knowing eyes, knew all he cared to know. He had no great and wonderful connection to any higher authority; no more than she.

All the crime commissions, at all the various levels, local, municipal, state and national, had all the information and the evidence and knew of all the connections and cross-connections, knew of the involvement of government, of big business, knew it all the way down to the pusher in the alley. And all of them pointed down to that alley: get the bastard off the street, the filth who is selling drugs to our innocent kids.

They all knew. All of them. And no one could or would do anything about it.

She felt herself sinking into despair: a sin. She knew this was a sin, and a sudden rush of awareness flashed through her.

She was not alive by mistake. Carlos Galvez did not make such mistakes: he could not afford to. Not even once.

She was alive for whatever reason he had *decided* to let her live, because she was no threat to anything. He knew, as clearly and precisely as she did, that there was nothing she could do to him, or to his operation.

The effort to think this all through exhausted her because beneath all her conscious thoughts there was *something*. Something elusive, something maddeningly important that she had forgotten and must remember. Something to do with him that she must, *must* clarify.

Miranda had no idea how long she had slept, whether it was late afternoon or morning or evening. She came instantly and totally awake when she heard the door open and close. Captain O'Connor pulled a chair up alongside her bed. His voice was flat and without expression: pure cop-voice.

"Miranda, have you been in touch with your family? Either directly or have you had anyone at all send them a message?"

"My family?"

"Does anyone, your mother, your son, your former husband, anyone at all, know that you've been . . . injured? That you're here, in the hospital?"

Her body went rigid. "No. No one at all."

O'Connor stared at her hard: penetrating, looking for signs. Then, satisfied, he said, "There was a phone call at the office about an hour ago. One of the guys took the message. Some new guy, who knows nothing at all about any of this, about you, your involvement. It was a man calling. 'A soft Spanish accent,' this young detective said. We're working on running it down." He shrugged. "The man who phoned said he was a friend of your family and would the message be delivered to you. At the hospital."

Miranda pulled herself up, her hand automatically touching the throb of pain across her forehead, then the stab of ice at the pit of her stomach.

"What message?"

O'Connor put on his battered old reading glasses, held the sheet of paper at a distance from his face and read:

"TELL MIRANDA NOT TO WORRY. WE ARE FLYING HER MOTHER AND HER SON UP TO J.F.K. FIRST CLASS. TOMORROW MORNING. PAN AM FLIGHT #611, ARRIVING 11:15 AM. WE'LL TAKE CARE OF EVERYTHING."

Captain O'Connor once again avoided her direct stare. "Miranda, we'll protect them. I promise you. They will be safe. And I'll find the leak: I'll find out who the hell let it out that you're alive and here. I . . . promise you. He left you for dead, and no one, absolutely *no one,* outside of a very tight group of people I'd vouch for with my life, knows you're here."

He was so upset that *she* tried to comfort *him:* It'll be all right. Do not worry. My family will be safe. Yes, you will protect them and protect me. Yes. Yes, I shall sleep now. Do not worry, Captain. . . .

There is nothing to worry about. Carlos Galvez will not hurt me or my family. He has no reason. Captain O'Connor would never understand this. She wasn't sure that she did herself, but she knew it was true.

Finally alone again, Miranda lay very still and carefully, systematically shut out all sounds and sensations. Her eyes closed lightly, her jaw muscles relaxed, she slowed her breathing to a deep, deliberate, carefully modulated exercise requiring great concentration. Within minutes, she felt disembodied, freed of her injured and aching flesh and growing despair. She drifted downward, toward a silent familiar place: her refuge, the very center of her being, the most private and inviolate dwelling place of her essential self, where there was room only for honesty. It was here that memory was stored, waiting.

It was here that she returned to Carlos Galvez and heard now what had been muffled to a soft meaningless stream of sound, the words lost against his body, obliterated by the strange, almost comforting pressures he had exerted on certain nerves by his knowing fingertips. He had not meant to kill her, or she would be dead. He had not meant to destroy her brain, or she would now be beyond thought.

He had meant to preserve her: to keep her. For himself and for his own reasons.

"Not all the money, not all the gifts offered to you, nothing tempts you, then so be it. For me, for my pleasure, you will accept the gift of your life. You have no choice, Miranda, you have nothing to say about this gift.

"But, you see, now *you are mine. Giving you life, I own you. You have no other life, for that life is over. Can be finished forever with the smallest pressure here—but instead, I touch you with love. Because you fascinate me: what you are is new to me and exciting and maddening. You did not bargain for your life with me, you remained as you have been and it is as I wanted you to be. Miranda, I whisper this to you, you can no longer hear me, perhaps, but you will know this: I am intrigued and fascinated, you have something I* must *know and understand and possess. I cannot buy you: that is part of it. But your life on your terms is over, because it rests on my fingertips, within the pressure I choose to exert, oh so carefully, so very carefully, and with love.*

"We are not finished with each other, Miranda. There are things about me you do not know, that I must share with you. The time will come. I will see to it. I will claim you and I want you to be just as you are, but I want to teach you things you do not know yet. You know so much, and yet so little. You are a woman and a child, and now you belong to me. I own you, Miranda. You are mine."

And then, the pressure on the back of her neck: his lips, a kiss and his words: *"Remember me, Miranda. Remember this."*

Then the sliding away, the slipping down, the darkness of nothing and . . .

Miranda felt her fists tighten; her body returned instantly. Pain recalled her to where she now was from where she had just been.

311

He had actually said those words to her. "I own you Miranda. You are mine."

She breathed quickly now, allowed herself to feel the pain in her ribs where she had been held by a booted foot; in her neck and throat which had been bruised by his strong though careful hands.

She was alive because of the absolute arrogance of Carlos Galvez. Her life was a tribute to his unshakable belief in his own omnipotence.

Miranda's anger turned cold and hard. How *dare* he assume the power of decision over her life? She felt a surge of strength and resolution, the dissipation of all remnants of despair. Her own reality returned, as exhilarating as a rush of adrenaline.

He had been wrong, this Carlos Galvez. He *had* made a mistake, and he would one day come to realize this. She would grow strong in every way possible. Patience was one of her greatest gifts. It was a matter between the two of them now. It had nothing to do with the great amorphous, untouchable power structure which controlled and devoured and bought and sold and destroyed anyone who tried to change things.

For all his worldly wisdom, for all his strange and terrible knowledge, Carlos Galvez had made a mistake many others before him had made. He had underestimated her.

She relaxed now. Gently, she slid into a soft, untroubled, dreamless sleep. It was just between the two of them now, as it should be, and he would find out the extent of his mistake.

Because Miranda Torres' life belonged to herself and to no one else.

Epilogue

He had been on Barclay Street many times. A lot of people did that: drove through, walked along, looked around, stared at people who came in and out of the buildings. They were angry, the people who lived there: What are you looking at? Get lost, get outa here.

There was that stupid ceremony on the television. The Governor and the Senator and a lot of important people, all saying about that girl who got killed last year with all those people watching. The Anna Grace Bill, they called it, and that was going to make people get involved and help. Sure.

It was a whole year ago and people stopped coming just to look. It was nice now, for him, to just sit in his parked car in the middle of a line of parked cars, across the street from the tennis courts, with the L.I.R.R. tracks to his right. Quiet and sort of settled down. He could look straight ahead and see the sides of the buildings where those Barclay Street people lived. Whole sides of the end buildings on both sides of the street: lights, shadows, grayish flicker of TVs, hum of air conditioners, sounds of music. Even people laughing sometimes. Or arguing.

He checked his watch. He knew she would come along in

a few minutes. She was like clockwork. That little fat dog must rule the roost. He didn't care about dogs, big or little or any kind. Not one way or the other.

It was funny the way she talked to that dog all the time, whether it was taking a crap or a leak or just trotting along. Fat little dog. She looked like her dog, that lady.

"Come on, now, Pudding, let's get this over with, there's nice cookies upstairs and . . ."

That dame must have a house filled with cookies. No wonder the dog was fat!

He watched. He watched. Tonight. This time. The feeling, the strange exciting angry happy feeling of becoming invisible, of disappearing into the dark air of . . . He came out of his car without a sound, crept around the back of the car, the stupid little dog too busy grunting, then yipping finally at him. It didn't matter. He didn't care.

The lady started saying, "Pudding, come back now, dear, and—"

He was clumsy and overweight and all the other things he knew he was, but he was also fast and strong, and he exploded with his power and her helplessness. He felt the dog at his ankle, and without thought he kicked backward, felt the impact, heard the grunt.

The woman was more worried, at first, about the dog, then she realized she was worried about herself.

The litany began: the words, the pleading. Why the hell did they always use the same words in the same whining begging nagging goddamn tone? Why didn't she just shut up? The power of his own deep strength lifted her, fat, heavy, into the back seat of his car, her legs hanging out toward the L.I.R.R. A train actually went by, people at the windows staring blankly, or reading, or whatever. Seeing? Seeing him and what he was doing? What he could do whenever he wanted to.

Something new happened. He had thought it might, sitting there night after night, watching the windows and the lights of the buildings on Barclay Street, watching them, wondering how it would be if *they* watched *him,* and what he could do whenever he wanted to. They couldn't see him inside the car.

He dragged the woman out, dumped her on the grassy dirt patch, mounted her. She screamed. The dog tried to bite him, but he just shoved it away with one hand while she made a lot of noise and he watched the windows on Barclay Street. He had never felt such power, such ecstasy, such excitement, in all his life. It was different this time, better. Not hidden: let them see, let them hear the lady scream!

He held the knife to her throat at the right spot, and as his force rushed from him the point of the knife plunged and her life force shot a red fountain on him, on his face, warm and thick.

When he was finished, when it was over, when she was dead, he crouched over her, pressed a nice small silver-colored key into her hand, rolled her fingers into a fist so she wouldn't drop it. He picked her head up a little so he could talk to her without crouching all the way down again, which was hard—he was much too heavy, he knew that—and he whispered to her, with a grin, "Hey, look, *I* don't know why the key, so how the hell can I tell you?"

He shrugged good-naturedly, turned, pulled his hand away when the dog growled and showed its teeth. He shrugged again. Poor dumb dog. No cookie tonight. He left it. He had no interest in killing dogs.

He got into his car and drove down toward Barclay Street and looked up at the rows of windows that faced the parking lane opposite the tennis courts. He knew they had been watching. He knew they had seen and heard.

But no one on Barclay Street did anything, as if they had not heard or seen or known a thing. For some reason, that struck him funny, and as he drove down Barclay Street he glanced up at all the apartment lights on both sides of the street.

He thought about that other guy: "Yeah, I'm the Beast of Queens." What a jerk! Why would he say a thing like that? Why would he take credit for all those women? It made no sense.

He wondered what the newspaper guys would call him now: Son of the Beast of Queens? He felt a little dizzy, a little high, a little hilarious.

He felt as if he had just settled something once and for all. But damned if he knew what.